Dear Reader,

Thank you for taking the time to pick up this book. This is a special book. We at Back Patio Press are calling it the 2020 OMNIARC.

It's like an omnibus of advance reader copies – for the Back Patio Press books 2020 season, all crammed into one fat tome.

We made it this way to give you, the advance reader, more bang for our buck. If we're sending you one book, why not send three? This way you can read 'em all, or just one or two. Get a taste of the Back Patio flavor for 2020.

We at Back Patio would love to support you in any way possible should you proceed with reviewing one of these books or interviewing one of our authors or editors. Please feel free to reach out to us at backpatiopress@gmail.com or tag us on twitter @patioback.

Thank you again for taking an interest in our humble little books and we hope you have a good time crackin' a beer, flippin' some dogs, and dogearin' some of these pages. We love you.

— Zac & Cavin

VENICE

T.J. Larkey

Book design: Cavin Bryce Gonzalez.

Cover Design: Zoë Blair-Schlagenhauf

ISBN: 978-1-7332757-4-3

33.9850° N, 118.4695° W

Venice

Venice

Venice

Venice

Venice

Venice

Venice

Venice

A novel by TJ Larkey

1.

I'm sitting in my apartment in Venice Beach, waiting for my heart to explode out of my chest.

I can picture it trying to leave me.

Prying open my ribs and performing the immaculate leap.

The perfect kill.

The perfect punishment for the decisions that led me here.

A few days ago, I was buying the usual from my dealer and she offered me something stronger. I don't have a job but there I was, spending money I don't have to meet some new White Girl that I "had to get acquainted with".

Now here I am, dying from the introduction.

Afraid that if I move, my heart will pop right out.

Move and there'll be two pops, punk — my heart *POPPING* through my breast plate, and my head *POPPING* against the floor.

Bring it!

The problem is I really have to piss and the bathroom is down the hall.

If I don't move, my dick will explode.

And I absolutely refuse to piss my pants then lose my dick then die.

Best to just do one.

I focus hard on not dying and/or losing dick.

Trying to imagine all my body parts becoming still and relaxed.

Relaxed and still.

But I keep having flashes of my neighbors walking in to the shared bathroom of our building and finding my lifeless body-- pale hideous look on my face-- in a puddle of piss with a big stupid hole in my chest.

I can feel the blood draining from my arms and legs and my heart is bouncing into my throat and off my skull now.

This is how I go.

Tonight, I have the stage.

I stand up slowly and walk carefully into the kitchen.

Then I drop my pants and start pissing into the sink, avoiding an embarrassing half-naked bathroom death.

Progress.

I take a deep breath.

I assess my surroundings.

Next to the sink, there's a nearly empty bottle of whiskey.

I look at it and decide that I should have some more.

That it will meet up with the cocaine in my body and smooth things out.

They'll come to a mutual agreement and decide it's best if my heart remains inside my body.

I take two big gulps.

And instantly regret it.

I feel dizzy.

The cocaine does not get along with the whiskey.

I imagine them fighting.

My organs begging and pleading for them to get along.

It's not working.

I can barely breathe.

My apartment suddenly feels like a wet hole in the ground and for some reason I start thinking about this kid back in high-school whose Mom had a boob-job and started doing porn. The kid found one of her videos online and his whole philosophy around life changed-- got tattoos, started lifting weights, routinely sent in audition tapes to the WWE-- and that makes me wonder if my death will make as much of an impact on anything as that fuck-film did.

I need to get out.

I need air.

I walk to my door.

As soon as I turn the handle, I hear sounds coming from across the hall.

Voices, people, people together, neighbors and laughing.

I shut the door and wait for them to leave.

The front door of the building closes, their voices getting smaller, but not fading away completely.

I tell myself it doesn't matter.

Why wait?

Your heart is throwing jabs at your chest cavity and you must go forth.

I walk out my door.

Oxygen enters my lungs.

I see the neighbors sitting on the stoop in front of the building, smoking cigarettes, talking, laughing, and it's not as terrifying as I thought.

I have an idea that maybe they can help me.

I have no choice anyway.

This is the consequences of having no friends!

I open the front door, trying to look normal, trying to look like a potential new friend.

And they immediately stop talking.

My presence sucks all the laughter out of them.

They look at me without really looking at me and I realize I'm unwanted.

But I sit down right in the middle of them anyway, my hatred of them instantly numbing my panic.

"Hey there," I say.

"Hello," one of them says.

And the rest disperse.

Some go back inside.

Some just walk off into the night.

Like, "This guy's here? I'm done, always."

Only one man is left.

The only man brave enough to respond.

He gives me a dead-eyed smile, puts out his cigarette, and walks back inside to join his friends.

The laughter starts back up again.

The sweet haha's of people that hate me.

I stand there hoping it will crawl inside me and live there forever, a constant reminder of whatever I want it to remind me of.

But it doesn't.

I walk away from the building.

Heading north toward Santa Monica.

I can hear music and in the distance I see bright lights and large crowds of people waiting to get in to the bars and clubs.

It makes me feel small.

Every single ounce of fun in the air crushing down on me.

I decide that's how I want it.

I do not want to be one of them.

Fun is for assholes.

I glare at the people of L.A. and dare them to try and be friends with me.

Nonsense.

I keep moving.

Walking ahead of me, there's a man yelling into his phone.

He looks lost.

No, he looks like he has purpose.

A place to be.

People to be with.

He walks quickly, his phone to his face.

"Why the fuck would you guys just leave!" he says. "You didn't tell me you were leaving!"

He slows his pace, jerks his head around.

He's looking at the street signs.

"I don't where that is. I'm not going to stand here looking it up like an idiot, and I'm not going to wait in line, alone, like a weirdo. NO!"

He starts shouting directions to the person on the phone.

He's angry.

He's a human.

Like me.

With the phone still pressed to his ear he walks around the corner.

I pass him and the laughter starts up again.

But the haha's are now my own.

They fill my ears, slow my heart.

And I breathe in deeply, sucking up the dirty ocean air and looking around at the palm trees and the fancy cars and my fellow humans.

Hello humans.

Living in the same time and general area.

But fated to be strangers.

It's perfection.

Their complete indifference toward my self-destruction is soothing.

And I can feel my heartbeat synching up with the entirety of Los Angeles now.

It seems important.

Something musical and romantic and full of death.

The shitty symphony of the city.

Sticking its hooks in me, re-animating my cardboard corpse and parading me around like the class clown.

I am alive.

2.

I'm lying on my floor, next to my bed.

My bed is this big padded mat that rolls up and can be moved very easily.

It's comfortable, but I like the floor better.

I believe that lying on the floor for a few hours a day will toughen me up.

I was a spoiled kid, very soft, so I'm always looking for things to toughen me up.

That's how I got here.

I got it in my head that moving to a big city I'd seen in movies and television, where I didn't know anybody, would somehow make me a tougher and overall better human. I was coasting around, not sure about anything other than wanting to live somewhere like that, when I lucked out and found the apartment online. It was cheap for being so close to the ocean and, even though I don't care about things such as close proximity to bodies of water or the correlating price of living in such places, I put down a deposit without even looking inside first.

I was on my way to becoming a tough guy.

It felt so badass.

For about a minute.

Then it transformed into panic.

A panic that remained all the way up until moving day.

I walked in to my new place with a laptop in one hand, a trash bag full of clothes in the other, and my bed/mat rolled up and tucked under my arm, hoping for the best. Hoping for a little more luck. Hoping for a place that would help me become... (something).

First, I looked at the kitchen/living room.

It had a microwave, a mini fridge, a sink, and a small couch that took up about thirty percent of the room. It was beautiful. I realized very quickly there was no bathroom (which I couldn't remember being mentioned online) and that was beautiful too. I felt stupid for panicking. I thought to myself, this is the essentials, this is beautiful.

Then I looked at the bedroom. It had old brick walls, little bits of it breaking off on to the creaking wood floors, and in the corner of the room the ceiling slanted down because it was right under the stairs. I could hear people's footsteps all day and night.

Then I noticed something very unusual.

The floor was wrong. It was crooked. If you put a pencil down it would roll to the other side of the room and disappear into the cracks between the brick wall. If I put myself down on the floor, however, no such luck.

At first, I thought the building was poorly constructed on uneven ground-- the first floor is street-level on one side of the building but not the other side. But later one of my neighbors told me that because of the age of the building, and the number of earthquakes it had endured, parts of the foundation had shifted over the years.

A building that could collapse at any moment.

My new home.

I threw my bed/mat onto the crooked floor and laid down next to it, like I'm lying down now, and thought, am I tough yet?

3.

I'm watching an old movie on my bed, holding my laptop close to my face to hear what the characters are saying.

It's loud outside.

Summer noises.

My apartment has no air conditioning or heat. But the weather is that breezy hardly-noticeable kind so my window is open and I can hear everything going on. The party down the block. The weekend traffic on Pacific Avenue. And the homeless man digging through the dumpster right outside my window.

Once a week he's been doing this, since I moved in a month ago.

I know this because every time I hear him I have this fantasy.

A fantasy about getting up the guts to talk to him.

I will discover he is actually a genius and that he wrote the greatest L.A. novel of all time. But lost it in a house fire that also claimed his wife and children.

After the incineration (his words) he took to the streets and started garbage sifting-- just as a form of therapy at first-- but then discovered it to be the purest form of artistic expression. An art form that he would then pass on to me.

That's my fantasy.

I pause the movie and put my laptop down on the bed,

then walk over to my window and watch him at work.

It looks funny.

He's bent over, digging in, and all I can see is scraps of trash being flung out onto the parking lot of our building.

This is my chance, I tell myself, speak.

Live the dream.

I sit on my windowsill and lean out.

"Hey man," I say. "How's it going?"

He jerks up, all sweaty and out of breath.

We lock eyes.

He says, "I just can't, no no no. Can NOT believe what you assholes throw out!"

And he's right.

"Yeah cool man," I say, like an asshole. "You want some water or a beer or something?"

"Nah, no, why, I got everything I need here," he says. "Look."

He holds his hand in the air and wiggles his pinky finger. A big fake-gold ring with an anchor on it, like you'd find in a cereal box.

"I found this last week," he says. "So you tell me, huh?"

"Nice find man."

"Yeah," he says. "I know assholes say this a lot, but it's true—that one's man trash is another man's booty. It's true."

"Truth," I say.

He nods and looks back down at the trash. I've done my part. And it's just him and his dumpster now, like it should be. It's almost sexual, the glare. I feel like a voyeur. Either that or I'm doing this thing I've been doing lately where I think everything is sexual.

Probably just that.

But it's intense.

We both stand there silently for a minute. Me watching him. Him watching trash. Then Dumpster Guy dives back in, out of sight.

"AhhHA!" he says, rising from the waste like a great murderous whale and holding up a pizza box with a few stale crusts rattling inside. "I told ya!"

4.

I'm in my kitchen.

It's very dark.

The rest of the city is asleep and all I can hear is my own footsteps.

It's usually my favorite.

The best time to be alive.

But tonight it reminds me of when I was kid.

I was afraid of the dark.

I remember looking into the darkest part of my room, restless and almost paralyzed, and picturing the worst things possible. I remember knowing that it was all in my head and nothing was happening other than my inability to stop imagining my own demise, but still I'd look in to those dark crevices and think, okay, just, kill me quickly please.

Then remembering that reminds me I'm still afraid of the dark.

I open the mini fridge.

What seems like blinding light pours into the room and I see something small move quickly away from it. Then I hear little scratching noises. It's coming from behind the fridge and then it's coming from behind the sink.

I make myself completely still. I tell myself it's in my head. But the sound gets louder and I move closer, silently, tip-toeing, so quiet that I start to scare myself, always scared, so scared that whatever is making the sound will pop out and systematically list all of my worst moments in chronological order, starting from age five, then murder me.

I open the cabinets below my sink and find the source.

A little family of mice looking up at me, terrified.

"Hello," I say.

"Don't be afraid," I say.

"Let's be friends," I say.

Then I reach over in to the fridge.

There's beer, eggs, a plastic bottle of vodka, and processed cheese I get from the convenience store across the street. I pinch off a piece of the cheese and set it down in front of the mice family, then I eat the rest of it in front of them so they know it can be trusted.

"My cheese is your cheese," I tell them. "Go on."

But they seem skeptical.

I leave it and walk back to bed.

I open my laptop, put in a DVD, and hit play.

As the intro credits start, I'm distracted by another creature darting away from the light coming from the screen.

I look over and see the little guy hiding in the corner of the room, between the cracks of the brick wall and partially hidden by my bed.

"Hello," I say, "You with them?"

I point to the sink.

The mouse looks at me for a moment, then runs away, up the crooked floor and back to the rest of his family.

"Nice to meet you," I say, and lie back down.

I watch the movie without any further interruptions.

I close my laptop.

I pull my blanket up to my nose.

I shut my eyes.

I whisper good night to my new roommates.

Then after imagining myself dying horrifically in an earthquake for an indeterminable amount of time, I force myself to fall asleep.

. . .

In the morning I wake up to something tickling my leg.
It's terrifying.
But it's nice to have things going on.
Distractions.
I lift the blanket over my head and see my new roommate burrowed under my knee. The same little guy that was near my bed the night before. He looks identical to the rest of his family, but I can tell it's him. Something about his movements.
"Hello," I say. "Good morning."
I want him to tell me everything is going to be okay.
Everything is fine, now that he's here.
But he doesn't respond.
Just runs out from under the blanket and back into the kitchen and behind the fridge.
Still friendless.
I sit up.
I get this cold sensation through my body and my left hand is asleep.
Then as I roll of the bed I feel something small like crumbs underneath me and it's terrifying.
Always terrified.
I yank the blankets completely off, wiggling like a little child, and see a dozen hard little brown pellets, about the size of a mouse's asshole.
It's right there.
Wasn't there last night.
But now it's there.

A declaration.

A black flag.

War.

I get up and check behind the sink cabinets but all I see are pipes, more mouse shit, and the cheese I left last night, untouched.

It's too much.

Shit on my bed all you want, but refusing my hospitality is a capital offense.

As I get dressed angrily, punching my arms through the holes of my shirt and kicking wildly into my jeans, I decide that's the rule, my one and only rule. I repeat it over and over in my head like a mantra, then walk out the door and into the convenience store across the street.

"Mouse traps?" I say. "They broke the one rule."

The clerk points me in the right direction.

I march down the aisle until I find what I'm looking for.

They have the non-lethal, sticky trap device, but I don't see the good stuff.

Give me the big bad lethal stuff baby.

I see the tag-- Tomcat Metal Mousetrap-- and the space where it should be.

But no mousetraps.

"Where's the good stuff!?"

"Huh?" the clerk says.

"The Tomcat?"

"Oh. We're out. But the Glue Traps work just as good."

"Hah!" I say. "If you knew the kind of mice I was dealing with, you would be singing a very different tune my friend!"

"Kay."

I buy the glue traps and head home.

I stick one behind the fridge, and one under the sink and wait, checking every half-hour while sipping beer and watching old Humphrey Bogart movies (a 4-in-1 DVD collection, to toughen myself up) that I'd bought a few days before.

But nothing happens.

· · ·

A few days go by before I see him again.

He's back in the corner where I had first found him.

"You!" I snarl. "Where's the rest of them?"

He crawls up on my bed, staring.

There hadn't been any more shit in the sink cabinet and the traps remained empty.

He seems lonely.

I look into his sinister little eyes, his little whiskers twitching, and I can't help it.

"You may stay," I declare. "But if you poop my bed again, I'll buy the good stuff. Tomcat. Metal. Very Lethal."

5.

I'm pacing back and forth in my apartment, psyching myself up.

My neighbor/drug dealer has invited me to a small get-together at her place tonight.

And the time for action has arrived.

Time to meet new people, have new experiences, new adventures!

I begin the journey by repeating "who cares?" in my head over and over, hoping the words will guide me out the door.

That's my mantra for the day.

Who cares?

Who cares?

Who cares if the people at this get-together come to the conclusion that, after getting to know me, I must be assassinated for the good of humanity?

Who cares?

Who cares if I don't make friends?

Who cares?

I'm confident that, at this point in my life, I'm not emotionally or physically equipped for friends. I barely even know my neighbor/dealer Annie. She's the woman that lives across the hall and sells me drugs and that was the extent of our relationship, until last week.

I'd gone over to pick up from her and we got to talking.

What I mean by that is, she talked. And after a few minutes of knowing me she decided my problem was shyness.

"You need to get out more," she said. "You should meet some of my people. Next week, when you need to buy more."

I told her I would. Said yes to something when I wanted to say no. Because yes is always easier. People like to hear yes. People like "yes people." But I'm a "no person" that is too afraid to say "no". A person who's even more afraid of going through the day without substances.

Yes yes yes.

I walk out of my room, into the hall, regretting everything.

The time for cowardice has passed.

But when I get to Annie's door I hesitate.

I can hear the group of people packed in to her tiny apartment, laughing, comfortable, carefree. The sounds of friendship and blissful ignorance of what awaits outside. What lurks in the shadows.

Me.

I lift my fist slowly to knock, shaking a bit. Then a series of scenes start flashing in my head like a horror movie.

I see myself kicking the door in and staring at the strangers in confusion/terror. Then I see myself running away, long Olympic-style strides out the door, sprinting past people on the boardwalk and children playing on the beach and straight into the sea face-first. The end.

I knock and the door opens immediately.

"Hey you!" Annie says. "Come on in."

She wraps her arms around me and I walk in to four faces looking up at me. Blank beady eyes. Sitting in a circle and passing around a bong.

"Everyone," Annie says. "This is Ty."

They all nod in unison.

I have an urge to declare, "I will NOT be your friend!"

But I just sit down and twist my face into what I believe to be a non-threatening, casual smile.

It doesn't work.

"You okay?" Annie says.

I tell her yes.

I lie.

I'm a liar.

It feels like everyone is staring at me and I start to see my movements through their eyes. Everything about me seems off. Something in the way I'm sitting or the way I'm avoiding eye contact. They suspect me, they know about me.

What they know exactly, I'm not sure.

"I'm glad you're here," Annie says, handing the bong over and lighting the bowl. "Wasn't sure you'd crawl out of your hole tonight."

"Me neither," I say, and pass the bong to my right.

Everyone has resumed the conversations they were in the middle of before I walked in. Conversations about simple things, people they know, places they frequent. The language of people who are generally okay with things. People who will never be friends with me.

For a moment this makes me angry, makes me hate them. But then I panic, imagining a life of never being okay with anything and realizing that my hatred of them only means I've lost, again.

Annie taps my shoulder.

"So," she says. "Whatcha been up to today?"

"Just walking around," I say. "Nothing really."

"Nothing?"

"Yup."

"Nothing at all?"

Everyone stops what they're doing, waiting.

It's still my turn.

"Well," I say. "Earlier today there was like, a minor incident. I was waiting at the light on Rose, smoking a cigarette, when this guy came out of nowhere and said, 'Hey man!' and I recoiled like an injured animal..."

I pause.

"...Has that ever happened to you guys? Like, forgetting you're there? Forgetting it's a possibility that others can see you and interact? Anyway, he asked me for a smoke and I gave him one. He was really drunk, swaying slightly, a little bit of vomit on his sleeve, and he couldn't even light the cigarette. So I lit it for him. 'Gah bless ya man' he said. Then walked off...."

The room is silent, all eyes still on me.

"It was sad. I definitely felt something like sadness as he walked away. He reminded me of my Dad, except my Dad doesn't drink or smoke or look anything like him. I guess I just felt sad in general and unfairly attributed my sadness to him. Anyway, long after the normal amount of time to respond passed, I kinda missed him so I yelled out "Thank You!" which was incorrect and made me feel even worse about the whole interaction. And then I went home."

The room is still for a moment until Annie does a sniff-laugh and the others join in, faking amusement to be polite.

I've failed the audition.

I'm a failure.

I'm fine with being a failure.

Failure cannot kill me.

But I can kill them!

I revenge-imagine grabbing the bong and breaking it over my head to fashion a glass sword.

Maybe ripping off my shirt to reveal the story I've just told freshly tattooed on my belly, still bloody and possibly infected, then murdering them.

Who cares?

I point to a bag with a few grams on the table next to me looking at Annie.

"That Mine?" I say.

"Yessir."

I pick up the bag, place my money on the table.

As Annie gestures toward her friends to try to start another conversation, I say, "I have to leave."

Then I leave.

6.

Annie isn't responding to my requests for more marijuana.

She says she's busy with her other job.

Some sort of self-help, shaman-yoga-instructor gig.

But I have my suspicions.

A few weeks before the ghosting began I'd shown up at her door uninvited and intoxicated.

Apparently, I was struggling to sit effectively on her bean-bag chair, then I threw up in her bong and demanded she sell me more cocaine.

I don't remember this visit.

She sent me a message-- emotionless, declarative sentences-- explaining what had happened, and hinting that maybe I should try out sobriety.

And then that was that.

The drug-dealer equivalent to a break-up.

I have to find a new dealer.

• • •

I'm out walking the boardwalk.

I don't like walking the boardwalk but that's where I was told I could find weed so I'm out walking the boardwalk.

It's noon on a Saturday.

There are people everywhere.

Men holding CD players keep coming up to me asking if I want to make a donation to their music.

Which means buy their CDs.

Which means I cannot say no.

Which means I don't have the strength to ignore them.

By the time I find a guy that can help me out, I'm carrying three CDs that I paid a total of three dollars for because I didn't want to talk anymore with the aggressive musicians peddling them.

"You broke under the pressure, huh?" the guy says after telling me he can hook me up.

"Broke hard," I say.

His name is Fresh.

He has these small face tattoos on his forehead and cheeks and he keeps calling me "bruh bruh".

Fresh is also a musician, a rapper, but he doesn't have any more of his CD's left.

"They're selling like crazy bruh bruh," he tells me.

"Yeah?"

"Hell yeah, straight fire."

I tell him I'd love to hear his music one day. As long as he doesn't pressure me into listening to it in front of him. Then I ask how the transaction will work.

"Oh yeah," he says. "You want that loud? Follow me."

After walking for a few blocks we get to a dispensary. Fresh goes in without saying a word to me and I just keep moving past the dispensary and into the alleyway next to it.

Waiting.

Nothing to do.

Nothing to distract me.

It's dangerous.

I start worrying about cops for some reason, like I'm a wanted man, then I try to act like I have something going on in my life other than waiting in alleyways for drugs.

Act normal.

You can do it.

I pull out my phone, start having a conversation with myself.

Saying things I imagine young men say to other young men on the phone.

"Yeah dude that party was nuts!"

"You banged her?!"

"No dude, Chad won't be pissed, he's so fuckin' solid."

After a while I start to worry that Fresh isn't coming back.

I'd gotten too deep into my character.

How much time had passed?

Should I take this as sign?

Should I be more like Chad?

After another fifteen minutes I give up and walk back to the boardwalk. I talk to a few more people but they look at me like I'm speaking a language not of Earth, like I'm an It.

Makes sense, It says to itself.

Finally, a man who says he'd been watching and laughing at me as I asked around offers to help. He's got a good look. Shaved head, wearing sweatpants and matching sweatshirt, and big fake diamond earrings.

I trust him.

"I got my card," he says. "How much you want?"

I tell him I want an eighth and he makes a motion with his hand like, "No problem."

He says, "But I will need a service fee though, that cool?"

I nod my head and hand him the money. As he counts it he keeps looking up at me and smiling, either reassuring me he's not going to leave, or testing me in some way.

"You're not from here huh?" he says. "You got that look."

"Arizona," I say.

"Oh shit, for real? I'm from Downtown Phoenix. But I

moved here a few months back. I sure as shit don't miss it. Fuckin, had to get outta there, ya know?!"

"Fuck Arizona," I say. "Yeah."

He tells me to stay put and points to where he is going. It's not too far but he is adamant that I stay put.

Five minutes go by.

Ten minutes go by.

Fifteen minutes go by.

And then I start to panic.

Without a plan or even a second thought I start walking toward where he pointed. Moving through the crowd. I pass a storefront with a man dressed like a doctor and holding a sign advertising quick and easy weed cards, and then I pass a shirtless man in a speedo, cruising on rollerblades and offering high fives to people.

It forces a thought like-- Venice Beach, baby.

Today's mantra.

A song for my city.

This is Venice, yeah. This is my new home, yeah yeah.

I already recognize some of the people.

The bodybuilders, the dog-walkers, the joggers, the homeless woman that threw a half-eaten yogurt at my feet on my first day here and hey hey hey, the largest gentleman I've ever seen in my life.

You can't miss him.

I'd noticed him a few days ago, harassing anyone that looked too weak to say "get away," while talking on the phone at a volume that could be classified as abuse. The kind of guy that you can't imagine being alone or not speaking, his huge body like a cancer consuming everything around him to survive.

I cut through the crowd trying to avoid him. But we make eye contact and it's awful. He walks right up to me, no hesitation. I'm one of the weak ones.

He says, "Hey, young man," over and over, and I know he's talking to me but I try to ignore him.

"Young man! You, walking away from me."

But I can't ignore him. He steps right in front of me and asks if he can help me. I tell him no. I tell him I just moved here and I'm taking in the sights.

"You sure I can't help ya?" he says. "Are you abso-fuckin-lutely sure?"

And that one does it. Without thinking, I break. I tell him what's going on and he starts laughing.

"I knew it!" he says. "I know everything goin on in this bitch. So you want my help or what?"

"I don't know," I say. "Maybe I should wait. Maybe he's just—"

"Nah nah nah. That's what I'm saying, you can't trust people these days. And I ain't motherfucking people. I can get you anything," he says, "Eh-nee-thang."

As soon as the very large gentleman says this, I see the man I'd given my money to. He's walking directly towards me until he sees the large gentleman talking to me. He stops, changes direction, heading for an alley behind a tattoo parlor and gesturing for me to follow.

So I follow.

And the large gentleman follows too.

"Thanks," I say, "But I see the guy."

"Who!?"

"Thanks for your help man. Have good one."

"No no no young man," he says. "Where this man at?!"

I walk down the same alley the man from Phoenix went down. I see him smiling. He looks like and old pal, my fellow Arizonan. I never should've doubted him.

He raises his arm out to do the exchange and we slap hands. Then I tuck the weed in my pocket as I walk away. Finesse.

"Hey, young man!"

I turn around.

The large gentleman is standing in front of the man that just made the exchange with me.

My fellow Arizonan looks terrified.

And the largest gentleman in the world suddenly looks like he's also the angriest man in the world.

"You know this punk-ass could get jumped for what he just did right!?" He points at the ground aggressively. "This my shit right here! You come to me!"

The man from Phoenix tries to walk away but the large gentleman towers over him, standing in his way. A shoving match ensues. And I can still hear, "You come to me!" as I walk back home.

My new home.

Venice.

7.

A group of homeless men hang out in front of the convenience store across the street from my apartment.

I do all my shopping there so I see them often.

They'll stand on the corner of Rose and Main, asking the customers coming in and out for money or cigarettes until the police show up and make them leave.

They're sort of my friends.

I mean, if I didn't give them change or cigarettes, they probably wouldn't speak to me.

Those kinds of friends.

The youngest of them is a man they call Sticks. Stringy hair that always looks wet and these huge boils all over his neck and face. He's around my age, I think, and he is telling me how he dropped out of high school in Alabama and took a bus to LA. How he's been here ever since.

"I know what you're thinking," he says. "I didn't wanna be an actor or nothing. Just thought it would be interesting."

He lights the cigarette I just gave him and smiles, showing off his front tooth that had been busted inward a few weeks before.

"I like it though man, can't complain. I always wanted to see the ocean and now I get to see it every day. Finding a job ain't happening, but I find ways of surviving."

"You'll find a job man," I say. "I believe in you."

He scratches at his face, at one of the boils that is really red and pulsating.

"Nah," he says. "I look bad. Like a child's nightmare of what might be under their bed. Shit! Even if I dress nice, I still look bad. Even if I finished school, stayed in Alabama, got a shitty job, I'd still be outside it all, just looking in. I don't mind being alone so this shit just works for me, except for the begging part."

"I can tell," I say. "The first time you asked me it looked like you were hurt. Like it was painful to ask."

"Haha! Fuckin' excr*oo*ciating. Gotta be careful, you don't want to end up like me."

He points at my clothes, my facial hair, laughing.

Sticks has been giving me a hard time about my appearance since I met him, because all of my clothes are at least three years old and I cut my own hair. If I cut it at all.

"I've been looking for a job," I say.

"Good for you. But you ain't getting a job looking like that. You got a good face. Just gotta clean up. You'll be parta the machine in no time."

"You find me attractive?"

"Handsome boy!"

He takes a drag of his cigarette, scratches at his chin.

He says, "Or, you know, don't clean up, don't get a job, whatever. My Mom always said do what makes you happy. She sure as hell did. It killed her, but she was the happiest person I knew."

"Shit."

"She had that addiction they made a TV show about," he says, and looks up, thinking. "Forget what it's called. Like, never being able to throw stuff away."

"Hoarders?"

"Yeah man." He slaps my chest with the back of his hand. "A hoarder."

37

"Ahh," I nod. "She died in a hoarding accident."

"No," he says, shaking his head seriously. "Diabetes, real bad diabetes. She'd sit around eating and drinking white wine, watching and reading all the shit she'd collected over the years. We're talking trash magazines, 99 cent romance novels, those 2-in-1 DVD's from the clearance bin at Wal-Mart. Just did that until she died."

"Doesn't sound bad," I say. "Maybe that's what I'll do."

"Fuck you wanna do that for?"

"Just kidding," I say, feeling inept. "I won't do that."

We go silent for a minute and then I hand him another cigarette for later.

He tucks it behind his ear and we say goodbye.

Until next time.

Sweet Sticks.

• • •

Once I'm safe inside my room, I take off my shoes and socks and throw them under the small space below the slanted corner of my room, under the stairs.

I take my pants off, my shirt, then walk around for a bit to keep my blood going.

I circle maybe a hundred times then stop in front of the mirror that came with the apartment.

The mirror is small and is hung up on the wall under the stairs so I have to sit down to see my face. To see what Sticks meant.

My hair and beard are long, scraggly, greasy.

I have deep dark circles around my eyes and I look about ten pounds lighter and ten years older than I did last month.

I laugh like a madman at this, this image of a new me, sort of forcing it out until it flows naturally. Then I whisper to myself, "the game goes on," and leap back onto my feet to walk to the kitchen.

I open the fridge and grab a beer.

I lift it to the sky and toast to Sticks, wishing he was here with me and not begging for his dinner.

At least that's how I feel now.

In a few hours I'll hate myself for forming any kind of connection, or setting myself up for any future obligations.

But for now he is my best friend.

I picture having him over for a beer next time I see him.

I'll get him drunk and we will tell stories.

He'll tell me more of life in the south, and I will tell him of my loud laughing neighbors that left me for dead a few months ago.

"Go on!" he'll say.

Then I'll tell him about the last time I saw them. A late night, coming home drunk, I'd dropped my keys then tripped over myself trying to catch them.

I laid there by the front of the door, my hand bleeding. I could hear the laughter. They were standing in the alleyway out front, watching, unable to contain their amusement, solidifying themselves as my enemies.

"How awful!" Sticks would say.

And I'd agree, share my plans for revenge, various pranks, and eventual homicide.

Or maybe we'd just tell stories.

Either way.

I walk over to my bed and stretch out on it, sipping my beer and listening to my neighbor's lives go on without me.

It is nice for me to be alone while all others around me are not.

If I think about it a certain way, it gives me power.

It's almost religious.

Like I wouldn't miss anything new and nothing would change if I just evaporated.

An inconsequential being.

I listen to the sounds of my neighbor's television that sits just on the other side of the wall, and I listen to the honking and general madness on the streets.

Then I listen to the little guy next to me.

My roommate.

I look over and see him munching on crumbs in his favorite spot next to my bed. He does not fear Man. He is my friend.

"Mouse," I say. "How would you feel about some company this weekend?"

He looks up at me, and I imagine he is smiling.

Probably smiling.

Most definitely smiling, as to say yes yes yes to all the company he can handle.

8.

I'm walking aimlessly on the beach.

Haven't been sleeping at all.

I lie in bed and drink beer all night, trying to drift off.

But it doesn't work.

I just run out of beer and then I get these headaches and then I pace up and down the beach and smoke cigarettes until the sun rises over the city, hoping I'll get tired enough to fall asleep.

After drifting around a while my legs start to ache so I sit down with my feet in the wet sand, head still pounding.

The rest of the world is just waking up. It's Wednesday or maybe Thursday or maybe I don't know and people start flooding the area. Joggers, morning people, beach people.

It's time to leave.

I can hear them breathing and talking and eating breakfast as I walk back to the boardwalk, hating them almost as much as I hate myself for hating them.

I start thinking about running the rest of the way back home, until I see Fresh.

And Fresh sees me.

I walk towards him, hoping he can help me out this time.

But he starts walking away.

"Hey!" I yell, waving my arms. "It's me!"

He continues in the opposite direction.

I can't take a hint.

I'm desperate.

I catch up with him and I can tell he remembers me, but pretends he doesn't.

"You called me bruh bruh," I say. "We had some good times, you and I."

"Nah," he says. "Fuck outta here."

"I'm serious. We went to the dispensary but you disappeared on me."

"I didn't take shit from you," he says.

"No, no, you didn't. I was just hoping you could help me out?"

"You a cop?"

"No. Do I look like a cop?"

He looks me up and down.

"Aight," he says. "Follow me."

We walk to the same dispensary he took me to a week ago. But this time I walk only a few feet away and then light a cigarette, still in sight from the entrance. A few minutes go by then Fresh walks out empty-handed.

He looks angry.

"You okay?" I ask him.

He walks right past me, like I don't exist.

Without turning around he says, "C'mon bruh bruh."

"What happened?" I ask.

"All garbage in there. I know a better spot."

We keep walking in silence. After a few minutes I start to feel like I should say something. I think to myself, this is a nice guy, to help me out like this. This is my bruh bruh. I should ask him about himself.

"How's the music going?" I say.

"Huh?"

"You said your CDs... you're straight fire."

He scoffs and says, "Don't say that."

We come to a cross walk and I can feel him looking me up and down again. Most of time, in my head, everyone one is always looking at me in this way—skeptical, uneasy, confused as to why I'm alive—but it hurts. I want him to like me. We could write hip-hop songs together and I could be his apprentice, rap on his next mixtape and make him proud.

So pathetic.

The WALK sign flashes and Fresh points to a small building with a neon-green cross painted on the window as we get closer.

"It's right over there," he says. "They usually got the loud."

"Nice," I say. "That loud."

Silence.

Fresh just looks at me again, pure hatred.

Then, more silence.

"Yeah," I say. "I shouldn't use the vernacular. I know."

"Shit you swear you ain't a fucking cop?"

When my new friend and I get to the dispensary I hand him the money with a smooth handshake followed by an even smoother fist-bump. I watch him go in. Thinking, "get that loud, bruh bruh."

A little while later he walks out of the building with the neon green cross. This time he's holding a little bag. He walks right past me again, through me almost, like I'm a ghost, then we keep walking and walking until we get to an empty alleyway that smells like rotting fish.

"Now this," he says, handing me the bag. "This'll get you there."

"Thanks. I really appreciate this."

"Uh-huh. Now give me your phone."

He reaches out his hand and I pull back slightly for some reason.

Fresh covers his mouth with his fist, laughing from his belly.

"Damn, you paranoid," he says. "I'll put my number in so you don't have to go wandering around looking like a zombie and shit next time you want weed. Or if you want something else, hit me up."

I hand him my phone. As he types the number in I stare at his face tattoos, feeling an urge to hug him. Just reach out, pull his face into my chest and hold him there, smothering him to death and then finding more like him and killing them one by one until I'm supreme drug kingpin in all of LA.

That is your destiny, I think to myself.

This is the way.

No, don't ruin this.

I won't.

He's putting his number in your phone, that doesn't mean you are friends, and it's no reason to get excited.

Ok.

Fresh hands me my phone and walks away, back towards the boardwalk.

The walk home is uneventful.

9.

I don't like the sound of it.

"Group interview."

But I need a job.

It's getting pathetic.

I'm living off a credit card and the very little money I have saved. Money I made working back home in Arizona and money my father gave me right before I moved here, in the hopes I'd make something of myself.

What I'm saying is, I'm broke.

Useless.

And still pretty soft.

I looked online, using my neighbor's internet, and found that a movie theater not far from me is hiring. I sent over a resume and the manager responded a few hours later, telling me to come in tomorrow for a group interview.

And the first thing that goes through my head is NO. I'm not ready. Can't handle groups, let alone group interviews. I don't even know what they are. Am I to become part of a group, or are they?

I type it in on my computer and read and read and read, preparing.

If I know what to expect, then I have a chance.

My favorite article that I find is called "How to Nail a Group Interview: Tips, Questions, and Work Simulation

Exercises".

I study it.

I let it become part of me.

I read it again and again until I know every question by heart.

"How do you work in a team?"

I grew up playing sports, so I am very comfortable with the concept. I live and breathe for the team. I love the team. I am the team and the team is I.

"If one of your team members asked you for help with their work, before you are done with your own, how would you react?"

Fuck yeah. You need me to sweep the floor? I'll sweep. I'll pick that popcorn up with my bare hands. I'll slurp that nacho cheese right up. You need help with the bathroom? On it. One of the urinals broken? Easy. I'm the new urinal. For the team, I will serve as a human urinal.

"What is your biggest weakness?"

Well, sir, I've got to be honest here. I am too hard on myself. A perfectionist.

"Why do you want this job?"

Ah! I'm glad you asked. One word: Film. I have been a student and lover of film my whole life. Just to be close to it — the magic, the prestige and pageantry — it would be an honor.

And I'm still playing it all in my head over and over as I walk to the interview the next day.

I'm wearing my best t-shirt and my hair is combed back.

I look like an asshole.

Hopefully though, an asshole with a job.

I can see the movie theater ahead of me and a mixture of hope and sickness fills my head like cold wet fingers pushing in through my ears.

Employment.

Responsibility.

Money.

I look down at myself, run my hands through my hair, inhaling that magical Californian air, and cross the street toward my destiny.

Ahead of me, a young man in a tucked-in button-down shirt is walking in to the theater. He's college age, my age, but he looks younger than me somehow, more alive. I watch him as he talks with an employee, smiling confidently, thanking the employee by putting his hands together and bowing slightly.

Then I watch as he walks through a door next to the snack bar.

He's here for the group interview.

He's my competition.

And I think, good.

If it were easy, I wouldn't want it.

Someone once told me that men are like sharks, that when they stop moving and competing, they die. And I am (essentially) a man. A shark. A competitor.

When I get closer to the theater door, I see my reflection. My nicest shirt isn't so nice and my eyes are sunken in and red and there is a big juicy pimple in the center of my forehead—couldn't be more symmetrical, pulsing and ready to explode on my fellow interviewees, so noticeable I feel like I'd have to address it.

But that's okay.

I've done my research.

I can do this.

I walk in and head for the door the nicely dressed young man went through. As I pass the snack bar, I can hear two employees talking. They're saying something about the actress in some new movie.

"If I was that hot," one of them says, "I'd be in movies too."

"Yeah, like, she's not even a good actress!"

"Fucking lucky bitch."

"Exactly. It's all luck," the other says.

And I start to feel physically ill.

The voices of the employees seem really sharp.

The smell of stale popcorn is all around me.

The floor is sticky and my shoes are making a crunching sound as they rip away from the soda-soaked tile.

My mind starts to drift off. The confidence is fleeing along with it. And for some reason my whole body feels hot and starts moving on its own. I'm walking out the door and then I'm on my way home and then I am home and then I'm on the phone with Fresh asking if we can meet up. I find myself in an alleyway behind a smoke shop. Fresh appears and he takes the cigarettes out of my shirt pocket and lights one, then sticks a small bag in the cigarette carton and hands it back to me. I realize it's my turn so I take out the money from my pocket and we slap hands and bump chests. He says, "later bruh bruh" and then I walk home with the image of the nicely dressed young man smirking at me, like he knows something that I don't and never will.

10.

I'm walking down Abbot Kinney, feeling embarrassed about something.

I don't know why.

It's just happening.

People knowing I'm still alive, giving it (life) a shot, feels humiliating and there's probably a reason.

I look around at everyone else walking and it seems like I've offended them by being in the same general area.

I want to ask them.

Why?

Have I offended you?

What improvements can be made?

But I know that's wrong. Egotistical to even think my presence could cause an emotional change in anyone. My existence is simply humiliating and it affects no one but me.

That's my mantra for today.

Existence is humiliating.

I continue walking.

In front of me, I see a family of four. They're snapping pictures and smiling and looking all around at the trees and the shops and the fast-paced traffic. They are on vacation. They are enjoying themselves and because of this they are walking very slowly.

And I'm walking just as slowly behind, because my

existence is humiliating.

The thought of cutting through them and making them look at me is unbearable.

It would ruin their day.

The last thing I want is to ruin this family's day.

But then I realize I am potentially doing just that by walking behind them. If they turn around and see me—boom, whole vacation ruined, children traumatized, Mother fearful for her safety and virtue and Father never allows the "Venice Incident" to be spoken of in his home ever again.

So, I'm torn.

Humiliation is a possibility either way.

We keep walking, together but not together at all.

Their pace speeds up and I feel like I'm safe, then they stop and I have no idea what to do.

I feel like I'm walking incorrectly, like my feet are lighter than the rest of my body.

But then I see an opportunity.

An old homeless man is in the distance. He is lying unconscious on a street corner in front of us, face down, his pants well below his ass cheeks.

I watch the unaware family get closer and closer to the homeless man like a head-on car collision is about to occur, feeling like this is my time.

I will save the day.

Prove my worth.

I pick up the pace and picture it playing out in my head. I'll take out a dollar bill and fold it up.
Then I'll skip merrily past the family and gently place the dollar between the homeless man's ass cheeks. The children will laugh and I'll take a bow and make a goofy face at the parents like, "Venice, huh, what can you do?"

But I'm too late.

The Father sees the homeless man and redirects his family

at the stoplight, and the Mother looks disgusted and shields the children's eyes.

They disappear.

I bid them farewell and good luck and I continue walking toward the homeless man, digging around my pockets and pulling out a dollar bill. I kneel down next to the him and tuck the money under his hand, making sure it's hidden and secure, then I linger there next to him for a minute, looking for signs that he's still alive.

He smells like watered-down gasoline and his skin is bright red and looks like it's shedding.

He's not moving.

I say to him, "Existence is humiliating," but still, he doesn't move.

I say, "Live a long life full of humiliation, then die," and I think I see him breathing.

A little louder, I say, "Death by humiliation. This is my fate," and now I'm not so sure he's breathing.

"Someone fashioning a noose made of all my humiliating moments and hanging me with it, yelling 'EXPOSED!' the moment right before my neck snaps. Last words I hear before the great dirt-nap. SHAMED or HUMBLED or something like that," I say.

And that one does it.

He jerks his head up, the rest of his body still limp and flat on the cement. We look at each other like predator and prey, but I'm not sure who's the prey. Then he solves that mystery by screaming wildly at me. Something I can't understand.

I try to calm him down but he just barks out these noises that resemble words.

The people around can't help staring.

It must look insane.

I look insane.

Of course they stare.

Watching the show.

Watching a face-down ass-out homeless man yell at me as I backpedal away with my hands in the air, looking humiliated.

Ask and you shall receive.

11.

I'm lying in bed, drinking beer and listening to my neighbors.

The walls are really thin and the floors creak and wail so you can hear every movement.

It's my only hobby.

Listening to my neighbors do the things they don't think anyone else knows about.

The most entertaining of everyone in the building are these drug-addicts above me. They are young and in love and they are arguing again.

I can only hear low groaning noises, so it must not be that bad. Usually they scream and throw things at each other for hours, bickering about money, drugs, making threats, until they calm down and apologize and promise they'll never fight again.

Almost every night they go through this.

And I've become invested.

Late last night they were arguing about who should get the last bit of the stuff they still had.

The woman was very calm as she pleaded, saying stuff like, "I'll get you well tomorrow baby," and kissing him over and over. But the man started crying before he could make his case.

"Spit it out," the woman said. "Say what you want to say."

He just hiccupped, snorted, and kept catching his breath. The woman became angry. There was screaming. Threats. Then the man finally spoke up. He told her what he had to do to get that last bit of dope. And how every time he's coming down now he can see it happening all over again.

The woman gave in at that and cried with him and they spent the rest of the night sitting near their window smoking cigarettes and kissing and making drug-free plans for the future.

That's how you know the fighting is over.

Whenever they smoke together out their window it means they've made up. It's a routine they'll probably never get out of, but when I see the smashed ends of their rollies falling from above I feel optimistic about things.

Or, maybe that's not the right word.

I only ever feel good about it for a few seconds.

A lot of the couple's cigarette butts end up on this old rusted black car that belongs to another neighbor named Beckett, an older man who's lived in the building longer than anyone. I first met him outside the convenience store across the street. He was talking with Sticks and a few others. At first I thought he was a part of the homeless crew that hangs out there every night because he was wearing a really beat-up old-looking leather jacket, and something about the way he spoke made it seem like he'd been separated from society for a while.

I walked up like I always did but this time Sticks didn't give me his usual greeting. He and Beckett were too busy having a conversation about the ballerina clown sculpture above the convenience store, this weird Venice landmark that had been there since the late 80's.

"The leg used to kick," Beckett said. "Then people started complaining about, ekh, the mechanical sound. But I love it. Just ekh, watching over us and keeping us safe."

When Beckett spoke he sounded like he was dying of thirst. He had to stop mid-sentence a lot, making this choking noise in the back of this throat.

"It was, ekh ekh, scaring kids too."

Sticks looked up at the clownerina.

"Damn dude," he said. "I kinda wish it was still kicking."

"Me too," Beckett said.

After the conversation came to the conclusion that, yes, indeed, it would be better if the clownerina was still dancing over Main Street, I gave Sticks my remaining change and walked toward home.

Beckett followed.

When I realized this, I wasn't worried or anything. It just felt like having a stranger's dog follow after you because he likes the way you smell. It was nice.

We walked together in silence until Beckett and I got to the parking lot of our building.

He stopped in front of his car and shook his head.

"This your car?" I asked.

"Yeah ekh, this old girl is mine."

He looked down at his beat-up old car like it was his child, then started picking up each of the butts on his hood.

"I just don't, ekh, understand why someone would do this?"

"I don't think they do it on purpose," I said. "Just careless I think."

"Yeah. But, ekh ekh ekh, it happens every night. How have they not noticed? I would notice. Wouldn't you notice?"

"I would notice," I said.

"Then why don't they?"

"Shit man, I don't know."

"But... ekh... why?"

After Beckett and I finished cleaning off his car we walked

into our building and talked some more, mostly about the cigarettes.

"It just drives me crazy," he said. "I know it's silly but, ekh, it's really making me crazy."

"Yeah," I said. "It was nice meeting you though."

"I'm losing sleep over it."

"Well, shit, I'll see you around Beckett."

"Keep an eye out okay?" he said, walking up the stairs to his apartment. "Please?"

"I will."

I immediately felt bad about not telling him I knew who the culprits were. But I think, for me, it's best to stay uninvolved. Being aware of my surroundings, yes, but never interfering. Like a chicken-shit God.

I take the last sip of my beer, walk into the kitchen for another.

As I drink, I start thinking about how and when I became the guy that listens in on others.

I wonder when I became the "creepy" guy, and how long it's been that way.

Then I think about past versions of myself.

No matter how insignificant the moment, or how depressed I was, I always prefer the past version of myself.

Feels like I'm only living in order to look back on the past fondly, or something like that.

So I think back to high-school, past-me, and how he would've interacted with my neighbors.

I decide he would not have been a "listener" or a "creepy" guy.

It was only three years ago, and I was still terrified of everything, but I feel jealous of him.

I think back to this time I'd thrown a party on accident and everyone just showed up. People that I'd went to school with for years but had never spoken to were treating me like I was an old friend, just because I provided them a safe place to get drunk in. One of them even told me he loved me. He'd staggered up and kept talking about how great it was to be hanging out with me after all these years. How he always thought I was kind of scary or appeared either "too weird" or "too crazy" to participate in any social gatherings. Then he did the love bit and I said it back, sort of laughing.

But that was past-me.

Current-me hides in the shadows.

Going backwards every day.

Less and less functional.

Drowning in cheap beer.

Fuck.

I take another sip and a really cliché thought like "liquid courage" jumps around my shitty brain, like the answer to nothing. Then I hear the stairs creak, slow footsteps, and heavy breathing.

"Ekh ekh."

I listen as the footsteps stop at the bottom of the stairs and then I hear a soft knocking sound coming from across the hall, next to the staircase. Apartment number 1. Where the building manager lives.

The door opens: "Hey Beckett how are you this fine day!" and the manager, Kevin, starts his routine, interjecting various forms of recognition like "Shit man" or "I hear ya" as Beckett complains about the cigarette issue.

"You said ekh, you'd help me Kev."

"I am," Kevin says. "I promise Buddy."

Kevin the manager is an aspiring actor. Long shiny hair and a perfectly trimmed beard. He rides a bicycle everywhere and is always smiling and I'm convinced he is some breed of psychopath.

"Buddy," he says. "Not cool."

"Yeah, and the other ekh day, one of the butts was put out in some kind of slimy material, and when I picked it up it got all over my hands."

"Oh, buddy, that's unacceptable!!"

Kevin also calls everyone "buddy". He makes all kinds of promises he never follows through on, peppering in the "buddies" to make you feel heard. I hate him. He should murder himself.

"You think you could ekh, ask around?" Beckett says. "Ask them to stop?"

"Buddy," Kevin says. "Consider. It. Done."

The door closes and I listen as Beckett makes his way back up the stairs.

It's the saddest footsteps I've ever heard.

It's hopeless.

No hope.

Consider. It. Hopeless.

Fuck you Kevin.

I light a cigarette and then sit on the edge of my windowsill.

Right below me is Beckett's car and I can't help but stare at it.

He's left the evidence on the hood, the butts all scattered over it like a crime scene, smashed and stained brown at the ends.

As I stare at it I start laughing silently at the absurdity of it, but also feel something like purpose. Like I've been put here to witness this. Put here to notice. Why don't people notice? They never notice. But I notice.

And in that moment, I am no longer the "creepy" guy.

I am the "noticer."

I can't remember when I became the "noticer," but I know why. I'm like that superhero. The blind one that dresses up like Satan. Except instead of saving people, I just spy on them.

I close my eyes, take a deep drag of my cigarette, listening intently to everything going.

On the adjacent corner of the building, my neighbor is playing reggae music and singing along.

This is Reggae Man.

This is the villain.

He sits by his window a lot, smoking joints while the music plays. My enemies in the building were temporary friends with him before they moved out. And I'm fairly sure if he were to see me and start talking to me right now, I would be left with no choice but to kill him.

That's part of the job of a superhero.

Justified killings.

But that would mean he'd have to know we are enemies.

I couldn't justify surprising him with something like strangulation or decapitation via my window slamming down on him repeatedly before he even had a chance to mentally prepare.

No.

I should tell him.

I'll tell him I hate him and see what happens.

I should've done it earlier.

Reggae Man, I hate you.

I hate that your body-suit and surfboard hang outside your permanently open window.

I hate that you're always home, making noises with your mouth, talking on the phone or singing or yelling down to other tenants as they walk by.

Reggae Man.

Sworn Rival.

Because of you, I walk around the other side of the building when coming to and from home.

You've inconvenienced me, I'd say. And therefore, I hate you.

"But why?" he'd ask. "I thought we were friends, I thought we were bros."

He'd beg just like that, and I'd shake my head, cross my arms, laugh a deep manly laugh.

But he'd beg more.

"Please. Don't you remember when I was moving in, I was standing out front, you remember, I was taking a break from carrying my things in. I said hey and you said hey and we shared a joint, man! A joint!"

Invincible Noticer—just standing there, arms on hips.

"I even told you about myself. About my dreams! How everyone in LA has some kind of dream and how I thought I'd fit right in!"

Immortal Watcher—looking valiantly into the heavens, smirking.

"I know you remember! I said I was a surfer and an artist…" Then he'd pause. "…I said I was writer… And you said you wrote too!"

Courageous Keeper—slouching and stunned now.

"You said you wrote too but didn't make money off it, or make any money off anything. Yeah. You said you still got help from your Dad!"

Inept Creepy Guy — suddenly and finally, embarrassed.

Reggae Man knew the weaknesses, he could not be trusted, was to be avoided at all costs.

Even in my dreams I fail.

And above all else, I wish things didn't bother me like this.

That I could just be above it, accept it.

I think the ultimate goal is to never react to anything, letting all the bad shit carve into you over and over until you are a lean mean living machine tearing through the absurdity. But I can't accept it.

The losses pile up.

I ash my cigarette out on the windowsill and lie back in bed.

I start feeling anxious, worried about Reggae Man seeing me, so I close my eyes and put my hands behind my head.

My senses are still at a superhero-level of operation, when a familiar smell wafts into my apartment.

I open one eye and see Reggae Man blowing smoke rings out his window.

He's smiling.

He's got evil in his eyes.

And he's bobbing his head to the music.

That music.

The music of the enemy.

I hear it in my head late at night when I'm trying to sleep.

I hear it when everything else is quiet and still.

The other day I was so sick of hearing it I wrote a note to him. Subtly hinting that he was bothering his neighbors and misspelling a word so he couldn't deduce that it was written by me. And then taped it to his door.

Reggae Sux Ass.

But Reggae Man carries that name for a reason.

The music fills the streets.

I picture him holding a boombox outside my window and mouthing the words "I'll make you love me" as I sit in darkness plotting his murder.

Reggae Man: surfer, writer, the devil himself.

But also and forever and always, fuck me.

He's probably a nice guy.

As I power through a new beer, I start to hear voices mixing in with the music.

Another neighbor is in the parking lot, walking home, and Reggae Man is yelling down to them over the sound of the crooning Jamaican.

The neighbor sounds annoyed and the music is finally shut off.

"Come join," Reggae Man says. "Just lit one up!"

The neighbor, who I can hear clearly enough now to know is Annie, says, "Nah. I've got some stuff to do," then everything goes quiet.

I move quickly over to the window and watch her walk toward the entrance. Then I press up against my wall and listen as she opens the door. Her phone rings. She answers "Hey, just got home," and I can hear the jingle of her keys and the creak of her door closing behind her.

It feels dramatic.

I think "to her, I'm the one to avoid."

Then I slap myself in the forehead, hard.

But not hard enough to make a sound.

The music starts back up.

12.

I decide to max out my credit card.

The limit on it, that I did nothing to deserve or be trusted with, is a lot of money for me, so I can use it to get drunk every day.

I decide I won't spoil myself with luxuries like new clothes or good food, just alcohol.

My reasoning being that thousands of people my age are going into large amounts of student debt that they'll have long after college, and all they're getting out of it is a degree and some party stories.

These are my party stories.

It's early afternoon and cars are whizzing by me as I walk to the liquor store.

A truck honks and I jump and snap my head to look around for possible predators.

My face goes red and my nerves are tingling.

I start walking faster, like someone is following me but I don't want them to know I know.

Then I see the sign — *LIQUOR* — getting closer and closer.

I feel hopeful.

I tell myself that the day is about to take a dramatic shift.

Once you get a drink, your life will take an upward climb.

And even it doesn't, who cares?

I do.

But hope is all you need!

Nope, you're the human equivalent to debris removed from a vehicular manslaughter victim's belly-button, and you're the worst kind of unoriginal.

Alright.

I keep walking.

The place I get all my booze is called Davey Jones' Liquor Locker. It's owned by a Russian family who drink all day and don't like people. Which of course means I want them to adopt me and pass on the store to me when they all die. I could change my name to Davey and wear t-shirts that say, "The Locker" in that block-lettering they use on sport's uniforms. "Give Up, With Us," written on the back.

The first time I went in to Davey Jones' Liquor Locker, the old man (the grandfather?) who owns the place was drinking straight out of a vodka bottle behind the register. It was late and the only other customers were a pair of young women that were heading to a party. They kept talking about the party and they were wandering around and checking their phones, only looking up to say fragments of a conversation to each other.

One of them would say something like, "Did you hear what (girl) did at (guy's) house?" And the other would say, "God, what a slut. I wonder if (other guy) knows." Then they would both look back down at their screens and just sort of coast through the aisles.

Finally, they picked up a bottle of white wine and walked up to the register together. The old man looked crazy-drunk and stupid-angry. He'd been watching the women too.

As they joked around and dug deep in their purses looking for cash the man's face started to tighten and his mouth was quivering. You could see years and years of anger that he'd stored up, ready to be heaved out whenever he pleased, just twisting around in his fat little pot-belly. It was beautiful. I wanted to kiss it (the belly). I wanted him to be my dad.

"Umm, do you sell ping-pong balls?" one of the women said. "Cause, I don't see them."

And that was it.

He started screaming in his native language—a lot of hard R's and Shk sounds—while alternating between pulling at clumps of his hair and pounding his fists on the counter.

The women left as quickly as possible, didn't even take the wine.

And then when I walked up to the counter, the man acted like nothing had happened.

This is my liquor store, my spot.

I walk past the "Never Trust a Man Who Doesn't Drink" sign that is written on a chalkboard out front and head straight for the cheap whiskey. I reach for a bottle but hear my stomach bark. I haven't eaten since yesterday morning, so I redirect to the cases of beer that are lined up on the bottom of the fridge

They look delicious.

It is the beginning of something.

This is how I'll turn it all around.

I grab two and head to the counter, where the man working today is sitting in a fold up chair and scrolling through his phone.

"This all?" he says.

"Yeah."

He scans the beer and my eyes dart behind the counter, next to his chair, where I can see the expensive Vodka he's been sipping from all day. A little shot glass next to it.

I hand him my card.

"How are we today?" he says.

"Good," I say. "You?"

"Very good today," he says. "Last night I watched Ape

movie. Have you seen Ape movie?"

"What?"

"World of apes," he gestures like I'm crazy for not knowing. "With James Frunko."

"Oh, no, I haven't."

"Ahh," he smiles. "You must watch this movie. Very good. New movie, the part two, is coming soon."

"Yeah," I smile. "I'll check it out."

I swipe my credit and I can feel him staring at me, then staring down at the beer.

"Can I ask something?" he says.

"Sure."

"Why you drink thees piss?"

I look at the cases of beer. They still look beautiful. Shiny and brilliant under the fluorescent lights of the store.

"I like beer," I shrug.

He puts his index finger up in the air and walks into the back room of the store. A few minutes later he comes out holding an unmarked bottle full of clear liquid.

"I like you," he says. "I see you often."

"Yeah. This is my spot."

"So," he holds out the bottle. "I give this to you as gift. I make this. Very good."

I grab the bottle and look at it.

"Drink," he says. "No one gives fuck."

I unscrew the cap and the smell hits me immediately. It reminds me of whatever they use to preserve body parts. I don't know exactly what that smells like but I think it'd smell like this.

"Go on," he says.

I tip it back and let it burn through my throat and into my stomach, trying not to wince. It tastes like it smells. Deadly.

"Good," he says. "Yes?"

"Fuck yes."

I stick the bottle in my jacket and grab the cases of beer.

Then walking home, I start to feel it.

The magic.

I'm smiling like an idiot the whole walk back, thinking about how far this gift will get me. I can get drunk for three days straight then charge it all to my card again when the time comes for more. Like plastic money.

College is for fools.

13.

I'm walking down the hall to the bathroom for a shower.
Because I haven't been showering.

It's too difficult.

I only take the journey through the building when it's very early in the morning, when I'm not too drunk and everyone else is asleep. Otherwise it's just depressing. Something about seeing a grown man walk out with an embarrassed smile, nodding at the people in the line that has formed as he shit out last night's microwave dinner. Just, bad for everyone. Not the worst thing, but pretty bad.

The real issue is the toilets. The never-ending battle between the toilets and my neighbors. The great war. Toilets breaking constantly, neighbors too ashamed to admit they've made a mess or that they shit at all, and on and on.

One of only a few things I know for sure, is that the world would be a better place if people acknowledged the fact that everybody shits.

I don't understand why people don't admit it.

We are animals.

And I embrace that.

This is my contribution to humanity. Walking out and looking at the next person in line and saying, "I just shit in there," or something to that effect. Then saluting them and wishing them luck.

No one ever laughs though.

No one wants to be an animal with me.

There is one other tenant in the building who shares my philosophy but I don't know their name. They just leave these notes. Notes of truth, honor, and courage, taped to the inside of the bathroom door.

The first one I saw said:

Please stop neglecting toilets.
If they need repair contact Kevin
or the building owner.
If I have to walk in and see yet
another strange bowel movement,
nestled around sheets of toilet paper and clogging the
mechanism, I won't be the one to
call and fix the problem.
Hopefully this teaches you all a lesson
about responsibility.
Don't be embarrassed. It's only shit.
Everyone does it.

I turn the key in the bathroom door and hold my breath, preparing for the worst.

But the toilet is clean, the window is open.

I strip off my clothes and turn on the shower. That hissing sound starts and stops and as I wait for the water to heat up, I accidently catch a glimpse of myself in the mirror.

It's really bad. It looks like I might snap in half. My skin is stretched tightly over my ribs and my chest is all sunken in.

I've done this to myself though. I accept it. And if I think about it a certain way it feels like I'm doing something necessary, suffering for a reason.

Or maybe I'm just a spoiled idiot and I accept that too.

I step in the shower. The water is still cold but I've already committed. The time has come, dirty boy. The weekly washing.

I scrub — nay — exterminate every last bit of filth on my body with lightning speed, trash talking the germs like, "don't come back bitch!" Then I step out, feeling a little less like a piece of shit.

As I dry off, I take another look in the mirror and flex my stringy biceps.

I throw a few punches, left left, big right.

Fuck you germs!

Fuck you neighbors!

Tell us about your shits!

Then I lean in close to my reflection and whisper, "Everyone does it," before walking out the door quickly.

So quickly, that I bump into someone that has been waiting.

Standing right in front of me, laughing, is Annie.

The line has already started.

I'd wasted too much time.

"Hey stranger," she says.

"Hello," I say, and adjust my underwear, making sure my dick is fully secure.

"Is it safe?" she laughs. "You look like you just did something embarrassing in there."

"Yeah. I mean no," I say. "It's all clear."

I look over her shoulder and indicate that I will be leaving now, but she keeps talking.

She says, "I'm glad I caught you actually."

And I nod and smile but feel intensely uncomfortable. I imagine my boxers falling down, my dick flapping about, prison time inevitable.

"What's up?" I say.

"I was just wondering if you had anything going on this

weekend? You know, other than hiding in your room?"

"Is that all you think I do?"

I imagine her fantasizing about me in my room, and also secretly wanting my towel to drop this very instant. Will the sight of my dick make her gasp and embrace me in the middle of the hallway? Is this considered a toxic/misogynistic thought? I don't care. How would we both react to my towel dropping? Would I run away, duck-like with my boxers around my ankles yelling, "It's usually bigger!" or would I play it cool?

"I don't *think* anything," Annie says. "I *know* you don't leave your room. "But me and my friend saw you the other day, talking to those homeless guys across the street, and she said she wanted to meet you."

"Who's your friend?"

"You'll like her," she groans. "Just, trust me. Meet us around ten o'clock tomorrow night, out front. We're going out drinking. It'll be fun."

I hesitate.

Just stand there like an idiot.

Not saying anything, but thinking the same old things.

I don't want to meet anyone.

No.

I want to drink in my room.

I want my hiding to be okay with people.

Can't I just hide?

Is that not acceptable?

Does this mean she doesn't want to have sex in the bathroom?

No.

"Look," Annie says. "I tried to tell her, like, to warn her. But for some reason she wants to meet you. Yes or no?"

"Yes," I say.

"Good," she says, and walks into the bathroom.

I feel tricked, but force myself to think differently.
A new mantra.
I will go out and meet people.
I will have fun.
This is what I need.
This will help.
Everyone does it.

14.

I'm standing shoulder to shoulder with strangers in a crowded bar, sipping a seven-dollar beer.

Everyone around me looks excited.

I am not excited.

I never get excited unless I'm alone.

Not even sure that counts.

I'm not a full human being.

That's what I keep thinking.

I'm supposed to be having fun.

But all I can do is think about how I can't have fun.

Fun is something you earn, I think, you're not entitled to fun.

I'm not entitled to anything.

I don't deserve this.

Not even sure I want this.

What I'd like most is to return to fetus state, or become a disembodied voice, reminding people that they are entitled to nothing.

I don't know.

Sometimes I get very dramatic and self-deprecating when I'm uncomfortable.

Other times I think that being self-deprecating is self-centered and pointless.

If that's true then I would have nothing not-self-centered

to say.

I should probably kill myself and take everyone at this bar with me.

I whisper, "Take em' out, me first."

Then I look around.

Annie and her friend are on the dance floor. Flashing red and blue and green and purple lights are illuminating their smiles. And about six feet above them, a DJ wearing big gold headphones is bobbing his head and waving his arm as he turns knobs behind a booth.

It's the most fun in one room that I've ever witnessed.

I imagine myself climbing on top of the turntables, doing fist-pumps to excite the crowd. Then jumping off head first into the hard dance floor, and repeating it until I'm no longer able to.

The people, drunk and unfazed, still dancing to some pop song—"I-I-I'm a champion, oh yeah!"—while I bleed out at their feet.

Juxtaposition.

I finish my beer and try to get the attention of the bartender. Everyone else is doing the same so it's difficult. I raise my hand as he walks by, calling out to him. But it doesn't work.

I lean in further, smile, almost begging, but a drunk man forcefully nudges his way in next to me and I trip, bumping into a man on the other side of me. Butt to Butt.

When I turn to apologize to him, fully prepared to offer my life for his forgiveness, he doesn't give me the opportunity. He's just yelling at me. Really close to my face. Spit flying. I can't hear him but I'm pretty sure he's saying something about respect. I'm reading his lips and his mouth seems to form that word over and over.

R-E-S-P-E-C-T.

As I stare at his lips, I start to imagine what would happen if I leaned in and bit the bottom one. Would it start a chain of events that ends in my death? Would they remember me? Sing songs for me?

But the man starts to calm down.

He's gotten it out of his system.

He lifts his drink towards me and I clink my empty bottle together with it, mouthing, "Fuck yeah," while he nods in agreement.

We are buddies now.

I picture myself challenging him to friendly chugging game.

Him agreeing and counting down.

Three.

Two.

Then right at the moment he says "One" I pull out a bottle cartoonishly labeled POISON and start guzzling it down.

I'm a champion, oh, oh, yeah!

By the time I get another drink, Annie and her friend are taking a break from dancing. They're standing behind me, trying to wave down the bartender. I tell them it's going to take a while.

"I've been in your shoes," I say, "I feel for you."

But Annie's friend just smirks, leans in toward the bartender, brushing up against me.

Within a minute she has two drinks in her hands.

"Thanks!" she screams, then turns to me and raises her eyebrows.

Her name is Veronica. Or Monica, maybe. Annie forgot to introduce us. I only remembered that it's expected of me to ask her name when we got to the bar. She shouted it at me as loud as she could over the music, twice, but I'm still not sure.

Monica.

Or Veronica, maybe.

She's got hair and eyes and a nose and ears. She's wearing

a sparkly dress and she smells so good it makes me self-conscious of my own smell.

She leans over me again, handing one of the drinks to Annie.

Annie say thanks and walks off, leaving Monica and I alone.

"Where are you from?!" she screams.

"Arizona! You!?"

"I'm from here, born and raised!"

"Nice!"

"You wanna dance!?"

"Okay!"

She grabs my hand and leads me through the crowd. We squeeze by a guy who's holding his shirt up and flexing his stomach, then we slink past a woman who's rubbing a man's dick-area with her thigh while dancing and sipping a beer simultaneously.

We get to the center of the dance floor. We start dancing. I'm a fairly decent dancer, but I lack conviction. I wish I was a great dancer. I think about that thing people say in regards to dancing, how you can tell if someone is good at sex based on how they dance, and it inspires me.

I decide to dance so far over my head that everyone in the bar will circle around and chant my name.

I'd like that.

It would be the beginning of something, a victory I never thought was possible.

Dance Champion of Venice.

I begin by raising my arms high, rolling my shoulders, shaking my hands slightly and moving my head left to right, just to warm up. And to smell my armpits without anyone noticing.

Then I go freestyle-- slight, sleek, unplanned movements.

Monica likes it.

She scrunches her face and makes an O shape with her mouth, in recognition of my ability. Then she gets even closer.

A new song comes on.

She looks excited.

She yells, "This is my song!" and starts rubbing her ass on me, her arms in the air, her hair all over the place, snake-like.

I switch up my style again.

Going for more of a relaxed, full-body swaying motion, and letting her take the lead.

I'm doing it.

From the outside perspective, I am having fun.

I'm built to dance.

Born to fuck.

A real boy.

As Monica dips up and down, I have full view of the bar.

I can see the other humans who are here to meet and potentially go home with other humans. I can see humans who are here to drink and forget about their job. I can see humans who are here because this is what they love to do. And then I can see Annie.

She's hidden in the corner, talking to a man I've never seen before. He looks very desperate and serious as he is talking to her. Annie just looks bored, at first. But as the man gets more animated and aggressive, begging and gesturing with his hands, she starts to look worried.

"Hey," I yell into Veronica's ear.

She's still facing the other direction.

"HEY!"

She turns around and brings her cheek next to mine.

"I think Annie needs help," I say.

She looks over in Annie's direction quickly, then turns back to me.

"Oh, she's fine," she says.

"No, I don't know, I think we should go check on her."

"SHE'S FINE!"

Monica pulls my face towards hers, hard.

Her teeth slam against mine and I feel her tongue sliding in and out of my mouth.

It's bad.

An image of myself flashes through my head, from the point of view of everyone around us, and it looks even worse. Like her jaw has dislocated itself to fit around my entire face.

I pull my mouth out from Veronica's, look back over at Annie.

But she's not there.

"What's wrong?" Monica says.

"Nothing," I say, "Let's get another drink."

She smiles and takes my hand again and leads me back to the bar.

We find a spot and she orders two more drinks.

There is some eye-contact.

Then she rests her hand on mine.

I look at it and it's strange.

Something like, "There's no TOUCHING!" runs through my mind and I want it to stop. Or maybe I want to bend her over the bar while everyone watches/hands us complimentary drinks/makes requests regarding our performance.

I don't know.

I look around the bar and try not to think about it.

"You okay?" Veronica says.

"I still don't see Annie."

"That was just one of her customers. He's a little crazy, but harmless."

"She sells in here?"

"Oh yeah," she scoffs. "Drunk people will overpay no questions asked."

"So, she left with him?"

"God no, I'm sure she's fine though. Annie wanders off a lot."

I nod, don't say anything.

She looks at me closely.

She's waiting.

Like I'm supposed to do something.

Lead her into the next phase of our lives.

But I don't what to say, except what I think she wants me to say.

"You want to go to my place?"

• • •

I'm lying down in my bed while Monica moves her ass up and down on me.

I don't feel much.

Maybe I'm too drunk.

But it's nice to look at, a very toned and soft ass.

Makes me want to take better care of my own ass.

Like do squats or trim my asshole hairs more frequently.

I don't know.

I'm supposed to feel like I've accomplished something in this moment.

I try to think back to the events of the night and pinpoint where I said or did something that made her want to come home with me, but nothing sticks out.

Maybe I was just there and that was enough.

That would be depressing.

Sometimes it makes me uncomfortable thinking about how easily people can get intimate with strangers.

No, that's childish.

I just have intimacy issues.

And, while intimate, I need to stop thinking about my intimacy issues.

I need to focus.

Focus on her.

I hope she comes.

I'm rooting for her.

I believe in her.

My chances of finishing are slim at this point.

Definitely too much booze, and too much thinking.

I can't stop imagining the obligations this might create going forward.

Will she want to text back and forth on a regular basis?

Will she think I am a bad person if I don't want to?

Am I a bad person?

I think I'll feel better about the situation if she comes.

She moans softly and speeds up her motions. Then I grab on to her hips and slightly lift myself up as she goes down. The sound of our bodies slapping together gets louder. She gets louder. But I don't make a sound.

I never make sounds.

Important to remember, when the opportunity presents itself, that I need to make some sort of sound so she thinks I've finished.

That is key.

I'm relieved she is facing away from me.

That this is the position she has chosen.

She is in her own world.

The rest of my body might as well not even be here.

I'm essentially a hairy dildo.

And it's working.

Her legs shake a bit and she goes all the way down, rocking back and forth and moaning softly.

My moment is here.

I squeeze hard on her hips, say, "Ahhh," in a way that I hope isn't creepy. Then she rolls off slowly and lies next to me, trying to slow her breathing.

"Hmm," she says. "I definitely needed that."

"Me too."

"Seriously. I know it's weird to say, especially now, but I haven't had sex in a while. My asshole boyfriend and I broke up a month ago and I don't know any guys that aren't friends with him. I've been like, such a loner."

"I hadn't either," I say. "In a while."

She looks around my room.

I'm embarrassed about my room.

But I don't want to make excuses for the state of it because that will only cause more humiliation.

"No offense," she says. "But your apartment isn't very welcoming. You might get laid more if you, I don't know, got some furniture."

"I don't think I can fit anything else."

"Yes you can," she says. "Doesn't have to be much. Maybe a desk? Dresser?"

"Your suggestion will be taken under consideration."

She pats me on the chest and stands up. The streetlight outside shines through my window and on to her naked body. I can't help staring. It really has been a long time. Too long. Because I have that sick, hopeful feeling as I watch her moving around.

She walks into the kitchen and pulls out a joint from her purse while I reach over and grab the whiskey bottle that's next to my bed.

She lays back down and we pass the joint and the bottle back and forth for a while in silence.

It's good.

If a relationship meant having sex then passing a bottle and joint back and forth in silence, I would be the best at relationships.

King of the relationship.

She passes me the bottle.

"What are you thinking about?" she says. "I know I'm not supposed to say that kind of stuff either but…"

"It's okay. I'm thinking that, if this was all a relationship was, I'd be really good at them."

"Me too," she says.

I take a sip.

"Is that why you and your boyfriend broke up?" I say.

"No, he asked if I wanted to be in an "open" relationship, which he knew I didn't. Then I found out from a friend he was on a dating app already, just to hook up with randoms, so I broke up with him. It also kind of ruined dating apps for me."

"Shit," I say, swapping the bottle for the joint with her. "That's bad."

"Yeah. I get that he like, didn't want to be tied down anymore but, just have the balls to say that you know?"

She lifts her leg and brushes some crumbs or dirt off my bed/mat.

I imagine it is mouse shit, that probably we just fucked in some mouse shit.

"Yeah," I say. "He should've done it differently. But I understand *why* he did it. Sometimes I'll pass an interesting looking woman on the street and think 'I love you' and genuinely want to be with her, or someone, for a long time. But then like five minutes later I'll be mad at myself for even thinking it. I'd hate myself for loving anyone because I know that I'm too selfish and afraid to be in a relationship. It's best if I'm alone and don't interfere with anyone's life or feelings."

"Dudes suck," she says.

"Yeah. But it's all in my head. So I really don't know

what would happen."

I hold out the joint in front of her.

"You can keep that," she says, standing back up. "I should go."

I look down at the joint, then take a drag and watch as she puts her clothes back on.

She puts on her underwear, her shoes, pulls her dress over her head.

Then gives me that look again.

What comes after this?

What is the next phase?

But this time I don't say anything.

"Okay," she laughs, walking to the door. "Text me. When you get some furniture, I mean."

"I will," I say.

She walks out the door.

And I feel relieved.

She never gave me her number.

15.

I'm walking to the sandwich place down the street.

I'm hungover.

I've been throwing up every morning, mostly bile, and my throat feels burned and raw.

I need to eat, need to keep the machine going.

I cross the street and walk pass the convenience store.

In front of the sandwich place, I see a homeless man pacing around and talking to himself. I've seen him before, hanging around Sticks and the others a few times, always jittery and looking up and down the street for something. But this time he seems scared.

I walk up to him, ask if he needs anything.

"Don't rat him out," he says. "Can't rat him out."

His eyes are wandering everywhere and he can't stop moving his head.

"I won't," I say. "I'm going in here to get a sandwich, you want anything?"

"Yeah, yeah," he says.

"You want a sandwich?" I say.

He makes a motion with his arms, waving them over each other back and forth.

"Chips," he says. "Just some chips."

"Okay. I'll be right back."

I walk in, tell the man behind the counter what bread

and meat I want, then move over to the toppings. They all look so colorful and fresh and nourishing and I have an epiphany. If I eat more vegetables, I will feel better. That's what I'm missing.

I picture myself picking fresh fruits and vegetables straight off trees and pulling them from the soil and skipping along eating them joyously, a fresh glow on my face.

"I want all of it," I say. "The spinach, tomatoes, peppers, everything. Give me all the greens."

"You got it," he says.

He piles it on, squishes it all together, then brings the sandwich over to the register.

"These too," I say.

He rings up the chips and the sandwich.

The price is higher than anticipated and I start to panic as I pull out my credit card.

I think back.

I know I haven't maxed it out yet but I can't help thinking the worst.

There is no foreseeable future in which I will be able to pay it back and because of this I feel guilty.

Always guilty.

So guilty that late at night I picture some big bad Credit Card Man staking out my apartment and taking notes on my daily routines, investigating me.

Monday 10:00 PM — Suspect is obviously unemployed. Bought two bottles of cheap whiskey from nearby liquor store and then didn't leave apartment for two days.

Friday 5:00 AM — Suspect wandered beach for hours, smoking cigarettes. Looks tired, possibly ill. He stares at ocean longingly, possibly suicidal.

Saturday 11:00 PM — Suspect walked around outside loud and packed bars, looking in at normal people. Suspect creeps me out, should probably drown himself in ocean.

After he pays debt, of course.

The card goes through.

"Here you go sir," the man says, sliding my sandwich toward me. "Have a good day."

I grab the sandwich, the chips, and walk out, looking up and down the street.

The homeless man isn't where I left him.

I walk slowly down the street in both directions, this dorky expression like, "nah wait a minute here!" until I see him huddled up outside the convenience store.

But when I get near him, he looks at me like I'm a predator.

He jolts up, starts walking away from me while shaking his hands and screaming.

"No man! Can't stay here! Can't rat him out!"

"Wait," I say calmly, "I brought you some chips."

I lift the bags of chips up to show him.

"I don't know man," he says. "I don't know, can't stay here."

"Me neither dude. Fuck that."

"Fuck that?"

"Yeah. I'm taking my sandwich and getting out of here."

He looks up at me curiously, making eye-contact for the first time.

"Yeah, yeah," he says. "Get the fuck out of here!"

He grabs the chips.

Our hands touch.

We're having a moment.

I picture myself forcing a gag and saying, "Ewww," really loudly, shaking my hand like it's infected.

But why?

The homeless man takes his chips and walks off.

I watch him stagger off toward the beach, talking to himself, eating quickly like he's afraid someone will take them.

Then I have another urge. An urge to join him. Just sit on the beach and eat my sandwich and never go back to my apartment or pay rent or my credit card bill. Ever.

I decide the lifestyle would suit me.

Going without a shower doesn't bother me and I don't want to be anything or accomplish anything and it's very possible that this is where my life is going anyway.

Why not get a head start?

I stop at a street corner and light a cigarette, weighing my options.

What kind of job could I do? What contribution to society could I make that'd help as much as completely dropping out of it? What job would suit me as well as being homeless would?

These are the questions that have been on people's minds for centuries, and there is something comforting in being a part of that.

I take a drag and decide my mantra for the day is, "centuries-old problems," and then I look at the world going on around me.

A shiny new sports car pulls over into a parking lot across the street from me.

An older woman steps out from it.

Her hair is long and gray and she's wearing big sunglasses and a warm coat.

Will she give me a job?

Could I be her servant?

Drive her around and answer her phone and clean her house and bathe her and be her confidant and sworn protector.

If required, I would be available sexually too.

Give me an honest wage and you may have me.

Do I have enough experience to put down, "Cunnilingus

Expert," on my resume?

I will practice.

In order to achieve your dreams, you must first hone your skills.

I imagine myself training, doing mouth exercises and trimming my mustache for the big interview.

I imagine being crowned.

The Golden Tongue.

America's Top Man-Whore.

The can't miss television event.

Maybe I could be a reality TV star.

Trying out to be the ultimate sex servant would be good TV.

Or I could be like those people that don't do anything but somehow end up being on TV, playing themselves.

The show would be called, "Trying to Not Be Homeless," and it would be about a bunch of eighteen to twenty-two-year old people just trying to find a job and make friends.

I would be the prototypical slacker, the comic relief, a loser, but America needs losers.

A professional at almost winning.

That's me.

Small victories, like deciding to get a bunch of vegetables on my sandwich in order to not feel like shit at all times, being my only taste of success.

I take a big bite of my sandwich.

It feels weird to be chewing and for a moment I feel afraid that I've forgotten how.

But the sandwich tastes bad anyway, like grass or something.

This is the price to pay for living a healthy lifestyle.

And I accept that.

Sandwich in one hand, cigarette still burning in the other, I start walking.

Without realizing it I'm going the same direction the homeless man went in, toward the beach.

I devour the rest of my sandwich, toss the wrapper in a trash can before I reach the boardwalk.

My stomach begins to hurt and I realize I ate too fast.

I always eat too fast.

I think about how, when I was younger, my Dad would make fun of me for eating whole meals without pausing to take a breath. Just shoving huge bites in my face and never leaving a scrap on my plate.

Could this be a skill needed for a job?

Charging people admission to see me fill myself with an unhealthy amount of food as quickly as possible.

"Will He Eat Himself to Death?!" being the big selling point.

So humiliating.

But necessary.

The necessary humiliation that must be endured to pay for things like food and shelter.

Will he explode?! Only five bucks, and that's what you might see!

Circus Eater Explodes While Trying to Pay Off Drinking Debt; Shits Himself.

I keep walking down the boardwalk.

I pass by couples and dog-walkers and I pass by restaurant after restaurant.

The smells start to make me gag.

My stomach now has this sinking feeling.

I have a very new, and very specific daydream of being sucked away by quicksand.

But then I see something magnificent.

A waiter carrying four plates at once out to a table on

the patio of a restaurant. Setting them down gracefully and without strain. Then the people at the table smiling and the waiter saying something that makes them all laugh and thank him.

It's perfection.

I look at him in awe.

He is better than me, a winner.

I could never be a waiter.

Convinced that I would do something to ruin the customer's appetites.

I picture myself trying to carry four plates at once and dropping every single one on the floor as the hungry customers look on in disgust. Then, like a shell-shocked war medic, kneeling down and scooping the food back on the plates and repeating, "I'll make it better! I'll make it good!" over and over.

I would need to be put in the back of the restaurant, unseen.

Could that be my career path?

Cleaning dishes and working my way up to a cook.

Would I be able to wash other people's dirty plates and cutlery without incident or soul-crushing defeat?

Very unlikely.

More likely that I would cut myself while washing a knife and decide right then to give up.

Just grab my gushing wound and slide down to the floor with my back against the sink, content with bleeding out right there.

Verdict: Dishwasher = Too Risky.

I ash my cigarette out on the ground and continue down the boardwalk.

There are a lot of people around.

Most of them are just walking.

And some of them are trying to sell things.

There's a man sitting behind a table full of his paintings, pictures mostly of Marilyn Monroe with tattoo sleeves and smoking joints. And there's an older woman selling home-made jewelry and there's a man with no shoes spray painting on a piece of sanded-down wood, his finished pieces displayed next to him with little price tags hanging off them.

It's tough to tell if all of them are homeless but most of them are.

I've seen them sleeping near the beach or begging all over Venice.

And at some point, during my time here, I've admired each and every one of them from a distance. Wishing I had the necessary skills to become friends with them or at least have a decent conversation with them. A conversation where I didn't come off like a spoiled little shit with delusions that being homeless is somehow an honorable choice, rather than a consequence of a cruel world I know nothing about.

In the distance, I see a man playing piano.

He has managed to set it on top of a large dolly.

I've seen him dragging the thing along the boardwalk under the hot sun before but I've never heard him play.

I stop in front of him and listen.

He's playing a sad song that sounds hundreds of years old.

His eyes are blueish grey and his hair is long and white and his clothes are filthy.

It is obvious he has seen much worse things than I have.

He's beautiful.

I wish I could give him money.

But I just stand there looking at him, listening.

After the song is over, it gets quiet and I don't know what to do next.

So I clap my hands.

No one else is clapping.

I feel like an idiot.

Most likely appearing to be an idiot.

I look around at the people walking and wonder if they are completely unaware of the piano man, or just unwilling to appear like an idiot.

It makes me want to scream at them.

Don't you see this man!? Do you not recognize beauty when it's right in front of you!? I'm not an idiot, promise!

But I just stand there, still applauding.

The man adjusts himself on the piano bench, then looks up at me.

We lock eyes.

He nods and says, "thanks," in a very soft voice.

Like I've embarrassed him.

He starts playing another song and I walk away in no particular direction.

16.

I'm standing on my toes, pissing into the sink again.

I've been doing it for a while.

The novelty has started to wear off and unforeseen consequences have arisen.

I've become paranoid.

Convinced someone will hear the distinct sound of piss hitting metal, then tell the landlord.

I'll be evicted.

Wherever I go, landlords, leasing offices, and even potential roommates will know of my sink-pissing.

The question isn't If.

The question is When.

If they haven't figured it out yet, then they will surely know when they see me in the hall.

They will take one look at me and know.

It'll be in my eyes.

They will see me for the disgusting cave-creature I am.

And the cycle will go on and on, until death.

I continue to sink-piss.

I've turned the faucet on and I'm aiming directly into the drain.

A sharp pain begins to build.

The worst and final consequence.

I'm pissing maybe thirteen to fifteen times a day but it

always feels like there's more in there. Then afterward I have this throbbing in the area between my balls and ass.

It's bad.

The only thing that helps with the pain is drugs or drinking.

But I'm pretty sure the pain is because of the drinking.

And you can't buy drugs with a credit card.

The cycle never ends.

17.

I'm sitting on my couch, hacking up phlegm and watching as Annie heats up soup for me.

I'm sick.

The soup is supposed to cure me, but it smells like it could kill. A smell that makes my head want to roll off my body, fall into my hands, everything feeling upside down, everything feeling strange.

I can't remember the last time someone made me food. Or the last time I was this sick. Like a really good bed-ridden illness. Illness that takes over your whole life. The best kind. The kind of sickness that I longed for as a kid. Begging and pleading for the sickness to strike in the middle of the night. Never expecting anyone to take care of me. Not wanting them to. Simply attracted to the idea of having no responsibilities or obligations. Sick and sedentary, a state of being. School out of the question. People avoiding me. Soup, nowhere in sight. Spoiled Brat Paradise.

Annie hands me the soup carefully, a paper towel underneath to keep from burning my lap.

"It's hot," she says.

I look down at it.

The soup is Annie's homemade bone broth and the bowl (my only bowl) hasn't been washed since I bought it. The combination of smells is bad. Like a farm full of animals all dying slowly together.

I take a sip and it burns my mouth and I have to gulp and clench my mouth to keep from vomiting everywhere.

"It's good," I say. "Thank you."

"You're welcome!"

Annie sits down next to me.

"Can I get you anything else?" she says.

"No, I don't need anything."

"Don't act tough," she laughs. "I know you're not tough. Let me get you some naturopathic stuff."

"What?"

"Let me get you some, oooh, some elderberry elixir or some ginger root. You'll feel like, instantly better."

She looks at my kitchen. There are empty bottles of booze and beer cans scattered all over, fast food wrappers sticking out of my trash can.

"Look at this shit," she says. "Your body needs more. You know, healthy things."

"I don't have the money to be healthy."

"Bullshit," she scoffs. "You're telling me this whiskey is free?"

"No. It's part of the plan."

"To drink yourself to death?"

"I need a job first," I say. "Then I can worry about elixirs and roots and things of that nature."

"It looks like your body is eating itself. That should worry you."

"I just need a drink. Not fancy food I can't afford."

"I have that shit in my apartment dummy. I was offering it to you."

"No," I say, hanging my head. "Don't be so nice."

"Why?"

"It makes me feel awful."

"You'd rather I be mean?"

"Yes."

"Fine."

She stands up.

"I won't offer you the job then."

"What?"

"No…" she says, walking to the door. "I'm not being nice to you anymore."

"What job? Like a runner? I can do that."

She stops at the door, sighs.

"No," she says. "Going out to the bars. I can't do it anymore. Too many broke dudes asking if I can smoke them out if they buy me a drink. I was just going to like, stop doing it, but I figured you could use the money."

"Isn't that kind of stupid? Dealing in public?" "Keep the drugs at your apartment and just go out and enjoy yourself."

"Annie," I say, and curl my lips inward, raising my eyebrows. "If I'm to be given a position in your business, my conduct will be just that. Business. I refuse to enjoy myself."

"Oh, fuck off. It's not hard. Just get drunk at a bar and find other drunk people who want to keep the party going."

"But the one and only appeal of selling drugs, other than always having drugs, is having people come to you."

"Most of my clientele are stoners," she says. "They don't mess with uppers. And I need to move this shit, like now."

"Why'd you buy it then?"

"Wishful thinking."

"Okay... I'll do it!" I say, like the job has already been given to me.

"Hell no. You don't want my help remember?"

I take the spoon out of the soup, glaring at her. Then I pour all the steaming hot liquid down my throat.

"Ahh," I say, breathing through my mouth to avoid the smell. "You're a miracle worker. What would I do without you?"

"Fuck you."

"Okay," I say. "I just realized that I don't want you to be mean anymore."

"So you want my help?"

"Yup."

"You want the job?"

"Yup."

"Good." She opens the door. "You start tomorrow. So I'll go grab my roots and elixirs and things of that nature right now. You don't want to be sick on your big first day."

"We can't have that."

Annie smiles, walks out.

As soon as the door closes behind her, I jump up and lean over the garbage. Waves and waves of it start pouring over fast food wrappers and empty beer bottles. An ocean of bone broth vomit.

I watch it flow out of me as if separated entirely from the act, like it's coming from someone else. Then after it's finished, I wipe my mouth.

"I'm employed," I say, staring at a chunk of celery. "I did it."

And a little bit of bile drips on to my beard.

18.

I'm standing at the bar, doing my job poorly.

Which means not doing anything.

I have moments when I think, "Here I go!"

But then something reaches up from under the bar and reminds me—You can't.

You will walk up to the strangers and they will recognize you as an other. Someone with too many thoughts that contradict their own. And then you will panic.

But I haven't panicked.

You will.

No I won't. I'm proud of myself. With a little luck, I will be a good drug-dealer. I have experienced panic attacks over things like doing my laundry, so I am convinced my nerves cannot tell the difference between every day obligations and criminal activity.

My superpower.

Which is also my weakness.

Which both eat each other and amount to nothing.

This is just more posturing.

This is more of the same.

This is the ABC's of Fuck Me Forever and Always.

Go get em' kid.

I look around the bar, searching for possible clients. It's packed. I don't know where to start.

Everyone here looks like their lives would not change in the slightest if I died right now in front of them.

I want to shake them by the shoulders-- "Weep for me!"

No I don't.

Maybe this is how it's supposed to be. If I reduce myself to something without thoughts or feelings, merely a vessel for money and drugs to pass through, maybe then I will succeed. Drug dealing, the anti-social way. The only way. If I stop referring to myself as a "drug dealer" every few seconds, then that might help too.

I drain my drink and take a lap around the bar, staring at each patron as I walk by and hoping they notice me. That's the plan. I don't know what my face is supposed to do, how I should walk, or anything that would convey that I'm a trustworthy person with hard drugs for sale, but this is the plan. Drift around and wait for confirmation I'm not a ghost.

The plan is failing.

Most of them don't notice me at all, and the ones that do avert their eyes quickly.

I circle the entire bar, accomplishing nothing, then sit down in the same spot, feeling inept.

The smell of failure and loneliness oozes out of me, while everyone else in the bar is clustered up and comfortable.

That must be my problem.

They are set in their ways and they do not want strangers (me) throwing off their dynamic.

I picture myself on a sinking ship, trying to squeeze into one of the life rafts and being denied by the other passengers.

I picture myself finally finding one that will have me, only to find out I was chosen as a sacrifice in case of shark attack/starvation.

Then I say to myself, "I'm expendable," and it makes everything clearer.

People that do not consistently enjoy other people's

company are expendable.

I'm expendable.

Tonight's mantra.

It plays in my head on a loop as I get up off the bar stool, and walk in to the bathroom.

At the urinals, there are two guys standing right next to each other.

They're staring intently at the wall a few inches from their faces while they relieve themselves.

Their bodies are so stiff and still it looks like they're consciously doing it.

Like, "Don't do it. Do NOT look at his dick."

I briefly think about putting my hands on their shoulders and whispering, "Want some cocaine?" and then trying to close a deal/conking their heads together and swapping the drugs for all their money while they're unconscious. But I just walk into one of the enclosed toilets and stand there, hiding.

I like it.

If I had to, I could stay here all night.

Make it a home.

The toilet is nicer than the toilet in my apartment building and there are a lot of carvings and graffiti on the walls for entertainment.

I'm set.

It's all I need.

I sit down on the closed toilet seat and read a few of the carvings.

One says, "Cops R Pigs."

Another, written in blue sharpie and in all caps, says "FUCK VENICE P.D."

It's very calming.

I imagine meeting the men who wrote them and telling them that I'm a drug dealer. Then becoming friends over the fact we both agree on the statements, "Cops R Pigs," and "Fuck Venice PD."

For the first time all night, I feel good.

Not right, but good.

I read a few more of the messages on the wall, then I stand up, unzip, and take a very painful piss.

I flush, then take off my shoe and dig out one the baggies to dull the pain.

Annie told me that I should leave the drugs at home, just to be safe, but I know myself.

If I have to go home to get the drugs I'll just stay there and do all of it.

This way, I'll only do a little bit of it.

I dig a little out with my keys and breathe it in, then I do it again, the sound of my snorts echoing off the bathroom walls and tile.

After I've done considerable damage to one of the baggies, I open the door and walk out of the stall.

Right in front of me, almost waiting for me, is a man in a blue suit.

He's smiling.

There is very little chance he doesn't know what I've been up to.

"Hey," he says.

"Hey," I say.

But what I mean is, I confess. I don't care anymore. I'm the only drug dealer in the entire history of drug dealing to be busted before he even deals drugs, but that's okay. You'll get no more trouble from me.

"Easy dude, relax," the man says. "Just want to know if you're sharing tonight?"

I take a deep breath, letting myself enjoy the numbness in the back of my throat.

I tell him I might be willing to share.

He smiles, walks into the handicapped stall.

I follow.

He pulls out his wallet and starts giving me his story. He says it's not for him. But he really appreciates this.

"I've got this girl with me tonight," he says. "One of those chicks that will go wherever the party is, if you know what I mean. And she's been on her phone for like, the last twenty minutes, asking around for a better scene."

I get into my character, which basically just means copying what I've seen in movies.

"I understand," I say. "But I don't have much on me."

"Please man. I'm dying here. This girl is too fuckin' hot to let go of. I swear. Dude. I'll buy whatever you have for whatever you want. Time is of the essence."

I nod.

I close the stall door.

I wiggle my toes, massaging the six little gram-bags that Annie weighed out for me that are lining my left shoe.

"How much cash you got?" I whisper.

He rifles through his bills anxiously and says, "Two-hundred, like Two-hundred."

"Ok," I say. "But I will need all of it. This is good stuff."

Now even I'm buying it.

I dig out one of the bags and hold it in front of him.

He looks at it closely, weighing it with his eyes.

We both know what's happening.

I'm ripping him off.

He's desperate.

And I'm just high enough to be okay with it, just out of my head enough to not screw this up.

"You're robbing me blind," he says. "But fuck it."

He hands me the money, takes the bag, runs out.

I linger there, counting it.

One-hundred and eighty-three American dollars.

Next time I'll count it first.

I'm learning.

I'm one of the unhappily employed. And I can't help but feel a sense of accomplishment. Maybe I've found my calling, maybe I'll get lucky.

Maybe.

I walk back to the bar and order some top shelf whiskey, a double.

19.

I'm on a website that lonely people go on to meet other lonely people.

I've been drinking all morning.

I feel invincible, yet deathly low.

After my third or fourth beer, I decided I'd go on the lonely people website for some laughs, and also for some research.

Research for what exactly, I'm not sure.

It just sounds better.

The first ad I see says: **Hipster Boyfriend Wanted**

And the desired effect happens.

I laugh, then click on the link to read further.

It explains what the word "hipster" means to her, sort of making fun of it, as well as a confession about just wanting a "friend" more than a "boyfriend".

It's a good ad.

I laugh again, for a different reason, then something inside me goes warm and I start writing an e-mail.

I have every intention of making it short and kind, just to talk to someone, but I end up writing a long story about the last time I was out at the bars on Main St.

I'd gotten too drunk and ended up dancing with a woman who worked at a strip club. She was a bikini waitress, not a stripper, and was very worried that I wouldn't understand the difference. But I would've liked her even if she was a stripper. Her hair smelled nice and I got a hard-on as we danced. Then we smoked a cigarette out back and I asked for her number. She gave it to me. But at the end of the night I tried to kiss her and she pulled away. So I went home and felt awful, like a rapist or something.

The end.

I send the e-mail and get a response immediately.

She thanks me for responding and says that I'm funny, and do I want to see a picture of her?

I say yes.

Thirty minutes later, I get a photo of a very young-looking girl wearing glasses, and nothing else.

Next to the photo there is caption.

It says: **U wanna to meet irl? I wanna know what yr hands feel like around my neck.**

I don't respond.

20.

"Well," I say. "What can I do?"

Mouse just sits there in his corner, looking up at me, not saying anything.

I don't expect him to say anything.

It's just nice to say things out loud sometimes, let the bad thoughts travel.

I'm in a bad way.

No beer.

No weed.

No help.

Annie left town with her friends a few days ago and she didn't tell me she was leaving until she was in the act of leaving.

She gave me the last few baggies to sell, said "see ya next week!" and then walked out the door.

That's a problem.

I've been relying on Annie.

Fresh hasn't been answering my texts and I can't go asking around today.

Just, can't do it.

The only thing I can do is talk to Mouse.

"What can I do?" I say. "Should I call Fresh?"

He looks down at the floor, probably just searching for crumbs, but I take it as a sign.

He's telling me, "Yes, you should call him."

He's daring me, "Do it, coward."

He's telling me, in his own inimitable way, "You got this, brother."

I pull out my phone and look at Fresh's info. Our conversations over text have been as brief and vague as possible and I suspect that he, like I suspect of everyone else, would rather I just leave him alone. But I decide to call him anyway.

I hit the button and press the phone against my ear.

No answer.

I hit the button again.

No answer.

Then a few minutes later I get a text from him:

Who dis?

Ty.

And?

You free?

Sry. Dunno what u mean.

Fresh, buddy. It's Ty. Your bruh bruh.

You got the wrong number sir. God bless you n yours!

Fuck.

He's found god.

I yell, "FUCK YOU!" Cursing him (God) and all he stands for. Then I throw my phone to the end of my bed and look down at Mouse.

He's frozen scared. His nose starts twitching and then his legs are moving fast, running along the side of my bed and into the kitchen and disappearing behind the sink.

I feel bad.

I shouldn't yell.

"I'm sorry," I say, addressing everything.

I'm sorry about my voice.

I know it sounds awful, painful to listen to.

I'm sorry.

I clear my throat, take a sip of whiskey, then reach for a cigarette.

A cigarette is what I can do.

The thought of smoking instantly makes things easier.

But I'm out of cigarettes.

All I hear is the residue flakes of tobacco rattling around the empty box and I can't even look inside.

It's too depressing.

Oh precious nicotine addiction I hate you.

I don't need you.

Oh yes I do, I feel you pulling at the back of my neck.

And I feel you too, sacred-fear-of-convenience-store-employees, you have been heard, you have been seen, don't you worry.

It'll be over soon.

• • •

Outside the convenience store, Sticks is asking around for change in his usual spot.

He looks like he's having a hard time.

"Whaddya know?" he says.

"Need smokes," I say. "Be right back."

Sticks nods and I can hear him politely ask the person behind me for change as I walk in.

Inside, the man behind the counter rings up my cigarettes and tells me a half-story about this woman he knew, way back, who smoked these same cigarettes, and now has cancer.

"Anyway," he says. "Enjoy the rest of your day."

I walk out and immediately light two, handing one to Sticks.

We drag deeply, trying not to exhale in passerby's faces.

"Thank you sir," he says.

"No problem. How's it going?"

"Well, I've been better. You remember Ron Ron?"

I puff from my cigarette a few times and hold it in.

"I think so," I say.

"He's the one that gets confused sometimes. Like, worrying about cops coming to get him."

"Yeah," I say, thinking about the man I'd bought chips for a while back. "I know him."

"Well, Ron Ron has some problems. And last night, when we were walking around, he started really losing it."

Sticks points in the direction where they were, by a busy intersection.

"He was accusing everyone of ratting him out. I don't know. He was just really going crazy and running around and calling everyone a snitch. So, the other guy with me, you don't know him-- hell, I barely know him-- he started yelling back at Ron Ron. Shit escalated. I was saying to both of em' real calm, 'Relax y'all. Relax' but they didn't listen. Ron Ron got right up in this guy's face screaming 'RAT! YOU FILTHY RAT!' and then they started shovin' each other. Meanwhile, cars are just whizzing by."

He makes a motion with the cigarette, demonstrating the vehicles speed.

"And I could just see it all goin' wrong. I tried to break it up but then Ron Ron got in *my* face. So I told him, and I feel awful about it, I told him 'Fuck you, Crazy-Ass!' And man, did he seem hurt, like I'd betrayed him. I don't know. He just looked really sad and then he ran off."

"Shit," I say.

"Yeah," Sticks says. "I didn't mean to, I just lost my cool. He *was* off his damn rocker, but he's my friend ya know?"

"Yeah. Where's Ron Ron now?" I ask.

"No one can find him," Sticks says, looking off into the

distance. "And his stuff is in the same spot as usual, where the rest of us keep it, so I'm worried something happened to him."

"Well," I say. "If there's a spot opening in your gang, please put me on the waiting list. I got a job now, kind of, but you never know."

Sticks doesn't say anything.

He just looks down, throws the cigarette on the ground and puts it out with his shoe.

"I'm kidding man," I say. "Sorry. Shouldn't have said that. If I see Ron Ron I'll do what I can to help."

"Yeah," Sticks says. "Okay."

I ash my cigarette out and offer him another to stick behind his ear, like usual, but he shakes his head.

"No thanks," he says. "Trying to cut down."

• • •

Back at my apartment, I lay on my bed and pull out my phone.

I start praying for a miracle.

Hoping for good news.

Hoping for anything.

But I remember I'd cursed the miracle-maker a mere half-hour ago, and there isn't any new messages.

I start re-reading the conversation with Fresh.

I try to picture what circumstances he must have been in to resort to the eternally feared "Who Dis?" text.

I can see glimpses.

Show me your world, dear Fresh, tell me what went wrong.

Yes, go on.

I can see you running for your life, being hunted by an army of tinted black SUV's, ducking around corners, time

111

running out on your freedom, when suddenly my message pops up, and you realize what must be done, suffering as you write those words, those words of necessary evil, setting me free the only way you can, the toughest of love.

Thank you, thank you Fresh, loyal Fresh, in another life we will be forever pals and together we will run LA, kill everyone.

But not in this lifetime.

Goodbye Fresh.

I look around my room, paranoid about everything and everyone, then light a cigarette right there in bed.

It doesn't calm me though.

I get scared about people smelling the smoke and kicking me out, vigilante style.

My paranoia increases and a very bland fantasy plays out in my head where my neighbors and the building manager Kevin conduct an investigation about where the smoke might be coming from.

Who could it be?

Who is the inconsiderate asshole?

It is I!

God bless you n yours!

I inhale from my cigarette, feeling slightly okay about being the asshole.

Then I pick my phone back up, staring at the names in the inbox for a while.

There are only three names though so it's not very exciting.

I click Annie's name and start typing.

I confess to her about the smoking inside and I tell her about my day, about Mouse, about Sticks, about Fresh finding god/being phone-tapped by the CIA. And on and on until I realize what I've just written down would make her think I've lost my mind.

I delete it all.
Then try again:

Hey, hope your trip is going well. Do you know when exactly you'll be back?

I send it off into space and close my eyes.
Hoping I'll fall asleep.
Sweet dreams, asshole.
But I don't fall asleep.

21.

I'm hunched over the bar at one of the usual spots.

I'm drunk, dressed in my finest attire, the baggies Annie left behind tucked safely in my shoe.

I wiggle my toes and look around for potential clients.

A woman I've seen around a few times makes eye-contact and walks directly up to me.

She's young and confident and also drunk.

"Hi!" she screams in my ear. "I know you. Don't I?!"

I shake my head, "No," and look around for the joke to reveal itself.

But all I see is a man with slicked back hair and a goatee on the other side of the bar.

He is watching the woman and I.

He looks familiar.

I try and remember if I've ever seen him with the woman before but my memories of the last few weeks are all half-dreams and hangovers.

The woman puts her hand on my shoulder.

"Did you hear me? I know Annie," she says. "She's a friend of a friend, and the friend told me..."

"Oh... yeah, I can help you out."

"Great! Where should we go?"

"In the back. Smoking area."

I tell her to wait here a minute.

I don't know why I say this. It just sounds like a drug-dealer thing to say. And for some reason I feel the need to play up the toughness.

As I get near the back door I turn and see the goatee man is still watching me, but I ignore it.

In the smoking area, four or five other people are on their phones or coupled up.

They're talking and distracted, completely unaware of me.

I light a cigarette and after a few drags, the woman walks out. The lighting is much brighter and I can see her clearly. She's my age, maybe younger, caked in makeup and wearing a dress that looks like it might burst.

"Can I get a light?" she says.

She pulls out a pack of menthols and I hand the lighter over.

"Thanks. My boyfriend stole mine earlier. Says I'm smoking too much."

I look around at the other people nearby again, then ask if I can see her pack.

"Yeah," she says. "Don't make fun of me though. I just can't stand the taste of regular cigarettes."

I tell her I won't, then I bend down to tie my shoe.

Before bringing a baggie back up with me I hesitate.

I have no idea why I hesitate but that's what is happening.

I tell myself it's okay.

I will be okay.

She is not a cop, too young.

She doesn't want anything other drugs, too skinny to murder you with her bare hands.

Okay.

I stand and slip the baggie in with her cigarettes.

Her face lights up and she quickly reaches for the small purse hanging from her forearm.

"What's this going to cost me?" she says.

I look down at my feet and drag my cigarette.

"Well," I say. "This is… the good stuff."

"Oh, cool. The thing is, I have like, no idea how this works. But it's exciting."

"Really?"

"Yeah, really."

I look at her closely.

She reminds me of someone.

Someone I knew a long time ago.

And then I understand my hesitation.

"How old are you?" I say, but I don't know why I say it. It just comes out and she frowns and I know I've made a mistake.

"Don't tell anyone, coke-guy," she slurs. "Just… shush."

I look around again, hoping no one heard her.

Then I play out my options.

I imagine selling to her, being locked away for life.

I imagine snorting it all right here and now, dying.

I imagine myself as the hero, dumping the baggies out on the ground and carrying her home to her parents, piggy-back style.

But it all feels wrong.

"Dude, come on," she says. "How much?"

I open the flap of her cigarettes, take the baggie out and stick it in my pocket, then hand the pack back to her.

"I'm sorry."

I toss my smoke and make for the door.

But as I pass her, she grabs my arm.

"Seriously," she says, in a way that makes me feel bad for her. "What's yer problem?"

"I really am sorry," I say. "But I'm retiring."

"What the hell does that mean?!"

"You're a child."

"Fuck you!"

She grips tighter.

I feel like closing my eyes and making really loud obnoxious noises so she'll go away.

But instead I just look around at the other people smoking again.

They're not moving at all.

Pretending we aren't here.

I can't be mad at them.

I would do the same.

When I turn back to face the woman, explain my way out of this by any means necessary, I lock eyes with the man with the goatee.

He's got his arm around the woman's shoulder, looking at me with intent to kill.

He says, "Everything okay Babe?"

And babe says, "This guy just asked me if I wanted to do coke with him back at his place!"

And I just stand there, watching them, feeling like they could be talking about anyone. Anyone but me. I'm just a watcher. An observer. They feel miles away in every sense. But no matter what I say, I'm the bad-guy. I can feel the man visualizing what he wants to do to my face and the woman just smirks, blood-thirsty.

This is their movie, and I am the villain.

The man steps closer.

"Motherfucker!" he says. "Did you ask my girlfriend to come home with you?"

His neck muscles are flexing.

His face is red.

His fists are clenched.

And now I picture him as the the hero, big fucking cape and everything.

But it's not quite right either.

"Yes," I say. "I asked her. And she was thinking about it before you showed up."

His left arm still around his girl, Goatee cracks into my nose.

Quick right jab.

My head barely moves but my entire face feels different and all I can do is stand there.

It never even occurs to me to hit him back.

I look deep in his eyes, watching the violence build, and I can see that he wants more, he wants mayhem, a fight to the death, good vs. evil.

But I won't give it to him.

"What's wrong?" I say, licking the blood from my mustache. "Finish him."

He rears back. Right before impact I think, "Victory!" Then fall back like a cannonball is blowing through my shins. Head bouncing off the concrete, feet in the air like defeated prey.

Finished.

I feel my nose go numb and through my blurry eyes I look up at the night sky.

From my perspective, it looks like home. I want to go home. I want my body hurled into space, orbiting the earth like a guardian angel. Yes, an angel. The ultimate hero.

I blow a kiss to the invisible stars and wait for them to summon me, their long-lost brother. But it doesn't happen. The goatee man walks over to me and blocks my view. All I can see is his face. The interchangeable face of my enemy. His mouth is moving but my ears are ringing like EEEEEEE so I can't hear what he's saying. I want to know what he's saying. What are his words of triumph? I want to learn from him. So I look closely at his mouth. He forms his lips into a small circle, then sends something wet and slimy on to my cheek before walking off with the girl.

A goodbye gift.

Thank you!

You're welcome.

I'll never wash it off.

• • •

I'm walking in to the liquor store.

I feel like laughing.

But something inside has taken a break and all I feel is coldness.

I head straight for the beer.

In the reflection of the door I can see my face.

The cocktail napkin shoved in my nostril and the swelling in my jaw make it look like one half of my face belongs to someone else. My evil bloated twin. It looks right. The universe evening things out.

I grab a beer, down it, grab another, then walk over to the whiskey.

I pick up a bottle with my unoccupied hand and walk to the front, trying not to think about the pain, and wondering what kind of mantra could block this out.

"There is no hero."

"Acting the villain out of fear of anything else."

"There is no villain."

But none of them make any difference.

Fuck mantras.

At the counter, the man rings up both bottles without looking at me. He's scrolling through his phone, shaking his head and paying no attention to me.

"That will be fifteen twenty-seven," he says.

I hand him my card.

He looks at it, then up at me.

"Hey! Oh… You were in accident?"

"No. Just the universe evening things out."

He's completely unfazed. This is normal. This is sameness. He looks back at his phone and says, "Listen, my friend. I have another question. Do you know Yeelp?"

"Like the app for restaurants?"

"Yes, the app. Do you know how to delete comment?"

The napkin slips out of my nose and I catch some blood with my tongue before sticking it back in.

"Like a review?" I say.

"Yes," he nods, squinting his eyes. "People here tell lies, all lies. I need to delete from page."

"I don't think you can do that man."

"Peermanent?"

"Unfortunately," I say. "I believe the yelp reviews are permanent."

He shakes his head and turns his phone towards me.

"Look at thees fuck, thees liar. Beely R," he says.

I grab the phone and start reading a comment by this "Billy R."

It basically talks about how he's suspicious of the owners because he bought an expensive bottle of Scotch and it tasted cheap and watered down.

"Shit," I say.

"Yes shit fuck Beely R. and his Scotch. If he comes in again…" He grabs the bottle he just rung up and motions like he's hammering something with it. "Kertains for him."

"Run the Billy R. show out of town," I say.

"Shaat it down," he laughs. "For good."

"I hope I'm here for that," I say. "Then we can kill him together."

He holds up his finger.

"Easy," he says, lowering his voice and looking around the store. "Keep coowal."

I put my hands in the air, keeping cool.

We laugh.

It is a mildly successful interaction.

He bags up my bottles and slides them over to me.

"Thanks man," I say.

"Very welcome sir."

He winks, waves goodbye with his phone still in hand.

"See you soon!"

• • •

When I get near my building, I see Beckett in the parking lot.

He's picking the fresh batch of cigarettes off the hood of his car and talking to himself under his breath.

I walk up next to him and flick one of the butts off the car.

"Hey Beckett," I say.

He stares coldly at his car and says, "Hello," like he could be talking to anyone.

It looks like he's about to snap.

He's approaching his breaking point.

The next cigarette might be the last before chaos ensues and he ends up killing everyone in the building. Me being first, of course. I can absolutely see that happening. Beckett busting in my door with a knife in one hand and a lit cigarette in the other, methodically stabbing me just to the point where I'm paralyzed but still conscious, then putting out the cigarette on my eyeballs and screaming, "Why!? Why me!?"

"So," I say, flicking another cigarette off the hood. "I've been meaning to talk to you."

"Yeah?"

"I know who's doing this."

Beckett looks up at me, a glimmer of hope in his eyes. "Are you ekh ekh sure?"

"Yeah. It's the people right above me."

I point to their window, right above us.

"I knew it!" he says. "I talked to them ekh but they swore! They swore it wasn't them!"

He looks happier than I think I've ever been in my entire life.

"Well," I say. "It's them."

"Thanks man—Whoah," He looks at me closely. "Are you okay?"

"I'm fine," I say, suddenly very aware that my head is throbbing. "I'll be fine."

"Okay, well, ekh, thanks again man," Beckett says. "Have a good night my friend."

"Goodnight Beckett."

I walk up the stairs and into my apartment.

The pain in my jaw is tightening and pulsing.

I can feel myself sobering up.

It's awful.

A cool breeze of panic blows over me, little bumps rising up on my arms and neck.

Then I quickly take out my lighter and pop the beer open and take a pull.

It doesn't work.

I lie down, unscrew the lid off the whiskey, then take turns sipping from both until I feel a little dizzy.

Still dressed, I roll over on my side and close my eyes.

My face feels like it's trying to slip away and hide.

My eyes are sore.

Teeth and gums are aching.

I slide my left shoe off using the right, pull out the baggies, rub a little all over my gums, tip the whiskey bottle into the side of my mouth, then curl my knees toward my head-- the cold glass of the bottle resting against my chest-- and wait for nothing.

• • •

I wake up to the usual sounds of the city, sweating and afraid.

Hallucinations/nightmares of the earth shaking and people coming to lock me away for reasons they won't share with me.

Always the same nightmares.

I rub my eyes, look around my room.

Before I can think about why or what purpose it would serve, I start nervously sipping from the whiskey and dumping a bit of coke out on a DVD case.

I take the tissue out of my nose and try to snort it.

But my nostrils are clogged and have crusted blood-snot all around the rims.

"Rectal consumption" pops in my brain and for a half-second I think something about "being bad-ass" in relation to "myself".

But it all just makes me sick.

I throw the DVD and the coke like a frisbee into the corner of the room, take the biggest pull of whiskey I can stomach, and lay back down.

• • •

Then there's knocking at my door.

I close my eyes tight and put my pillow over my head.

But the more I try to ignore it, the louder it gets.

My heart starts bouncing around my insides, hard, and the knocking just gets louder.

I get up out of bed and walk to the door, half-expecting it to just explode and send me through the window where armed men await to take me away. Just lock me in a basement somewhere. With the mice and the darkness and the silence. Where I belong.

I open the door and see Annie standing there.

She's wearing a sundress and has a little redness on her shoulders and she smells like not here.

"You're back!" I say, immediately hit with my own dog-shit breath.

She looks annoyed.

"What the fuck happened to you?" she says.

"Got punched."

I walk back to my bed and sit down, feeling like my whole body is shutting down, like I could sleep for days. Then I reach for the whiskey bottle. Knowing it won't help. But not having anything else to do.

As I start to unscrew the lid, Annie swoops in and snatches the bottle away from me. She starts yelling at me. Really loud. Saying things that I know are about me, but sound completely unrelated to me. Saying things like, she can't sit around and watch me kill myself. Things about a friend of hers that had a problem, things about regret, things about friendship, things about helping me out.

And finally, she says things about rehab.

She knows a place, very cheap, very close.

She can even help me pay for it.

"Rehab is for people with real issues," I say.

Annie motions to my face, my surroundings, putting her arms in the air.

I watch her closely.

The thoughts in her head are aligning themselves for another speech.

She's hurting, she cares.

And all it does is make me uncomfortable.

If I'm uncomfortable then it must mean she really means it.

Or she's just helping me out as a defense mechanism against guilt.

Either way, she needs this.

"Okay," I say. "I'll go."

"Really?"

"Yes."

She hugs me.

We are hugging.

Then we are packing.

I pack as little as possible, knowing I won't be there long.

Annie doesn't notice.

She's on the phone already.

She's done her part.

She's off the hook.

She tried.

Even if I fail, she can tell others this story, how she gave an emotional speech and convinced me to seek help, even helped pay for it.

And then she can forget.

She can live her life without ever having to think of me again.

22.

The rehab building is right on the boardwalk, the front door just a few steps away from the sand.

"We know how easy it is to find drugs around here," the woman in charge of the program says. "But we think the ocean view is more inspiration to start living a healthy lifestyle."

I look outside at the people walking the boardwalk.

They seem, to me, like they are on an entirely different plane of existence.

It's depressing.

I don't want to be them but sometimes they make it look easy and that makes me feel embarrassed about involving anyone in my problems.

"Yeah," I say. "I like it."

"Good!" the woman in charge says, and glances out the window smiling. "That's a good start right?"

I nod and smile.

She nods and smiles too, then begins to ask questions that get more and more personal.

I answer all of them.

I feel really phony and embarrassed about it, too on the nose and everything, but I even tell her about the counseling sessions when I was a kid, and the pills they wanted to put me on.

She writes it all down, nodding.

Then she says, "Now, when your friend called she said you mostly have a problem with alcohol. Is that right?"

"Yeah."

"But you have issues with cocaine as well?"

"Well, I don't—"

"It's okay, you can be honest, no judgement here. But we will have to take a urine sample. It's policy. We don't allow anyone to admit themselves while intoxicated or under the influence of anything."

"I'm sober," I say.

"That's great. But it's policy. We'll also have to check your bag."

The woman stands up from her desk chair and walks out of the room.

I don't know what to do.

I think about leaving but the idea of moving hurts my brain so I just look around her office.

There's the usual stuff.

A framed degree, books about self-improvement, and a bunch of photos.

One of the photos is of her and this really crazy looking guy (a patient?) with eyes that would make you think he has taken many lives with his bare hands.

It makes me wonder, if a few really traumatic things happened to me when I was young, would I be a serial killer.

Ridiculous.

A few minutes later the woman returns.

Walking behind her is a large intimidating man dressed in a button-down white shirt and freshly ironed pants.

The muscle.

He's completely silent as he digs through my stuff-- just a few books, dirty clothes, toothbrush, my 3-in-1 shower gel-- then gives the nod to the woman in charge.

"Okay…" She slaps her hands together. "Now you'll follow Maurice here to the restroom for the urine test. Then he'll show you to your room."

Maurice walks out the door, still not saying anything.

I follow him down the hall to the restroom, where he hands me a cup and tells me to leave the door open.

"Okay," I say, feeling the kind of sadness where you want to make life easier for everyone around you. "You got it Maurice."

I walk to one of the urinals and unzip.

I try to relax.

But the pain betwixt my ass and dick is inflamed and it takes a while for me to start peeing.

"I'm trying," I say, craning my neck and looking at Maurice. "But I have a prostate slash bladder issue because of all the beer. And I think peeing in the sink is bad because I have to stand on my toes and point it straight out."

"What?"

I manage a few drops, like a broken squirt gun, and a pain like tiny box-cutters travels from the tip of my dick up into the bottom of my spine.

"Almost done?" Maurice says.

"Yeah. Sorry."

I finish pissing, screw the lid on the cup, place it in the designated area, then follow Maurice down the hall, deeper into the building.

The rehab building.

My new home.

We walk by the kitchen and the high-school cafeteria smells, then we pass a group of men outside on the patio smoking cigarettes before stopping in front of one of the many doors in the hallway.

"This is you," Maurice says.

He points into a small room with three small beds

crammed inside.

"Thanks."

"Uh-huh."

Maurice walks away and I place my bag on the only unoccupied bed.

The other two beds have various personal effects on the bedside tables, and the bed in the opposite corner as mine has a bunch of posters of 90's hip-hop groups taped above it, like he's made himself comfortable for a long visit.

Like, this is it.

Like settle in.

Like fuck.

A cold feeling goes through me and I sit down on the bed, nervously reaching for my bag, looking for something, anything.

But nothing in there will help.

Nothing anywhere will help.

I know this.

I tell myself to forget it.

Keep moving.

Just keep moving and nothing will stick.

I stand up, walk out of the room and out to the patio, where I'd seen the other patients smoking cigarettes.

A few of them are still out there though, standing in a circle talking.

I do that half-step-limbo thing to re-direct, almost falling to avoid being seen, but the embarrassment of almost falling shakes me and I lose all rational thought.

I walk outside, standing on the other side of the group.

The one who's leading the conversation, an older guy with a shaved head and no eyebrows, is speaking so loudly that I can't ignore him.

He's describing some new TV show that has dragons and lots of nudity.

"The best part about it," he says. "Is that I was fucked up when I watched it, so when I get outta here it'll be like watching it for the first time."

"Yeah, you're right," one says.

"Never thought of that," says another.

And then me, standing there like an idiot, says "Pfft" way louder than I intend to.

I've avoided eye-contact to this point but now I can feel them staring.

"Hey!" the man with no hair says, "You ever seen it?"

I shake my head, doing that inverted smile thing that isn't really a smile, then light a cigarette and turn my back to them.

They say a few more things, similar to, "Hey! You ever seen it?" but I remain facing away.

I'm a coward, but I'm okay with that, and I think they are to.

One by one it goes:

"He's in a mood."

"Probably feeling like death."

"Yeah. Look at him. He's a kid."

"And a real heartbreaker too, hehe."

"Sheeeeit."

Then they toss their cigarettes and step inside.

I'm alone again.

I walk to the edge of the patio and look out at the boardwalk.

There are people everywhere.

The sun is giving them it's last bit of light, that pink and orange tint over the ocean before it moves on.

I try to enjoy it without any pretense, or comparison, but I can't.

I watch the people, thinking.

These are happy people, in a happy place.

They've done it.

I'm proud of them and feel glad that the whole world isn't like me.

The world only needs people like me to balance things out, so people like them can appreciate what they have and be happy.

Happy to be alive.

To be near the ocean.

Where movies about happy people just like them are made.

Where unhappy people wish they were.

Where beautiful women migrate to.

A place for dreamers, desirables, people in love, people with enough courage to come here and dig in. People like Sticks and Annie, who welcome all, in this beautiful city they call home.

Venice, L.A., Southern California, America.

I take a drag of my cigarette and think, you can have me Venice, I love you. Then I look back out at the beach, trying to "find inspiration" like the rehab lady said.

Through the crowd, I see a woman in a bikini walking by.

She has sand stuck to her ass-cheeks.

Her sandy ass-cheeks are attached to long tan legs.

And she is the most beautiful person I've ever seen.

I don't feel inspired, but I am in trouble.

Oh, yes, just like that.

I'm in love with not just the city but everyone in it, especially her. Her golden hair, her golden skin. My golden sand princess, I love you. My loathsome romantic city, I love you. I love you so much I want to cry!

I haven't cried in so long but now is the time.

Go on.

Let it out.

Fall to your knees, raise your arms into the clouds!

No, stop that.

Sorry.

You're just horny.

Ok.

Don't you realize you haven't jerked off in weeks?

Yes, I realize.

And when was the last time you had sex, to completion, with a woman?

I don't remember.

What do you remember?

I toss my half-finished cigarette into the wind, feeling sick, then walk back inside the building.

The rehab building.

My new home.

23.

When I get back to my room both of my roommates are there.

They're lounging around like they've always lived there.

Laughing.

Completely content.

But then they notice me standing there at the doorway and immediately the mood shifts.

It feels like war.

Territorial.

They ask me a few questions, coldly.

I give them short answers and then they ask a few more questions before I get to part where I tell them I'm the new roommate.

"Oh shit," they say. "Come in and relax man!"

Everything becomes very brotherly.

They are excited to have someone new, someone to mentor.

It's very difficult to not puke as they speak.

"Today was good though," the man who sleeps in the bed next to mine says, "I think there was some good progress. But fuck it, right? What do I know?"

His name is Buck.

He has a face that looks about fifty but everything else about him seems young.

His hair is spiked up, his clothes are tight, and he sounds enthusiastic about everything he's saying, even if he's talking about something very sad.

"Man, for me," he laughs. "I'm just glad I'm fucking breathing. When I got arrested, I thought I was stroking out, thought I was dead. Can you imagine? Big dude like me, fucking crying like a baby and clutching my arm, screaming 'I don't wanna die now I don't wanna!' over and over. Man, I never want that feeling again."

"No, that sucks," I say. "And you got arrested?"

"Yeah," Buck says. "I was way too fucked up in public, making a scene."

"So they made you come here?"

"This place or jail," he laughs, slicking the sides of his hair back. "Easy choice right?"

I nod, but don't know what to say.

I look around the room, trying to look okay with everything, trying not to come off as uncomfortable, trying not to vomit.

I smile at both of them.

The roommate with the hip-hop posters is lying on his bed, listening to music on a CD player with just one of the headphones over his ear.

He notices me smiling at him and says, "Most of the dudes in here had to come. Court ordered rehabilitation, you know?"

"Oh. It's all guys in here?"

"Sausage-fest," Buck says. "I don't why, but I had this fantasy of like, meeting a bad-ass bitch in here and falling in love. Like some Sid and Nancy type shit."

"Me too," I lie, picturing Buck and a "bad-ass bitch" stabbing each other with knives and bleeding out together.

"My brothah," Buck says. "I knew I would like you."

"I like you too Buck."

"Hell yeah."

My roommate with the headphones gets out of bed and walks over to me.

He says, "You'll do just fine here. Welcome to Phoenix House." Then he slaps me on the shoulder as he walks by me and out the door.

I look at Buck.

He's still smiling really big.

"Judah is cool," he says. "That's Judah by the way. Doesn't talk much but he's cool."

"Cool," I say. "You guys both seem cool."

"Fuck yeah," Buck says. "This place ain't bad really. Good people."

After talking more about the place for what seems like hours, but was probably just a few minutes, Buck stands up and tells me it's dinner time and to follow him.

"Shit man." He looks down at his watch. "Time is all fucked up in here. We're missing pizza night."

We walk down the hall and then up the stairs to a big room with collapsible tables lined up like a cafeteria. Around thirty guys are in there, eating pizza and watching a playoff football game on an old big-screen TV in the corner of the room.

Six of the guys are sitting in chairs separated from the tables, right in front of the TV, wearing football jerseys and moving around nervously as they watch the game. But the rest of the guys look like me.

Exhausted.

Nibbling at the pizza and staring off into space.

"You hungry?" Buck says, gesturing to a table with about ten greasy pizza boxes on it. "You should probably eat."

I nod my head, follow him to the table where he picks up three big slices topped with everything and slaps it on a styrofoam plate.

"You picked a good night to show up. Playoffs AND pizza," he says, walking toward the TV. "Lucky motherfucker!"

I grab a slice and sit down at a table in the back, away from the group.

I start eating.

The pizza is cold and I feel cold and I'm sweating and sick.

My stomach is making sounds like it needs food but also feels like it would reject anything put inside it.

Lucky motherfucker.

I chew slowly and look at the TV.

The team that's behind is making a last drive in the final two minutes of the first half, and three of the six guys wearing jerseys are now pacing by the TV and yelling after each play.

Stuff like, "Throw it to (best receiver)!"

And, "Why the fuck aren't they feeding (best receiver)!"

While the other three guys, wearing the other team's jersey, are sitting quietly and sighing in relief when a pass is incomplete.

It's good to watch.

It makes sense.

There is one team trying to score, and one team trying to stop them.

It's simple.

The offense completes a twenty-five-yard pass on the sidelines, stopping the clock, and the three men standing up all high-five and fist-bump each other.

"We still got time," one of them says. "Take a few big shots before settling for three."

"Nah man," another one says, pacing back and forth and pulling on his jersey to air out his armpit sweat. "We should just kick now, go into half-time with momentum, then ride that till the end. We got this."

I take another small bite of the pizza and think about being a part of a "we".

Brotherhood created out of similar interests.

It feels like I would enjoy being part of something like that, even if there were no real emotions attached to it.

Then it just feels like I've reached a new low.

We.

A man walks into the room from behind me.

He's balding, barely any teeth, and wearing a black t-shirt with skulls on it.

He seems angry.

He grabs a slice of pizza, looks around at the scene with furrowed eyebrows, and eventually locks eyes with me, smiling a fleshy pink smile like we're old friends.

I can't do anything to stop him.

He walks over and sits down next to me.

We don't speak.

I'm happy about this and suddenly I feel very invested in the football game.

I pretend he's not there, staring at the TV as the offense is about to try one more play before bringing out the kicker.

The quarterback takes the snap, scrambles around, pump fakes, then throws a long pass into the end-zone that's juggled in the air by the receiver and then the corner before falling to the ground.

Incomplete.

The men in jerseys alternate sighs and screams of frustration, filling the room with chaos and imbalance.

I too feel disappointment.

But it only lasts a few seconds.

"Fuck this," the man with the skull t-shirt says. "It's all meaningless you know?"

I look over at him, in case he's addressing me.

"Don't get me wrong," he says. "I love these guys, but

they're kinda missing the point."

"What is the point?" I say.

He turns toward me, like he'd expected this, and says, "Bettering yourself. I came here to force myself away from all distractions. Bettering my mind. But, this? This is just meaningless."

"Meaningless," I say. "All meaningless?"

"Yes! Finally. Someone who gets it."

He sticks out his hand.

"I'm Toby," he says.

I wipe the sweat from my palms and shake his hand. "Ty," I say.

"Well, Ty," he says, crossing his arms. "What brings you here?"

"Booze."

"Ahh, the drink," he laughs. "And what else?"

"Just booze. I probably shouldn't be here wasting anyone's time or effort really. I don't why I agreed to this in the first place."

He shakes his head, smiling like he knows something I don't.

Then I turn my attention back to the TV.

The kicker is lining up.

Silence spreads over the room.

The snap is crisp, the kicker drives into the ball and sends it up and up and up, but hooking left.

"OoooOH!"

No good.

The men in jerseys get loud, yelling at the players, then each other.

"Oh come one, just shut up," Toby says under his breath, then nudging my shoulder. "All this is, is wasted energy. I almost died. I mean, I did die. My heart stopped for two whole minutes and you know what I saw? Nothing. I had no eyes because there was nothing to see and I had no ears because there was nothing to hear. Who cares about men wearing tight pants and playing a child's game after that?"

"Not I."

"I know," he says, looking deep in my eyes. "It's been nice talking to someone else who knows. I'm happy you're here. And not dead."

"Me too."

Toby walks out of the room and I continue eating my cold pizza slice, listening to the men in jerseys talk shit throughout the game.

One team scores.

You suck.

Then the other scores.

No, you guys suck.

Then it ends.

24.

"So, if you think about, it all started because of her," Buck says. "Everything that led to this moment could've all been avoided, if we just never fucking met."

He's telling me about his girlfriend.

Or ex-girlfriend.

I'm not sure.

I'm tired and I want to go to sleep.

I keep yawning, trying to end the conversation, but Buck keeps going.

"That bitch," he says, under his breath. "Just, never should've met her."

He'll get close to the point, what his girlfriend did to him when they last saw each other, but ends up thinking of a different thing she did in the past, or repeating a story he told me earlier on.

"She knew things though," Buck says. "That's why I stayed with her. That fucking bitch. She knew how to do things you only see in porn..."

He shakes his head and then looks over at Judah, who is laying down with his headphones on and his eyes closed, asleep.

"I probably shouldn't be telling you this," he says, lowering his voice. "But she knew porn stuff because she actually did porn when she was younger."

"Well, that makes sense then."

"Yeah," he says. "She's a *fuh*-reak, you know? There was this one time, we were out at the lake, jet-skiing, and she was holding on to me, like from behind." He holds his arms out like he's hugging someone. "And I swear dude, it was the time of my life. Jumping the waves from the big boats driving around, mist in my face, hair in the wind. When suddenly she-- boom, like it was nothing-- just pulled down my trunks."

"Uh oh."

"Yeah. Just started jerking me off. On a jet-ski. In the middle of a crowded lake."

"Nice," I say. "I gotta get *me* an ex-porn girl."

"Fuck no," Buck says, getting very serious. "They're all crazy. Never ever date a porn chick. Ever. If you start dating a porn chick, I swear to you, I will find out, somehow, someway, and then I'll come beat your ass."

"Okay," I say. "I will not *get me* an ex-porn girl."

"Good. If you learn anything in this place, let it be that."

Buck gets very quiet.

I can tell he's thinking of all the years and years he spent with this woman.

"Anyway," he says. "The tug-job she was giving me was like, really slow at first. I must have been going like 40. And the lake was packed. Fucking families everywhere. I could still focus on what I was doing, sort of, but then she really started tugging on me. I thought, 'this crazy bitch is going to rip my dick off'. I really thought she was, man. It might've been the drugs but I just started freaking out. I yelled 'STOP' as loud as I could but, have you ever been on a jet-ski? It's really loud. She couldn't hear me. She just kept tugging and tugging, jerking and jerking, and without realizing it, I started to accelerate."

"So you crashed?"

"I fucking crashed it man."

"Shit."

"And the worst part was--"

"You didn't finish?"

"Oh no, I finished. I came so much. Probably impregnated half the fish in that lake. No. The worst part was, it ruined hand-jobs for me."

"Like PTSD?"

"Yeah," Buck says. "Post Traumatic Stroked Disorder."

He laughs.

My eyelids ache and my head is splitting and I can't stop sweating but I laugh too.

"So yeah," Buck says. "What I'm trying to say is, as funny as it sounds now, meeting her was the reason for all of this. Seriously. Everything could've been avoided, if we just never fucking met…"

Buck goes on to tell me more about his girlfriend. Or his ex-girlfriend. Until Maurice, the muscle, appears in the doorway and tells us it's time for bed.

"Lights, gentleman," he says. "It's time."

"You got it Boss," Buck says.

Maurice moves on to the other rooms and I say goodnight to Buck.

"Goodnight man," he says. "Tomorrow will be rough. It was for me at least. So try and get some sleep."

"I will," I say.

I turn off the lights and try to get comfortable. Flipping the pillow, pulling the blanket up to my nose, immediately throwing the blanket back down by my feet because of the moth-ball smell, then moving on to my side.

Only a few minutes go by before Buck starts whispering from across the room.

His voice hovering over me in the darkness.

"Hey, you awake? I just remembered," he says. "I

completely forgot to tell you what she did. My ex-porn ex-girlfriend. Before I came here. That bitch."

I don't answer.

25.

I wake up to a warm sensation.

It's mid-afternoon.

No one's around.

I'd been having dreams about beautiful women in bikinis, sandy-assed, riding jet-skis, and I kept forcing myself to stay asleep as the morning noises went on around me.

I've been in and out of consciousness for close to thirteen hours, but still feel half-asleep. Half-asleep and feeling that child-like embarrassment about sleeping longer than everyone at else at the sleep-over.

I sit up and notice that the warmness is near my thigh and upper dick-area.

Then I lift my boxers up and look down at myself.

I've cum in my pants.

I don't feel disgusted or sad or embarrassed, I just feel separated from myself.

Like the real me is up there in my head, laughing and doing a bit where he pretends to be angry.

Pathetic child, he says, hiding his laughter.

Sick monster.

Reigning fuck-up.

You fucked up so much that you ended up here, in a place designed for fuck-ups who want a second chance, and what did you do?

144

You jizzed the bed.

Pathetic.

I look around the room, then peek out the door into the hallway, checking if it's safe to walk to the bathroom.

It's a large building but we share the bathroom with the room next door that's occupied by three other men.

If they were to walk in and see me changing out of semen covered underwear, I imagine my time in here would not be as enjoyable as it could've been, if they didn't see me changing out of semen covered underwear.

But I don't see or hear them.

I grab a pair of semi-fresh boxers and walk in.

There's no lock so I walk in to the stall, close it behind me, and quickly get to work.

I peel off the slimy underwear and put on the fresh underwear and then walk to the sink with the slimy underwear and begin washing them, feeling like it might be time for me to leave.

I still hear the real me, up in my head, saying, Do it.

Just run.

When you find yourself in a rehab center, covered in your own cum, it is certainly time to pack your shit, call it a life, and run away.

I wring out the boxers and clutch them in my hand, trying to hide them, then walk back to my bed.

As I pack, I start to playing out my exit in my head.

What needs to be said?

Do I need to say anything at all?

If I simply walked out, would they chase me?

Would alarms start ringing?

Would I hear the alarm and start running wildly, screaming at passerby's that I had to leave, I came in my underwear, so I simply had to go?

No one cares.

I place my bag on the bed and grab my keys and place them in my pocket.

As I zip up the bag with everything inside I see Buck standing in the doorway.

He's smiling, bad coffee breath, reeking of cigarettes.

"You're up?!" he says. "Just in time, group is about to start so I came to see if you were feeling up to it?"

I don't feel up to it.

I want to tell him what happened and that I don't belong here. That I'm wasting everyone's time and wasting everyone's time feels worse than how sick I feel.

That's me.

That's who he's talking to.

A person that wants to curl up in a dark corner, cat-like, not bothering anyone with their own death.

"I don't know Buck," I say. "I don't—"

"Oh come on."

He pats me on the back and pushes me out the door and towards the stairs.

I start walking.

Through the hallway.

Up the stairs.

And into the large room where the playoffs and pizza were set up.

Everyone from last night, and a few guys I haven't seen before are in there, sitting in chairs arranged in a large circle, almost like they were waiting for me.

Amongst the worn-out faces of my fellow patients, there's a woman in her mid-twenties there.

She's holding a clipboard and wearing a t-shirt with the rehab centers name on it.

I haven't seen her before but it is obvious that all the guys really like/are hopelessly in love with her.

She says, "Alright, should we get this rolling guys?"

And everyone nods and says things like, "Let's giiiiit it."

I sit down in the circle and don't say anything.

From across the room, Toby, who's wearing the same skull t-shirt from last night, gives me a wink and leans back in his chair.

I have no idea how I keep from puking.

"So, how's everyone feeling?" the clipboard woman says. "Can we just go around and give a quick 1 out of 10."

Everyone goes around and, without context or explanation, says a number.

"Bout a... 8."

"Shit, like 2, maybe."

"Definitely a 10."

Until it gets to me.

I look around the room and ask myself, based on everything, in comparison to my entire life that came before this, what number would accurately represent my state of being today.

"I'm gonna go with a funky fresh double zero," I say.

But no one acknowledges me or laughs.

The rest of the men just follow by saying their own number, and I'm amazed no one is laughing.

"Alright, good," the woman says. "Now who wants to speak first. Anyone?"

Toby raises his hand.

Before the woman can call his name, he starts talking.

"I'll kick it off if you don't mind," he says.

The man to his right rolls his eyes and there is some low groaning from the others.

Buck elbows me softly.

"Shit," he whispers. "This fucking guy always goes first."

The woman with the clipboard quiets everyone and tells Toby to carry on.

"Thank you." Toby says. "Just wanted to say, real quick,

before we get started that—and I know I've talked about this before—but I really think we should step up this whole process. Talk about some real stuff, instead of just sharing stories about how bad we all fucked up. I want to be able to share what kind of internal changes I'm going through, and I'd like to feel like you guys are open to that. But I don't. We just try to one up each other on the crazy shit we've all done."

Toby looks over at me.

"I was talking to Ty here," he says. "And I think he'll agree."

The room gets quiet.

Everyone looks over at me like I've betrayed them.

Betrayed the balance.

"What the fuck," Buck whispers.

I stare at the floor, cross my arms, adjust my pants, scratch at my hardened crusty pubes, anything to avoid and ignore this.

But I can't.

I end up thinking about all the possible things I could say.

If this were one of those movies they make here it would be the moment I'd realize a change must be made, and participating in this group, participating in anything with other people, would be the first step. If I had any opinions or morals or beliefs, this is the moment people would be forced to listen to them. I'm supposed to say something like that. That I've realized my problem, I've figured it out, drinking is bad, avoiding everything is wrong, and Toby is right. We should take this opportunity to reflect, dig deep, fuck this addiction stuff up.

But I don't have any beliefs and drinking isn't my problem.

"I have to go the bathroom," I say, and walk out.

Down the stairs.

Through the hall.

Into my room.

I throw my bag over my shoulder and walk out the front door and onto the boardwalk and back to my life.

Back to more of the same.

No one chases me.

26.

On the way back home, I stop at a restaurant on the boardwalk.

I sit at a small table on the patio, underneath an umbrella with a beer logo on it, and wait for a waiter to notice me.

It's nice out.

Clouds overhead blocking just enough of the sun.

And not many people around.

I pick up a beer list and look at the options. Under the "Imported" list there is a beer I recognize. A German beer with a German name that my parents used to keep in the back of the fridge, for when my German grandparents would come over.

But they never came over.

It was always in there, waiting.

I'd look at it and think "that's beer." Then I'd have a strong urge to drink it, just to see what it was like, but also knowing my Dad would kill me if he noticed one missing.

"I'll have one of these," I tell the waiter when he walks up.

"What size?" he says.

"The big one."

"Okay," he says, sort of examining me. "Do you have any money?"

"Did I just order a beer knowing I didn't have any money

to pay for it?"

"Yes."

"No."

"Good."

He nods and walks away.

I look around to see if anyone noticed.

But as usual, no one noticed.

Everyone is on their phone so I make a point of soaking in my surroundings demonstratively, as to say, I'm living and you're not, you fucking nerd.

In front of the restaurant I see a small group of old homeless men.

Two of them are setting up a drum set, a speaker, a mic, and the other one is tuning a guitar.

I try to get excited about this.

I pre-meditate a positive reaction to whatever music comes out of these old, beaten-down homeless men.

They are ready and I am ready.

After it's all set up, one of the men starts speaking into the mic, addressing everyone sitting outside at the restaurant.

He's wrinkled, wearing a Lead Belly t-shirt, and his voice is raspy.

"How we doing folks," he says. "We're going to play a few songs while you eat your lunch, if you don't mind."

A group of women sitting near me all "whooo" and clap.

I clap too, almost knowing, but mostly hoping, that it will go well for them.

They play a few covers of old blues songs, pausing in between to explain a little about the song, and then they start playing their own original songs.

"This is one of ours," the singer says. "Hope you like it."

The guitar player starts strumming and the singer gets into the first verse.

He's singing about being a strung-out teenager, then he's

151

singing about living on skid row and waking up to death around him every day.

I can tell it's about him.

It's a true story.

After the song is over, a few of the women sitting near me walk over and drop money in a guitar case that's in front of the singer.

The singer says, "Thank you, and god bless you." Then the women walk back to the table near me and continue eating their lunch.

I stare at them for a bit, not knowing why.

They cause no emotion in me, positive or negative.

But I do have an urge to follow in their footsteps, by putting money in the guitar case.

I want the singer to say, "God bless you."

I want that "God bless you" so I can take it home and think of it whenever I feel down.

And mostly I want to stop constantly picturing myself doing violently anti-social things, or glorifying every little daily thing I see others do, just because they appear to be doing them with little to no effort.

I don't know.

The waiter walks up.

"You want another one?" he says.

"I'm good. But can I bring a beer over to the singer," I say. "Like, if you put it in a paper cup or something?"

"You want me to put a beer in a paper cup so you can bring it to that homeless man?"

"Yes, can you?"

"No."

"Okay then, I'll just have a cheeseburger to go then please."

The waiter walks away.

I turn back to the homeless men.

They're finishing their last song.

I feel anxious, tapping my heel on the table and waiting.

The singer says, "Thank you for listening" and they start packing up.

A few minutes go by and the waiter brings the check and the cheeseburger and I hand him my credit card nervously, hoping it goes through at least one more time, but mostly hoping the band doesn't leave.

I watch them closely, anxiously.

The waiter returns and says, "Thanks for coming in," like he'd prefer I didn't anymore, then places my card on the table.

I sign quickly, add up the tip, and walk over to the homeless men.

The singer is handing out the profits to the drummer and the guitarist, maybe five dollars apiece, and they don't notice me standing there at first.

"Hello," I say.

The guitarist looks up at me briefly, then puts his guitar in its case.

"Yeah, anyway," I say. "I liked the show."

"Thank you kindly," the singer says, but doesn't look at me at all.

I'm still just standing there.

It feels like we should all be very familiar with each other because of how many times I've imagined this interaction in the last few minutes, but now I'm just standing there like a cold unrequited high-five.

"Yeah it was awesome," I say again. "I actually wanted to put something in the case there but I don't have any cash, just this, if you want it."

The singer looks at me now and notices I'm holding out the to-go container in front of him.

I tell him it's a cheeseburger and he takes it from my

hands, smiling big before bestowing the eternal "God bless you" upon me.

"No problem," I say. "I asked the waiter if I could bring a beer out to you as well, while you were playing, but I guess they can't do that."

The guitarist looks at me as soon as I say beer.

"Next time we'll join ya," he says. "I get thirsty out here you know?"

The singer sucks his teeth and says, "You're always thirsty man!"

Then we all laugh.

"No but, seriously," I say. "If you guys play here often I'll buy you guys some beers next time."

They all agree and seem really surprised by my insistence.

Internally I acknowledge the fact that this was slightly nauseating charity for the purpose of instant gratification, but then I shrug it off and cherish the "God bless you," replaying it over and over in my head.

The singer and I shake hands.

I tell the other bandmates goodbye and start walking toward home.

As I get closer to my apartment, I start to feel anxious again.

A good anxious.

I want to see my bed/mat and Mouse and my crooked floor and even my neighbors.

I've missed them.

I run up the steps and bust in my door and start looking for Mouse, starting with his spot in the corner by my bed, then searching around the kitchen.

But he's hiding.

I open the fridge and crack a beer and start to feel safe.

I feel content.

I've built a home here and laughed here and almost died

here.

I've done all the things a real human does.

I look around the room, nothing but love in my eyes, and tell each and every item in my apartment how I feel about them.

I love you couch.

I love you sink/toilet.

I love you disintegrating wall.

And you, Mouse, I love you too, wherever you are.

I open the sink cabinet and he's not there.

I look behind the couch and he's not there.

Then I look behind the fridge and there he is.

He's sitting in his own shit, stuck to one of the glue traps I'd forgotten about.

He looks terrified and he's making little squeaking noises.

I don't have time to think.

I just rush to my computer and type it in.

How to get a friend out of a glue trap?

The first thing I see says that I need nail polish. That's it's the only way to go, the only option. So I run out and cross the street, striding into the convenience store with purpose.

"Nail Polish!?"

The cashier points me in the right direction and I find it without issue.

"This it for ya?" the cashier says.

"My friend got caught in a glue trap."

"Kay."

I rush home.

Mouse is where I left him.

I had a small fantasy of him busting out of the trap as soon as I left, but how could I expect such a thing? These traps are designed for his kind. Designed to track and trap at will, no questions asked.

Barbaric.

I slide the trap out from behind the fridge and open up the nail polish, then I scrape the shit out from under him so I can have a clear path to his feet. Just like the internet instructions said.

"If I follow the rules," I say. "You should be just fine."

I begin the procedure.

Pouring a small amount on his back feet first, and gently pulling his legs up.

But it's difficult.

As soon I touch his legs, Mouse starts squealing and trying to run.

It only makes things worse.

It's what the trap is designed for.

A slow painful death, brought on by his own struggle.

Then I have an idea.

I pour a little more nail polish on his back legs then hold and slightly push down on the glue as Mouse tries to rip his feet away.

He's nearly free, when he starts doing something I didn't expect.

A pool of the nail polish has settled in the corner of the trap and Mouse starts drinking from it. I don't know what to do. And he doesn't know either, except what all creatures must do. He's in survival mode. He thinks it's water.

"You idiot," I say. "That'll kill you."

I make one last attempt to rip all four feet from the glue but I'm too late.

Mouse jerks around slightly, almost like he's dancing, then he's gone.

Goodbye Mouse, you fucking idiot.

I pick up the trap and walk outside to the dumpster and just stand there, feeling very sad about most things, but not all.

From around the corner, Dumpster Guy appears.

It's his time of the week.

"Hey what'd ya find?" he says in a territorial tone.

"Nothing, it's just a dead mouse," I say. "It got caught in a glue trap."

"Look at that," he says. "Those things are everywhere. Last week I found six of em' in there."

He points to his dumpster.

"Yeah," I say. "You mind throwing him away when you're done looking?"

"I think I can," he says, still staring at the dumpster. "But I forget stuff easily."

I put Mouse down on the street, between the dumpster and the apartment building wall.

I give him a silent goodbye, then imagine myself eating him and drinking the remaining nail polish in order to join him in mouse-heaven.

"I'll take a walk and come back," I tell Dumpster Guy. "So if you forget, I'll see him and throw him in before the truck comes tomorrow."

"Good thinking kid," he says, then immediately hops in and gets to work.

I walk down the alleyway and cross Pacific Avenue and head toward the beach.

The sun is going down and people are starting to leave.

They pass me without a thought, while I look at them and imagine what every single one of them thinks about when the silence comes.

I get to the sand.

I take off my shoes.

Put my phone and keys inside them.

Then walk to the end of the ocean.

The water goes over my toes and I feel cold.

My nerves are fried.

My senses start waking up.

I wade further into the sea and turn around—letting the waves smack up against my legs, my ass—watching as the streetlights start flickering and the neon signs of the smoke shops and bars light up.

Beyond that I see the fancy beachside condos. The old rejuvenated houses with the big gates and the beautiful gardens. And the people that live inside them, those happy people again, living in a happy place.

But this time I see them alone.

A different kind of alone.

An alone that they can't talk about, that they're ashamed of, or that they don't even have a name for.

But I do.

Right there with my feet sinking into the sand and the salty ocean taste on my lips, I decide that that kind of alone will be called loneliness.

The worst kind of alone.

An alone that can't be cured.

Not yet.

What must be done is this.

I will build a great home for the rejected and the poor and the sad and even the rich who suffer from this loneliness, right here on the beach.

That's what I'll do.

I will be the architect of a new kind of living.

I'll rally all the homeless in Venice, paying them with beer that I put on my credit card, and instructing them on how the great home should be built.

There will be bathrooms for everyone, even floors, and thick, sturdy, soundproof walls.

Of course.

But this home will have something other homes don't.

They will start the foundation by placing the brick all around me.

I will feel the weight of it slowly crushing me to death and I will smile.

My dead body part of something to shelter living bodies.

The perfect sacrifice.

The perfect end.

I put my hands into the ocean and splash around, as to say to all of Venice that now is the time to join me.

Live together inside of me, sweet city of mine!

Let me help.

Please, I say.

I want it more than anything.

But nothing happens.

I walk out of the ocean, my feet dragging through the seaweed.

I slip on my shoes and head for the boardwalk.

On the way I think about tomorrow but it scares me so I light another cigarette, finish it, light another, decide to grab a case of beer from the liquor store, do that, then walk back home, the me from ten minutes ago seeming more and more laughable.

THE END

Acknowledgements

First, a big n' sweet thank you to Cavin. If not for him this book would be rotting on my computer. And secondly, but just as importantly, thank you to the writers that wrote books so good that I had no choice but to steal from them.

About The Author

T.J. Larkey lives in Arizona. He is doing much better now. Also his name really is T.J. He has been called that his whole life. It's not abbreviated to hide something dorky like Timothy.

Twitter: *@tjlarkey*

Selected Work: *neutralspaces.co/tjlarkey/*

Time. Wow.

Cosmic Observations by Neil Clark

For Taylor, my cousin.

Contents

Time.

Wow.

When It's Time to Go

This time, you just wanted a simple life. Go to work. Watch kitten videos and food vlogs before bed. Overorder Chinese food at weekends when the hangovers bite.

But wherever you go, there's always something.

Your first ever room had rising damp. The next had moths that ate your clothes.

Your last place had a switch in the cupboard under the kitchen sink, with 'NOT IN USE' written above it in red pen. Your head would constantly be in that cupboard, oblivious to your phone pinging in your pocket with concerned texts from family, stern voicemails from work. You'd stroke the switch for days on end, applying tiny and tinier amounts of pressure. You'd trace the letters with your fingernails and wonder if you'd discovered the reset button for the universe.

When it was time to go from there, you flicked the switch,

put the keys on the table and left the flat for the first time since the day you moved in. As your plane took off, you saw an earthquake below, just how you'd imagined.

The new house smelt of fresh carpet and just-dried paint. It felt efficiently put together, like it wasn't passive aggressively wired to the fault lines of the universe.

But you couldn't figure out how to turn the power to the shower on. Your first morning, you had to wash yourself over the sink. It was cold, and the floor got sudsy and wet. Your shivering made you late for your new job.

Then later.

Later still.

Too late.

Absent.

You put a towel over the puddle and spent the next year sat in the bathroom, watching rings of mould circle the loops of fabric, witnessing ecosystems turn from green to light brown, dark brown to black.

You wondered if this was what God was doing. Sitting naked on His bathroom floor instead of turning up to His day job. Shivering. Watching the hues of the globe shift a little each time we loop round the sun.

You found out about your nickname at work. 'Jesus'. You

thought it might be because everyone was waiting for you to turn up. That wasn't it. It was because the suit you bought for your first day was getting holier and holier.

You'd never seen a single moth in the flat. You asked the internet if moths can lay eggs underneath human skin. Took the year off to read all 365,000 results.

After you finished reading each article, you inspected your skin so closely, looked so deeply into every pore that every pore became a black hole. Your body became a network of rifts in the space-time continuum, through which the moths were travelling via the ice age and the space age and the stone age, only emerging into the present day to feast on your suit when you were asleep.

Today, you got a letter from the bosses, asking if you owned any other suits. "The holes are getting ridiculous," they said. "They leave you exposed in places that shouldn't be exposed. We see red marks all over your body, like a toddler went mad with a permanent marker."

"We can see right through you," they said.

You knew it was time to go when the earthquake caught up. Shook your flat so hard the towel crinkled on the floor, sent ecosystem crashing into ecosystem. Shook the moths out your pores. Shook open the cupboard doors. Revealed a switch under the bathroom sink that said 'SHOWER'.

You flicked it and left the keys on the table.

Outside, low black clouds touched the tops of derelict buildings. People ran naked in tight circles, bumping into one another.

As you fled on a stolen scooter, the heavens opened behind you. Flooded the town. Swept your towel into the sea like a magic carpet in the middle of a nervous breakdown.

Your next place will be at the summit of the highest mountain on Earth. The locals will worship the roar and smell of your battered scooter. Feed you. Paint red patterns on your chest and forehead.

You'll be above the clouds, where you can watch the rains wash away the world underneath until you feel your sense of scale floats out of your skull. Until you're standing over a sink, tap running.

You'll see a plane on the horizon, with red writing on the side that says, 'NOT IN USE'. There'll be a glint in the window of the cockpit.

Raise a finger, see if you can beckon it over. The locals will love it if you can.

Different

When you returned to Earth after a decade in space, I took you to our favourite restaurant.

It was the same restaurant as before, except the sign above the door had changed colour and font, and the toilets had new touchless flushes, and the table we always sat at faced another way. All the waiters from before had left and become mortgage advisors and been replaced by the mortgage advisors of tomorrow, and what used to be called a burger was now a locally sourced grass-fed beef patty on a bed of foraged vegetables, served in an artisanal bun.

Over mains, you told me about cells in a human body and how they replenish every seven years. "No fibre of us remains from seven years before," you said.

Over dessert, you told me you were leaving me.

"It's not you," you said as your tentacles played with your food. "It's Earth."

I Fought The Lawn

(And The Lawn Won)

I accidentally drove my lawnmower down a black hole in my garden.

It scrambled time and space, spaghettifying me into a state of perpetual lawn mowing.

That's how I mysteriously disappeared from the face of the Earth, yet my grass remains so immaculately trimmed.

Mirror Tunnel

Somewhere in the universe, someone else is typing these exact words. Such is the vastness of existence.

They're thinking of me, typing these words too.

I'm thinking maybe the universe is an illusion, like a hall of mirrors.

"Interesting thought," we're typing.

Shattered

You came back from space with a box marked 'FRAGILE'.

I was six years old and mischievous. I found it and shook it until the contents turned to powder.

You caught me and told me what was inside: a voodoo replica of the whole entire universe.

Everyone has been living in a meteor storm ever since, and nobody knows why.

It's our little secret.

Unnatural Selecion

As a child, I found a shell on the beach. I held it to my ear and heard the sea gently lapping the shore.

Centuries later, an alien found my skull on a barren Earth. It held it to its antenna and sensed the *bleep* *bleep* *crash* *bang* *wallop* of capitalism and the apocalypse.

Old Light

As flames scorched the Summer air, the barbeque went bad.

We were laughing. We were chatting about holidays. We were saying how nobody cares if the burgers got a bit burnt. It makes the flavour more interesting.

Someone was explaining the maillard effect. Someone else was saying what a beautiful day it was. Clear blue skies.

Your chat always gets all cosmic after a few beers and too much boring conversation around.

You told everyone the sunlight we're feeling on our skin is not the sunlight of now. It's the light of eight minutes and twenty seconds ago. That's how long it's taken for it to travel from the Sun to Earth.

Then I said something. It just came out. Sometimes I get snippy after a few beers and too much of your astrophysics bullshit. I said it also takes less than eight minutes and twenty seconds to fuck up a marriage. Know what I mean?

The silence that followed lasted from Mercury to Venus.

You broke it by asking everyone to please leave. Now, please.

Now you're inside, washing dishes loudly. Now I stand in the garden, old light from eight minutes and twenty seconds ago burning my skin and forming the only shadow left in the garden.

I want to convince the light to turn around. To start its journey again from the beginning, from right before either of us opened our mouths.

Time Lake

We had our first kiss on our minus 100th wedding anniversary. You were a duckling, I was a fish. We dived in for the same crumb at the same time, and our mouths met. At that moment, our future selves were sat in our garden, throwing bread into the pond whilst discussing reincarnation and whether that blemish in the water was in fact a rift in the space-time continuum.

There's No Place Like Home...

Our universe has an extra star that doesn't exist in any other dimension.

We call it the Sun.

I've travelled across space and wormholes my whole life.

When I'm asked where I'm from, I glance at the void in the starry sky, where home should be.

"You wouldn't know it," I say.

Sometimes It Takes 65 Million Years to Find 'The One'

I found everything about you so fucking sexy from the beginning of our date. Your T-Rex watch. Your yellow and green 4x4 vehicle with the film's logo stenciled on the side. Your walking stick, topped with the mosquito encased in the sap.

Before the starters arrived, we were already humming the John Williams theme tune together, getting all kinds of satisfyingly bitchy glares from the other tables.

By the end of the mains (you had the rack of lamb) you'd told me the key points of your life story:

Age ten — going back to the cinema to see the film another twenty times in the opening week;

Age eighteen — going travelling, obtaining DNA from the Jurassic age;

Age twenty-two — getting kicked out of your biomedical engineering degree for conducting a series of morally dubious experiments.

"And what did these experiments entail?" I said.

"So what is it you do?" you replied. "I saw on your profile that you work in the zoo?"

"That's right," I said. "They say I'm a real keeper!"

When you laughed, there was something crocodilian about your grin. A reptilian glint in your eye.

We enjoyed a comfortable few seconds of silence. To me, it felt like a real *moment*. I think you felt the same. You took me by the hand. Your palms were dry and scaly and made me want to buy you some good moisturiser. Your fingernails seemed to be getting sharper and pointier by the millisecond, but I didn't mind.

"Can we skip all this small talk?" you said. "I don't have time for small talk. Maybe not even desert or coffee."

"Shall we go somewhere else?"

"Do you have the keys to your workplace on you?" you said. "The thing is…"

"Oh, here comes 'the thing'," I said. "There's always a 'the thing'. Alright, put me out of my misery. Tell me what 'the thing' is."

"The thing is, I've managed to replicate a lot of the film's science stuff in my home lab, on myself. The biomedical engineering stuff. The DNA stuff, with the fossils and the old mosquitoes. But... I didn't have the time or the money for the other stuff. The infrastructure stuff. The safety stuff. The ethics stuff. You know, the Dickie Attenborough stuff. The cages to keep the dinosaurs away from the general public stuff. The Park stuff."

"Just the Jurassic stuff."

I looked into your eyes. They appeared to be moving round to the side of your face. Your jaw was starting to jut out. Your teeth were getting longer. It reminded me of my college days on acid and mushrooms, feeling the trip kick in. You made me feel like I was nineteen again.

I could have left you right there, to take care of yourself. I could have jumped into the nearest vehicle and headed for somewhere safe. Sat with a big bowl of popcorn and watched from afar as everyone in your path got viciously mauled, all silhouettes of half-eaten torsos flying through the city skyline against the backdrop of a full moon.

Maybe I should have paid for my share of the meal and left. Never seen you again. Kept searching online for The One. Plenty more fish in the sea. Genetically stable fish, a few geological periods closer to my own age.

But by that point, it was too late. 65 million years too late. I was already in love.

Seam

The music video becomes a cultural milestone.

The song is about keeping on dancing no matter what.

The video looks to have been shot in a single, spectacular, sweeping take.

In reality, the video was shot in two takes.

There is a seam.

During the break between shooting take one and take two, a message pings in the band's family group chat: *Sad news. Call home.* They read it separately, in three different dressing rooms. They meet in the middle to make the call. They listen to their mother's voice. They put their hands on each other's backs. For the first time since their journey to stardom began, they feel flesh and blood underneath designer clothes. They hang up and pause, then decide they will finish the day's work. Crazy money had been spent on this production. If major streets can be closed down for this: if traffic can be redirected, tears can be suppressed. They do the second take. They do it with aplomb. Their private jet takes them home and they get fed like they have hollow legs. In the bedroom they shared as children, they fight over who gets what bed. It's irrelevant. "Aunties and uncles are coming," they get told. "They get the beds. You all get the floor." They get granted compassionate leave. The execs tell them the most important thing is that they're back and ready for the promotional tour. They put on weight for their mother, then lose it for the label. The video gets released. The video goes viral. The video gets talked about by the world. Wannabe editors and directors and film-school lecturers dissect it. They know it was shot in two takes and two takes only. Debate rages in comments sections. Industry boffins speculate on where the seam between the two takes is. If there is a seam, nobody can conclusively find it. They question whether there is one at all. The video's director vows never to reveal this secret, even to the band themselves.

The band members know exactly where it is.

Two minutes in, they are dancing.

They keep dancing.

They don't miss a beat.

Two minutes in, their steps get a lifetime heavier.

A Date with A Time Lord

"You look different from your profile picture," I said. Your face was the same, but your clothes and demeanour were drastically different.

In your profile picture, you were a 1980s throwback and I liked it. Swiped right on it. Thought you looked cool and retro.

"That picture was taken in what you'd call 'the past'" you said. "About thirty-five years what you'd call 'ago'."

"And what would *you* call it?" I said.

"I wouldn't call it anything. It's just me. It's just a picture of me in 1983."

You told me words like 'ago' and 'soon' and 'then' make very little sense to you. You told me concepts like 'late' and 'early' are stupid. To you, getting worked up about punctuality is like an Amazonian frog getting riled about a tiddlywinks competition on Mars.

"Know what I mean?" you said.

"Not really," I said. "Not when I'm too hungry to think straight and we haven't even ordered yet."

"But we *have* ordered," you said. "We've ordered. And we've eaten. And we've fucked. And we've not messaged each other. And we've gone our separate ways. Met other people. You, someone who understands and values punctuality. Me, a fellow Time Lord who knows what I mean. It's all happened. Just not what you'd call 'yet'."

You droned on and on for 'forever'. Told me what I call the 'future' is, to you, like walking around a museum you've visited several times before. You said that sometimes it can be nice to be around someone who's not a Time Lord, because you get to see their reactions to events afresh. But overall, you're bored. Bored of the Time Lord life. You told me a part of you envies me and how I live life the linear way, how I'm so caught up in the 'present'.

When I tried to attract a waiter's attention, you stopped talking and said you were sorry.

"For what?" I said.

"I'm timelordsplaining again. So... what do you do?"

"Don't you already know the answer to that?" I said.

"Being an all-seeing Time Lord? And if you already know we're going to fuck and that it'll be nothing more than a one night stand, what's the point in even making an effort?"

You grabbed my hand and looked me in the eye for what a non-Time Lord like me might call 'an eternity'.

"It is what it is," you said.

And that was the moment I'd always remember from our date.

In the end, we ordered and we ate. And we did indeed fuck, and it was what it was. When we went our separate ways, I did meet someone else. I grew old. I died. I went into the ground and became the land. My minerals cultivated other life, which eventually died and cultivated other life again. Earth died, too. But parts of it and remnants of me migrated to other planets, from which new alien species spawned. Before any of that, others died and went into the earth, which produced me.

Theoretically, you were there for it all. You were there when the only remaining remnants of human existence were the plastic bottles and shards of glass we produced. You were there when our towns and cities became fossilised underneath sheets of ice, and you were there when my ancestors were wearing animal hides and painting on cave walls. You always 'were'. You always 'will be'.

But to me, a mere non-Time Lord, that moment you grabbed my hand and you said the fuck we were about to have that you knew was going to happen anyway "is what it is" was the moment you became dead to me.

What Would Happen If The Speed of Light Simply Changed

I knew the speed of light had slowed down to a snail's pace when I looked across the street. The people I saw on the other side were from weeks ago.

I knew it when I looked down at what I was eating and saw breakfast, even though I was actually eating dinner.

I knew it when I first laid eyes on my true love, even though our children were already born.

Skyscraper Head

At school, they call me Skyscraper Head, due to the skyscraper growing on my head.

No doctor will operate on it. They say the plumbing, from top to bottom, is connected to the part of my brain that operates my heartbeat and breathing. One burst pipe and I'm dead, they say. It's a lot of guesswork. There is no precedent. No person has had a skyscraper growing on their head before.

The skyscraper is mainly occupied by office workers. In the evenings, I hear them leaving from the underground carpark that seems to have appeared somewhere deep in my skull. I hear their vehicles whooshing away via the tunnel that drills through the part of my brain that controls my sense of time and space. During the rush hour, those senses get scrambled by all the burning rubber and horns and exhaust fumes.

Know what's cool about having my sense of time

scrambled? I get to see the future every evening.

Do you know how tall the building gets in the future?

The building gets three hundred million miles tall.

The building has the universe's highest nightclub, restaurant and aquarium. All the craziest adult shit in existence happens up at the top.

The building has a pad on the roof for space stations from far and wide to dock.

The building is the only skyscraper visible from other galaxies.

Right at the bottom of the building, there's a memorial. They put it there so the universe can always remember where this amazing cosmic skyscraper took root.

The memorial has the date I was born and the date the pipes burst.

At night, when the building is empty and the streets and roads and tunnels are silent, everyone I ever knew gathers at the memorial to remember me; the schoolkid they called Skyscraper Head.

Drifters

I volunteered at peak apocalypse.

When you watch your pension go to shit, then your job prospects fizzle to nothing, then you don't know if you're going to eat again, then you literally don't know if the sun is going to rise the next day, you get to the point where you just think 'fuck it'.

A few days later, the forms are signed and you're getting launched into deep space with a hundred thousand others in the same boat.

We all watched Earth from the spacecraft's viewing deck. We watched it stretch the limits of our sight as we drifted further out.

It was a curved surface of toxic clouds, frozen seas and derelict land.

It was a scarred sphere getting smaller and smaller.

It was a microscopic speck, dwarfed by the other dying planets.

"I still see it," I said to the people round me – strangers, yet suddenly brothers and sisters in arms.

"I still see it too," they said.

"Now I don't."

"I still do."

"Now I don't either."

Then the alarm went off. It was time to begin our cryo-sleep.

• • •

Waking up in space after a thousand-year sleep feels like jolting upright from a dream in which you're constantly falling. Except, the sensation of constantly falling doesn't ease as you realise it was just a dream and now you're awake.

The sensation of waking up and looking at the clock and realising you've slept in. That's another thing that took hold. Except this time, you haven't slept in by an hour or two. It's been a millennium. And it's not like the consequence is getting a little telling off from the boss, or getting mocked by your colleagues for being late. No, the boss is dead. Your colleagues are dead. Your friends. Your family. All of them, hundreds of years dead.

We gathered together, us strangers in arms, and made awkward quips about having slept like a log. After breakfast, we caught up on the news from the time we'd lost to hibernation.

The last transmission from Earth was nine hundred and eighty-four years ago. They told us that humankind was doomed. They thanked us for our service. They told us we should fend for ourselves out here. Not to worry about reporting back, because there would be nothing to report back to. By the time we watch this, they said, the only life left on the planet will be the bacteria that can survive near geothermal springs.

So there it was. We were the drifting log from the tree that fell in the forest when nobody was around to hear it fall.

We gathered on the viewing deck and we looked out to the stars.

We knew its light would have faded too much to be visible from where we were. Still, a group of us tried to pinpoint where the Sun would be.

And we could have sworn we saw it winking back at us, like the ghost of a loved one in an unfamiliar crowd.

Swipe Night

Midnight & Noon were a match on each other's Tinder.

One messaged the other as the other was going to sleep.

The other replied as they got up.

The world got in the way of them ever meeting.

Midnight gazed and lusted at Noon's light reflecting off the moon, forever pining for what might have been.

Sleeping with The Fishes

A black hole opened in my ceiling and swallowed my bed.

My landlord refused to replace it, claiming I was liable.

When I moved out, I hid a fish in the black hole.

The stink it made transcended space and time, ruining his property portfolio forever.

Our Rhythm

When you fell to Earth, you promised to teach me how to navigate the universe. In return, I said I'd show you how to dance.

Together, we spent the rest of time waltzing through the cosmos —

1-2-3-moon,

      1-2-3-star,

            1-2-3-moon,

[Unfinished]

Every morning, I'd ask this barista how he was, and he'd always say the same thing — "I'm here."

Then one day, he wasn't.

That was years ago. But I still think about that guy, all the time.

Apple Juice

As a kid, he'd drink apple juice on the rocks out of a tumbler to be more like his dad.

As an adult, he drinks apple juice out of a tumbler to be less like his dad.

The More The World Got Damaged

(The More You Cried)

You collected your tears. First in a jar. Then a bucket. Then a pool. A lake. An ocean.

Soon, you flooded the whole world in salt water.

Earth became a giant teardrop, streaming down the cheek of a sobbing universe.

Glue

At the Chinese takeaway, I order my food and I get it handed to me in a steaming hot paper bag. In the time between ordering and receiving my food, I have these conversations with the lady who runs the place.

We talk about next to nothing. We talk about the weather. We talk about funny or annoying habits her other customers have. We talk about stuff to do with my work. We talk about China. We talk about the days we've had, how things change with the time of year because of the climate or holidays or whatever. One time, when no other customers were around, she gave me a tutorial on how to chop a carrot so the pieces look like little goldfish. Our conversations are a million tiny dots, but over the years, they've become a huge canvas you take a step back and see something whole and beautiful.

One time I told her how my boss was a massive dick, and how everyone was quitting because of it. She told me about her chefs. How they'd been there for decades.

How staff stay with you if you treat them right, which saves you so many headaches in the long run. She told me that's why the food here is so good.

I go there whenever I have a bad hangover or I've had a shit day at work. Something about their wonton soup glues me right back together.

This time, I was both things. Hungover and just had a shit day at work. I'd made a mistake. A customer called me a fucking cretin. Said I couldn't organise a piss up in a brewery. Said he was going to take this right to the top so the people who were paying my wages would know all about it and would replace me with someone who wasn't some bleary-eyed waster. He stormed off, only to storm back and grab my ID from around my neck to get my full name.

Sometimes I go into the takeaway and she's busy or not there for whatever reason.

This time, one of the chefs came out from the kitchen to take my order. I'd never seen him, but I felt like I knew him. I felt like his hands had pieced me together a million times. I told him so.

Then I took my steaming hot bag of food home and I ate, and I felt this cruel and shattering world become something whole and beautiful again.

Relaunch

One day you woke up and told us you'd just returned from space, and that Earth was a globe-sized allergen that was suppressing your ability to think straight.

You said the stars were your epinephrine injectors.

You said you were a prisoner to gravity.

So we got you a trampoline and put it in the garden.

You slept through the day, then we'd hear you on it all night.

You told us you were going to keep improving on it. Keep upping those seconds in the air to minutes.

Then hours...

...Days

... Years

...*Eternity*

What We Can Learn
from The Death of Mr McKenna

They found my old high school history teacher, Mr McKenna, dead behind a bookcase in his home. Neighbours had complained about the smell.

I looked into his cause of death. Apparently if you drop something behind a bookcase or a wardrobe, you should never lean into the small gap between it and the wall to retrieve it. If you lose your balance, you might get stuck. If nobody finds you, you might die. Apparently, this is very much a thing.

Instead, move the bookcase or wardrobe first. It might be a bit of a pain, but then again, so is slowly dying alone.

I don't remember many lessons from school. Only those from Mr McKenna's.

I remember him spending a whole afternoon convincing us 'however' and 'therefore' are two of the most powerful words in the English language, and we should always consider using them in any conclusion to any essay. I remember someone asking him what the point in learning history was. He told us, amongst many other things, history presents us with an opportunity to learn from our mistakes of the past.

It must have been awful for Mr McKenna. All alone, lodged against a wall as his last breaths left his body. The bookcase that killed him must have been stacked with so much amazing literature. Books about wars, scandals, revolutions, migrations, all kinds of hardship.

In all those pages, I bet there was nothing warning about the potential perils of getting stuck behind a bookcase. Maybe if there was, he'd still be alive today.

These words are going to be in a book. These very words, right here.

Maybe this book won't stop any wars. However, maybe it will end up on someone else's bookcase. Maybe when that person gets old and they live alone, they won't die stuck behind it as a result. Therefore, these words about Mr McKenna's death would have saved someone's life.

I think Mr McKenna would have liked that.

Italy

I went to Italy alone this time. When I returned, you asked me why I hadn't taken a single photo.

I told you the older I get, the more I enjoy the ephemeral nature of memories.

"The memories would still be ephemeral if you took a photo or two," you said. "It'd also mean you could share them."

"Share them with who?" I said.

I turned to look at you.

You weren't there.

Hadn't been for years.

Star

I befriended a sad, dying star.

By the end, I had to hold it to keep it warm.

"Hey," I said. "Light years away, someone is gazing at the night sky, seeing you in your pomp. A radiant, fiery ball of energy..."

It sobbed a neutron sob.

Then I felt it go cold in my arms.

Scars Are Decorations

For forty-three years, I globetrotted with that leather suitcase.

When everyone bought the one with the wheels and the retractable handle, I kept carrying my life around in that bulky old thing. When both my arms got too dead to lift it any further, I'd drag it along, sweeping all kinds of dust bunnies and gunk off airport floors, train station steps, puddled potholed streets.

When rips appeared, or when the handle got worn-in, I sat in my hostel or motel room and put plasters on my fingers, then I'd patch the case up, sewing a miniature flag of whatever country we were in on top of the holes.

I don't remember who, but someone somewhere once told me scars are decorations.

Then in Riga, I pulled it off the baggage carousel and it just collapsed, like some frail old dude having a cardiac arrest. Spilt its guts out everywhere. Shed half its flags. Caused a bit of a scene, people rushing down to their knees to help out. In the end, I had to scoop everything up and fireman's lift it out of there. I've taken painkillers for my back ever since.

Whatever home means, I took it back there. Home. I opened it up and sat it empty on my front doorstep. Filled it with compost and turned it into a flower bed. Closest thing I ever had to a garden.

I have the suitcase with the wheels and the retractable handle now. It's spared me a few dead arms and gunk bunnies, I'll give it that.

And when I'm back here, back at whatever home means, I sit out on my doorstep at night. Sip a beer. Tend to the flowers. Chat to them about the past, like some old dude talking to some dead dude.

The Boy in The Jacket

I found a note in the inside pocket of this amazing jacket I just bought from a vintage clothes shop. The paper was a pinch away from crumbling between my fingers, but I could still make out the phone number written on it. Underneath were the words—

'Call me'.

I called. I told you how I got your number.

You remembered the jacket. "That jacket is over fifty years old," you said. "I wrote that note forty-eight years ago. Forty-eight years and seven months. And two weeks this Saturday."

You told me what it was like to dance with the boy who wore it. "We were like a pair of figure skaters who already knew our gold medal was in the bag." You said that sometimes, you still think you see that boy.

He'd be old by now. Old as you. But sometimes you see a young man in the middle distance and, for a split second, you convince yourself it's him, and he hasn't aged since that night. You convince yourself your eyes will meet and he'll say he's so sorry he never called. Then he'll take your hand and you'll glide into a parallel last fifty years in which you'll wake up next to him in the present day, and the real last fifty years will all have been a mundane dream that will fizzle from your memory within seconds.

"Are you wearing the jacket right now?" you said.

"I am."

You told me not to talk anymore. To keep the jacket on. To stay on the line with you while you hum a little tune. To sway my hips to your rhythm. To keep swaying. To keep swaying until you were ready to hang up.

I'm still swaying.

I think you've fallen asleep, but I won't hang up.

A Date without Small Talk

I hate small talk, so I thought it was cool when we hugged and you said, "Hi, nice to meet you. Do you think that time existed before the universe was formed?"

We went mini-golfing. I asked you if you thought it was possible that a miniature Earth, maybe the size of one of these golf balls, might exist somewhere inside this normal-sized Earth.

"How do you know we're not already inside this miniature Earth you speak of?" you asked. "How do you know giant clones of us aren't walking around out there, having this same exact conversation?"

"Except I guess they'd be calling it just golf," I said.

The rest of the date might have lasted a minute or a million eons. I don't remember, because you made me feel dizzy, like my world was a vortex on course for a black hole.

Whenever it ended, I asked if I could see you again.

You told me this was inevitable, because the universe is expanding and will continue to expand until it begins to collapse. Then it will collapse until it has collapsed to nothing. From there, it will start expanding again, and it will expand in exactly the same way it expanded before. All events will be exactly the same. Eventually, it, and we, will arrive back at this exact moment. This has already happened a trillion times before, and it will happen a trillion times again. The universe is trapped in this cycle.

"So yes," you said. "You will see me again. In this iteration of existence or the next."

A day later, I messaged you. I said the weather was nice. I asked how you were doing and what you were getting up to.

I waited for you to message back.

I waited and I waited.

I waited more. I waited longer than it takes for the universe to expand and collapse and then expand again until the moment we first met. I waited for so long that I now have a definitive answer to your question:

No. Time did not exist before the universe got formed. If it did, surely by now I'd have seen you again.

Talk

I'm calling the emergency line but my ear is drowning in dark currents.

Through the flow I almost hear myself telling them I just need someone to talk to and can they please talk to me because I think I'm dying and I don't want to die alone.

They tell me we're not alone.

I'm trying to stop blood leaving my head from behind the lobe but it's like plugging a monsoon with a cork and my hand only pushes the crystals lodged in my skull further into my skull.

They tell me they're sending the aliens and who am I and where am I and where have I been.

I'm listening to myself telling them I need the aliens to get here quick.

They ask me what happened and I tell them there was trouble out here and I went to stop the trouble.

I'm telling them just as I thought I'd stopped the trouble something smashed the back of my head and I didn't see anything but it feels like the whole universe got condensed into a snow globe that collided like a species-shattering meteor into the back of my head and are the aliens coming soon?

They tell me I need to keep talking and they keep asking questions that relate to the real world and I'm not in the real world.

I'm watching those deepening dark currents from my ear flood the ground beneath my head like a black hole and I feel the black hole sucking me into a portal to the future past.

They ask me if I'm still there and tell me to say something just give them a signal because it's really important that I keep talking because I'm getting sucked in.

Once I'm inside time is going to get stretched and warped.

They ask me something else but I don't hear because

I'm sucked in. And time *is* stretched and time *is* warped. I see the future. The future is me waking up in a hospital bed. I'm peeking at my family through bandages. They're telling me I was apparently talking a load of gibberish when I got here, "But what's new?" It hurts when I laugh but I don't mind. The physical wounds heal within weeks. The future future is more painful. The future future is not being able to go out in public without hearing crunching glass coming behind me instead of innocent footsteps. The future future is dark and rainy nights seeing jaggy shattered vodka bottles covered in blood falling from the sky. The future future is standing in a crowd and looking at the back of someone's head and seeing gashes open up behind their earlobe like black holes that now suck me into the past where

I'm a child. I'm in therapy because I have this compulsion to hit people. They don't do anything special there. They just talk to me. I stop doing it and I grow up and I stop a fight and I get bottled and sucked into a black hole and back into the future future where I'm back in therapy. They ask me if I've considered getting out there. Spending time with other people in the same hole.

He and I talk because there's nothing else to do but talk because it's not like we can go out. He talks gibberish about space even more than I do. Says he's 99% sure he's an alien because that would explain a lot about why the world to him is so fucked up but every cunt else is able to just get on with it. I tell him it got better for me when I started writing down my thoughts. On good days I can get it down to a solid 98.9%.

One time I turn up and he's written something. What he's written is a story about me and what happened to me and of course it's got black holes and aliens in it.

At the end of the story the aliens arrive and pull me out the puddle of black hole and as expected they are green and shrouded in blue light. I don't know who I am or where I am or whether it's the past or the present or the future or future future. What I do hear is myself talking into the phone that's still connected to the emergency line that's lying in the puddle of my blood.

I'm saying thank you

Thank you for just talking to me.

A Whisper from The Sea

I heard about a black hole somewhere in the ocean.

I packed my easel onto a boat and went out there to find it and draw it.

I got too close. The black hole swallowed me up. Turned my canvas into a unit of time. Trapped me in eternity.

You'll never see me again, but do not fret.

I'm always sketching. When you miss me, look out to the horizon. Follow the pencil lines. Your future is all mapped out for you.

The Promise

You asked me to bury you in space, away from gravity.

"Promise?" you said.

"I promise."

When you died, the rest of the family insisted you got put in the ground.

I grew up and became an astronaut. I carry a spade on every mission.

Each time I return, I put a handful of stars on your grave.

I feel the weight lift, bit by bit.

They Cry and Shriek

We can't hear it, but Moons make noises as they circle their planets.

They sing and laugh if their planet is in harmony. They cry and shriek if it is not.

Our Moon has been crying and shrieking for centuries.

We gaze up at the night sky.

"Isn't it beautiful," we say.

Moving The Dust Around

I fell down a trap door in the floor of the universe.

The cellar down here is full of disused stars, old gravity and musty time, all coated in layers of moon dust.

The only thing I can do to alleviate my eternal boredom is to shift that dust, using the vacuum of space.

The Looping

My soul left my body.

With no body, you can't do much except wait.

I watched my children grow up and die. I waited for time to end and loop back to the start. I waited more. I watched my parents get born, grow up, meet.

Then I went back in my body and I started again.

Tides

The Moon is drifting from Earth.

Eventually, we'll lose contact.

We'll gaze at the sky and see it joining the orbit of another planet.

They'll make tides of their own. Not better ones, just different.

Tides that seem right as we watch them lapping those faraway shores.

+0

You've gone solo to another wedding.

It's the section of the day straight after the service, before everyone goes and sits for the speeches and the food. Everyone stands around waiting and drinking sparkling wine and talking. Waiting. Talking. Waiting. Talking and waiting. Everyone, waiting and talking, talking and waiting in couples and in pairs. Everyone, in pairs and couples, talking. Except you. You're alone. Waiting. Drinking. Waiting and drinking.

You're standing. You're hovering. You're taking anxious sips. You're floating between groups of two and groups of four and six. Wherever you float, wherever you hover, you're turning even numbers odd.

$1 + 0 = $ You

You've done the right thing. You've gone and you've locked yourself in a toilet cubicle.

You're locked in the toilet cubicle. You're quaffing

complimentary champagne, flute number five, waiting for it to morph you into some sort of social butterfly or some shit.

You've already used the toilet and flushed the toilet, but you flush the toilet again. The sympathetic groan of the cistern masks the breathing exercises you're now doing — the ones you were taught to do when things get a bit much at work — by the occupational health therapist who later went off for six months with a nervous breakdown.

The cistern's final hisses fade to silence. You flush again. It's the fourth time you've flushed. You contemplate your options. The chatter out there sounded as loud as ever. The talking and the waiting shows no sign of letting up.

You see two ways out.

The cubicle door is Option 1. Back out there to more people talking while you stand and you hover and you wait and you scramble that gentle equilibrium of even numbers.

Option 2? An escape. Down the toilet, Renton from Trainspotting style. Through the sewage pipes, finale of *The Shawshank Redemption* style. You picture it, elation, as you stare back at the venue, now a distance away. You're covered in shit, but you're out. You're alone, but no longer odd.

Did you know that the average person spends six months of their life waiting for a red light to turn green?

The above has nothing to do with anything. I just told you it to pass a speck of time, maybe calm you down a bit.

Hi.

I am your +0 for the rest of the day. I am your future self, from just far enough ahead to tell you this: after two more flushes and a few more deep breaths, right down through your belly, it will be time for you to take Option 1.

That's a nice suit you're wearing. You look far too amazing to get it covered in shit. Plus, you're not that skinny.

I'm here to tell you you'll go out there and, maybe something to do with all those empty champagne flutes you've left around the edges of the room, you'll butt into the first even numbered group you see and… it'll be…

fine.

They'll be glad to have you butt in. Their conversation

was drying up before you came. Nobody really likes the talking and waiting bit.

You'll get chatting to a nice lady. She'll be the auntie of the best man who feels like she is, by extension, the auntie of the groom and now therefore, by extension, the auntie of the bride. Something like that. She'll be a town planning consultant. She'll tell you a very interesting fact about how long people wait at traffic lights in a lifetime, then she'll tell you it's actually made up and probably not true, because how could anyone actually know that?

Then the waiting will be over. For the speeches and the food, you'll be sat next to another odd number. You'll ask him where he's been hiding this whole time. He'll tell you he'd found a cloak room. He'll tell you he'd spent at least an hour there, burying his face in people's jackets to smother the sound of his screams of anguish and existential dread. You'll tell him you wish you'd thought of that. You'll tell him you'd spent that whole time looking for a rock hammer.

"To maim all the other guests?" he'll say.

"Something like that," you'll say.

Then you'll agree, the best way forward is to keep drinking.

You'll drink.

You'll dance. With him. With town planner auntie. And the groom's granny. And the bride's uncle Jimmy. And everyone else. You'll belt out the wedding band's versions of 'Livin' on a Prayer' and 'Wonderwall' and you'll invade the stage and encourage everyone else to do the same and even though nobody will, it won't matter, because…

It'll be fine in the end. You'll be sad when it's over.

Anyway.

I'm exhausted now. All that dancing. All that singing. The bruises from the stage dive. I'm going to bed.

I just thought I'd drop in on you before I call a taxi, because I've been where you are now. It was brutal. Really tough. Could have done with somebody like me there in my ear.

So there it is. Have another flush or two. Finish that champagne. Breathe in through the nose and out through the mouth. Get yourself out there. Act amazed when you get told that fake fact about traffic lights and waiting. Dance. Sing. Invade.

And in a few hours, don't forget to check back in on the you of the past.

Snooze

I ran a bath and went for a lie down while I waited.

The smell of lavender made me drift off, and I fell asleep for centuries.

When I woke up, the floodwaters on my floor contained all the sea life in the world.

I waded through fish and whales, seaweed and shipwrecks to turn off the tap.

Then I climbed back onto my floating bed and went back to sleep.

Then We Soar

Whenever I see a comet in the night, I know it's you winking at us.

"Grab on," you whisper through the dark and cloudless sky.

I hold my thumb and forefinger up to one eye and I pinch the tail.

Then we soar between the stars and the universes, shedding gravity and time, sadness and death.

The Grass Is Always Greener in The Stars

"I want to be an Earth child," said the alien who abducted the boy.

So, they swapped lives: UFO for bike.

Nobody told the alien that Earth children grow up, or that he would grow up sad, always staring at the sky, always contemplating former lives and bad decisions, always writing about what's smiling down from the stars.

Silent Grunge Street Disco

Every Saturday evening, I walk to my night shift. As I get to the centre of town, I pass a group of about twenty drunk people. They all have earphones in. They're singing 'Smells Like Teen Spirit' by Nirvana as they mosh out-of-tune down the street, led by a lady wearing a t-shirt that says 'Silent Grunge Street Disco'.

This happens every week.. Same time, same spot, same song, same lady.

Apart from the lady, I never look at the individual faces. They probably change from one Saturday to the next, but I like to think of them as the same; like my life is a repeating groundhog week and I have therefore not aged another seven days since the last time.

When I pass the group, moving in the opposite direction, I don't go round them. I go through them. I imagine their dancing bodies crushing the pent-up angst out of me. In their ears, they hear 'Smells Like

Teen Spirit' and feel nirvana. In mine, I hear noise pollution and feel fear.

Surely an inverse scenario is unfolding in some parallel universe –

Every week, they stomp to work through a concrete jungle soundtrack of capitalism. I'm drunk, moshing in the opposite direction with a group of friends, Nirvana in my earlobes. I'm back in the moment I heard that song for the first time. I'm thirteen years old. Their music is what tells me maybe I am wired into this life ok after all.

At work, I stay tuned to this scenario. The clock ticks. The seconds stretch and linger and make me too exhausted to ever get myself out of this rut. I close my eyes. I'm drunk, in a parallel universe. And I'm thirteen years old.

And I will never be a week older than the Saturday before.

Tonight, I Fall From The Sky

My blood absorbs into my body. My bones heal. The airbag sucks into the steering wheel. The car uncrumples and veers onto the road.

I drive home, backwards.

I unkiss you goodbye and go into the house, where I haunt you until the day we meet.

Neil Clark is a writer from Edinburgh, Scotland. He didn't discover his love for the written word until his twenties and never thought he'd be writing a bio for his first print collection. But here we are, people. Here we are. He has flash fiction stories published in various online journals, has been nominated for awards such as *Best of the Net* and *Best Small Fictions*, and has placed in some competitions. You can find out more about it at **neilclarkwrites.wordpress.com**.

Twitter: @NeilRClark.

Acknowledgements

Eternal thanks to the Back Patio Press boys, Cavin Bryce Gonzalez and Zac Smith, for making this with me, for your energy, for the journey. Cavin, thank you for your encouragement, your faith in me, for making me realise this was possible in the first place. Thank you to my two best friends, Richard Jacobs and Stephen McLaren, for being exactly that. Thank you to my parents, for every reason in the universe. Thank you to you, the reader.

NUMBSKULL

No Glykon

Beneath the respirating sky, someone sits in the grass. The details of details take her attention for the moment. She decides to leave. She goes somewhere. She goes somewhere else.

With a section from a newspaper under her arm, someone else sits on a curb in front of a convenience store. A tattoo on her arm reads, 1...2...3 Instant Triangle. The font is minimal and sans-serif.

$$\triangle \text{|||} \triangle$$

Something about her thoughts is different, the pulling sensation on her mind and everything in the back of her mind being pulled to her face and thinking of all her thoughts and thinking of all of her thoughts on her thoughts. A radiating pain starts in her head. She starts experiencing nausea-type feelings. She does whatever she can to feel okay, but the pain and nausea linger until her remedies wear off.

Text message from Lela: What are you doing?

Text message from Goya: I have dry socket from getting my wisdom teeth pulled. What are you?

Text message from Lela: I am a piece of trash. Wanna hang out?

Text message from Goya: I'm putting my life on hold until Thursday via pills.

The wavy lines of refracted light reflect on Lela's arms and legs and body and other people's arms and legs and their bodies. She walks down a city street in one-point perspective. The perpendicular planes create the condition for the unsubstantial vanishing point, and the parallel lines around her allude to that point on the veiled horizon.

At home, Goya crawls into her blanket cocoon, closing her eyes and finally her thoughts becoming dreams of simple shapes.

Lela researches dry socket. The complication follows tooth extraction, and it involves a dislodged blood clot. The wound appears to be dry, and it is not dry. Exposed bone creates the illusion of being dry. There is a list of symptoms.

Severe throbbing

Continual bleeding

Radiating pain

Foul odor via putrefaction

There is no treatment. It will improve or disappear with time.

Text message from Lela: Dry socket seems brutal.

Goya responds by text messaging a photo, and Lela watches her phone's screen change to show the thumbnail of the image. Lela feels reluctance at the idea of opening the image, but she opens the image anyway. It is of a newspaper advertisement for deconstructed jeans. It shows a woman performing a crystal ritual to turn herself into mist.

Text message from Lela: On Thursday, let's go to the park and drink beers from paper bags. I fly to my dad's on Friday.

Lela stares into an out of focus space. She is not paying attention. She ignores everything. Her jeans fit tight to her legs, acid-washed and cuffed at her ankles. The left leg of her jeans is torn at the knee and lower thigh, white thread crossing the mouths of the holes and more white thread hanging from their mouths like vomit. The right leg of her jeans is torn at the upper hip, the pocket showing through the tear, the pocket's trigonometric print showing through the tear. She wears an oversized, gray, V-neck shirt with Space Brace written across the front, and the words are written in bleach, and the A's in Space Brace are triangles.

Lela bites into a hamburger, thin paper enwrapping half the sandwich with parallel pink and yellow stripes. She chews quietly, and her mouth is closed. She swallows the bite.

Her hair hangs across her face and down to her chest, and it is straight, and it is a faded pink. The color is natural, but no one knows why it grows in that color, not even doctors know, not even her parents know. The faded-pink hair is her most distinguishing quality. Sometimes it seems to be her name, That Woman with Faded-Pink Hair. Most people think it is fake. That seems significant for no reason.

Behind a fledgling shopping center is Lela wandering the alley. A plastic bag floats. A piece of paper slides. She stumbles upon an abandoned warehouse. It is constructed with red, midcentury brick. The structure can only be seen from behind the shopping center. Lela glances around. She is alone. A sign hangs above the door. It is weathered. It is discolored. It reads, Warehaus. The A's in the sign are triangles. Lela inspects the entrance. The door hangs on rusted hinges. It is slightly open. It is oddly welcoming.

KURTHUN THUN

As Lela approaches the door, there is a flash of lightning and a delay and a roar of thunder echoing its way behind the shopping center. She peers into the curiously-open door. A rusty lock and chain keep her from opening the door any further.

Lela examines the opening's width. Thinking she might be able to squeeze in, she lines up her body. The air pressure drops, and the wind hisses through the alley, thick and swarming. Another flash of lightning cracks the sky.

KURTHUN

Again there is the delay and another roar of thunder echoing around Lela. Before trying to squeeze through the door, she changes her mind. She decides to avoid the rain. She decides to go home.

‡‖ — ‖‡

Below the first article is the same image Goya sent in a text message, the supermodel surrounded by crystals and looking upward and wearing deconstructed jeans while she is turning to mist. Goya reads.

Anchorite Observer

4

SUPERMODEL TURNED TO MIST

Supermodel Unfolding Berlin, who starred in a string of high-profile campaigns for top designers, has turned to mist in at her luxury flat in Anchorite. No one knows how to communicate with Unfolding or if that's possible. Her body was discovered a floating haze after she left a series of messages on her website saying she was "slender limbs tottered with weakness". Unfolding, a regular on catwalks in New York, Paris, and Anchorite, has modeled for leading designers. A friend found American-born Unfolding muting her apartment as water vapor. She filmed herself committing the ritual on her cellphone camera. The ceremony was uploaded to her popular blog. In her last blog post, she requested that the footage of the ritual be used in the next Tight Violence campaign. In a press release, Tight Violence said, "Our hearts and support go out to Unfolding's family. In some way, Unfolding turned us into mist. We have decided to respect Unfolding's wishes and use the footage in our next campaign. We expect the campaign, a new line of deconstructed jeans dedicated to Unfolding, to be our most successful yet." Clothing is considered to be deconstructed when it is intentionally torn, ripped, or cut. This often creates the illusion of being worn out or worn in. The press release goes on to say that part of the proceeds will go to found a new nonprofit wellness promotion program titled You're Worth It.

After only reading one report, Goya closes the obituaries.

While Lela stares at a lamp, she realizes the storm subsided.

Lela returns to the warehouse with the curiously-open door. The sun's light is diffuse. A mist hangs in the air, and it tints everything gray. Lela squeezes through the door.

As she penetrates the structure, she seems to already know her way. All the colors are pallid and grave. She walks cautiously. On the far side of the warehouse, she finds an office. She gazes at the floor.

A dusty flannel shirt lies on the ground. It has a name tag pinned to the pocket, the kind someone who works retail would wear, and it reads, Lela Pierce. Though her last name is Jarvis, Lela enjoys the novelty of the original owner sharing her first name. The flannel appears to be clean enough to wear, so she puts it on. It fits well. She brushes dust off the sleeves.

A nullified sentiment precedes a nebulous period and an unconfirmed, disinclined insignificance and a hazy void.

While Lela is on her way to meet Goya, a few people seem to stare at Lela for slightly longer than usual. People usually stare. She is accustomed to it. She has faded-pink hair. But they never stare for this long. This seems more intense. They seem to resent her. She hunches forward, and she enters the park where Goya is smoking a cigarette and reading a section of the newspaper.

"Hey," Lela says.

"Hey," Goya says without looking up from the paper.

"How's the dry rot?"

"The 'dry socket' would suck," Goya says, "but, you know... drugs and stuff."

Lela sits across from Goya. She assumes smoking is particularly bad for someone with dry socket, but says nothing about it.

"..."

"..."

"People seemed to be staring at me with a lot of intensity or something while I was walking here," Lela says.

"Well, you are the woman with faded —" When Goya looks up at Lela, Goya pauses.

As Goya folds the paper and shows what she was reading to Lela, Goya smiles, and she feels self-conscious of a slight overbite, and she covers her mouth with her hand. Goya holds the section of the newspaper out to show Lela. Below the report Supermodel Turned To Mist and below the image from the advertisement for deconstructed jeans with the model turning herself into mist in them, Mom Claims Two Teens Also Turn To Mist titles the second article. Goya's finger points to two black-and-white, side-by-side photos.

In the photo on the left, a slouching boy smirks knowingly like he is getting the joke of everything, and he is looking into that space in the distance reserved for people to avoid looking at a camera, and his distressed jeans have a large tear in the right thigh. In the photo on the right is someone in a dress printed with a pattern of patterns, and she has a timid smile, and her jeans are acid-washed with rips in the knees.

Although the photos are in different frames, their subjects are standing in front of the same wall with geometric wallpaper. It is like they are cut out of the same photo. Their names are written under the photos. Under the photo, it reads, Lela Pierce. Goya reaches over and holds the nametag on Lela's flannel. It reads, Lela Pierce.

"According to this, you, Lela 'Pierce' and your boyfriend turned into mist, and drifted off," Goya says. "Or that's what your mother chooses to believe, but they probably just ran away."

"I choose to believe they did the mist thing too." Lela unpins the name tag. She places it in the flannel's pocket. She places both hands over the pocketed nametag like she is holding it to her heart.

"I can just imagine David and I turned into mist and drifted off," Lela says, thinking this is funny, but she does not laugh.

"Yeah, David would be like, 'How do you want to do it or whatever.' And you would be like, 'I don't care.'"

"And then it would never happen."

"..."

They digress to something else.

They digress to another something else.

They digress to Lela negotiating getting some of Goya's pain medications.

They digress to Goya negotiating using some of Lela's crafting supplies.

They digress to talking about Goya's plan to do nothing.

They digress to talking about Lela's upcoming trip.

Lela is going to be visiting her dad, and she is going to be working with her dad, and he works as an archivist in Endless Summer. The work is challenging and emotionally significant, but Endless Summer makes her feel particularly alienated because she cannot relate to the people who live there for no reason she can think of.

⅃ ⅃⅃ L

While Lela and David stand in an airport terminal, someone's name is called over the intercom. Someone else's name is called over the intercom. The lights fluoresce. Lela cannot focus, and her hand is in her pocket, and she fidgets with two halves of a broken crayon. She pulls the two halves out of her pocket. She shows them to David in an open palm. One half reads, Ultra. The other half reads, violet. The letters are all capitalized, and the industrial-style sans-serif font has gentle and full curves, and the terminal strokes in the letters are cut diagonally. He picks the Ultra half from her hand. He smiles.

"This is like one of those things where when we are old and don't recognize each other, we can put the crayon halves together, and I will know you are you, and you will know I am me," David says. The Ultra half of the crayon is between his fingers. He holds it up. "Like a friendship locket or whatever."

Lela holds the violet half between her fingers. Slowly they move the halves toward each other, unhurried and synchronized and rotating. David feels a welling of anticipation for no reason. Lela feels calm. She smiles. This seems funny to Lela. This seems funny to David. The pieces begin to come together. The joining halves eclipse a fluorescent light.

David and Lela push them together softly, and they turn them until they fit snugly, and they turn them until it reads, Ultraviolet.

David notices Lela crying and smiling at the same time. Someone's name is called over the intercom. Lela Jarvis is called over the intercom. Lela looks off into the distance, and she laughs one breath of a laugh.

"Lela, your plane is boarding," David says.

Lela blinks. A tear path runs from her eye. It runs past her nose. It runs across her lips.

David memorizes her features for later, hoping to remember the world as it is. Lela has faded-pink hair, and she has black eyes. She blinks.

From her left eye, a rectangle grows. It starts tiny. It starts as close to being nothing as possible. As the rectangle becomes larger, a hint of a border on the rectangle becomes visible.

Inside the rectangle, David is driving home from the airport, and it is raining. The rectangle delineates Lela crying at the airport and David driving home.

Inside, the road is empty. It is lined with trees. It is freshly paved. The lines are freshly painted, and the line-space-line-space pattern is mesmerizing.

Everything outside the rectangle is diminished as the everything inside continues to grow. The rectangle fills almost everything outside of the parallelogram, and a little bit of Lela leaving David frames him driving. Lela boards the plane for Endless Summer.

In the rectangle, there is a town ahead. A house goes by. Two signs go by. There is a bright-indigo glow. It shines in front of him. It shines in front of his car. He thinks, Shit. But he feels calm. He thinks, Deer.

And he slams into a drippy, fluorescent, mushy deer-type thing, and pieces of the deer-like thing and pieces of the car fly at the window, some pieces quite large and some quite long and others small shards.

A cube floating above a circular pool of black water. One corner of the cube touches the center of the pool. Inky ripples in the water extend toward the edges of the pool. An equal-and-opposite reaction at the edge of the pool pushes the ripples back toward the center. The equal-and-opposite ripples collide with the new ripples radiating from the center.

The deer-type creature is in the mud. Its faceless head is warped, sludgy mush. Its body is inferred by drippy-indigo outlines that glow. One of its antlers is broken off, and David can tell its neck is twisted around backwards by the direction its other golden antler is facing.

David stands over the deer-type creature. His car

11

is parked on the side of the road. Smoke rises from it. The creature's front leg kicks. It seems like it is trying to run, but only one of its legs is moving.

David paces. His shoulders are hunched, and he covers his face with his hand, and he looks through his fingers, and the deer-like thing's indigo glow starts to fade. The moving leg quivers, and it pulls the deer's body forward just a couple inches. Gradually the glowing outline fades completely.

Surprised at how little he feels about the accident, David watches the lights of a plane in the distance. Is it the one taking Lela to Endless Summer? Is it taking her to the archivist work that is life affirming and enjoyable? A car drives by.

The rain is soaking through his gray slacks and his cardigan and his shirt. The water vapors in his breath create a smoke-like puff. He is underdressed for how cold it is. He runs his fingers through his hair and grabs a handful. With his mind going in every direction is David sighing. He lets go of the handful of hair leaving a large poof sticking up on his head. He sits on the trunk of his car and occasionally looks at the horizon.

Sometimes the image of Lela seems like it will frame everything forever.

■ ■ ■ ■

Evenly spaced on the geometric-patterned carpet in front of her, Goya spreads out her supplies for crafting, including what she borrowed from Lela, a bottle of super glue and a bottle of PVA glue and a glue stick and a stack of all the magazines she could find that feature ads for deconstructed jeans and a pair of scissors with a white handle and an energy bar with gold packaging and her laptop.

The tow truck pulls away. It leaves the mechanic's parking lot, and it leaves David, and it leaves David's car. But the mechanic's shop will not be open until tomorrow.

David inspects the hood of his car. Blood and piss and shit and pieces of the car form a gradient from the hood to the trunk. The hood is covered in cartoonish gore, and the trunk is relatively clean. In a shit-I-just-hit-a-large-woodland-creature mindset, he has the urge to prod the gore. He decides against it.

The mechanic's shop has a fenced in lot. Two dogs watch David from inside the fence. They snarl. They bark. They do not faze David. The snarling and barking enter David's perspective as though muted and distant. Behind the dogs, cars are stacked on one another. The stacks are like gateways. A nameless mist rolls through the gateways. The dogs are losing interest in David. The mist is beginning to envelop the dogs. The dogs turn, and they walk further into the mist. Everything has a vintage tinge. Everything fades out.

Text message from David: Can you give me a ride? I hit some deer-type thing.

On the other side of Goya's room, her phone vibrates on top of her dresser. She stands up from the evenly-spaced crafting supplies, her walls covered in collages of deconstructed jeans. She gives her hair a suburban touch. While holding her phone in her hand, she furrows her brow. She is wearing a sleeveless, one-piece outfit with a geometric pattern with various textures inside the shapes with fluorescent pink and fluorescent green and black outlines. Showing her slight overbite, she wears a calm expression. Her motions are awkward in a calculated way.

Text message from Goya: Where are you? Are you okay?

Goya's phone buzzes again. She grabs her keys off a stack of magazines and flips the phone over. The message is not from David.

Text message from Hunter: You can buy a gun at walmart for $500.

Hunter and Goya and David are friends. More than friends, they are roommates.

THUNK

David closes the passenger door. Goya puts the car in drive.

"Let's go somewhere. Take me anywhere but here," David says.

Goya is wearing a sweater over her jumpsuit's

geometric pattern of textures. It is large. It is black. She smiles to herself. As they drive, David develops fantasies of how her driving could take their lives. They are complex. They are detailed. She drives them somewhere. She drives them somewhere else.

David sighs throughout the drive. He has seen these streets a hundred times, and they look nice for the first time, and they look nice for no reason. Everything has a film-type grain. Everything is a little blurry or out of focus or whatever.

Text message from unknown number: Mic check mic check 1 2 1 2 is this thing on?

Text message from David: Your landing gear is down. I repeat, your landing gear is down.

Text message from unknown number: I wanted to fly this baby into the sun.

Text message from David: Please tell me who is this person that doesn't know babies aren't allowed in the sun anymore?

Text message from unknown number: If 9/11 taught me anything, it's that the sun is the only good place to fly a baby.

Text message from unknown number: Haha... I'm Karen. Goya gave me your number.

David does not know any Karens. He holds images in his head of all Goya's friends he has seen but does not know their names, the woman with a bloody nose smoking a cigarette beneath an asymmetrical haircut and someone with hair covering their face and three people in fluorescent colors with masks knit with geometric patterns.

Text message from David: Witch Karen?

Text message from Karen: We met at Lela's going

away party. You made a sad face at me.

Text message from David: Ahh sorry autocorrected you into a practitioner of dark arts.

Text message from Karen: :)

Text message from Karen: Do you want to meet up for a drink tomorrow?

Text message from David: Sure.

— ■ ■ —

Goya parks, and she runs around the car and opens the door for David. They walk up steps lined with dense forest. They can only see a few feet into the dark woods. The steps lead to a landing leading to more steps leading to a gate that leads to an overlook. The steps and gate and overlook are made of gray stone. Goya walks ahead of David. Before she can see the view from the overlook, she sits in front of the gray gate.

"The overlook is supposed to have a beautiful view," Goys says.

"Yeah," David says. "I bet it is amazing."

The night lingers around them, and they linger in the night. David walks up and sits beside Goya and looks at the gray stone gate. Goya feels a certain-sorrow-type emotion. Under someone's lost sweater, she tugs at her jumpsuit's geometric patterns of textures and shapes and outlines.

"Not looking seems romantic," she says.

They smoke cigarettes. The Tight Violence label on David's pants fills Goya's perspective. She is having trouble not thinking about the deconstructed jeans, the mouths of the rips and the acid wash and the model's mist coming up through the holes of the jeans and her legs losing their shape. She wants to talk to David about it but does not bring it up.

"I just want to stay on the edge, never witnessing that amazing view," she says.

David laughs. "The precipice of the precipice," he half says and half asks.

Goya laughs one beat of a laugh, her top front teeth showing on her upper lip.

David likes her overbite. He likes her coarse mannerisms. He likes her awkward features. He likes her strange outfit. To him, these are some of her most attractive qualities. Why did she use the word romantic? When will he be on the precipice of the precipice of Lela's return? He wonders about something else. He forgets that thing.

"Out of sight, out of mind," David says.

"Yeah," Goya says. "That's where we are."

"..."

Leaving vacant ground, David stands. He begins walking back to Goya's car, and Goya waits a moment before following.

David stops, and he studies the spaces between the trees. Is that an indigo light bouncing deep in the forest? When Goya walks up beside David, the light disappears.

"What's up?" Goya asks.

"I thought I saw something moving in the forest."

"You probably did," Goya says, and she puts her hand on David's back to say, Let's go.

"..."

"I mean... it's a forest."

17

Just before the rain picks up again, Goya and David arrive at their house, the modest three-bedroom structure sitting on the hill. Steps lead from the street to the front porch. They leave the car, and they walk to the house without talking until they arrive on the porch.

"I am going to hang out on the porch for a bit," David says.

Goya watches him sit on the edge of the porch. They spend a lot of time on the porch smoking cigarettes and watching clouds pass over and watching the wind in the front yard and talking about nothing.

"..."

"..."

Goya walks up to a speaker they use as a table. The speaker is covered in graffiti, Killer Perfume and Buy a Gun and an upside-down cross inside of a triangle on the forehead of a skull inside of another triangle with upside-down crosses above it that look like eyes with the triangle as a mouth and New Heavy. The letters are capitalized. All the A's are triangles.

Goya touches a beer can resting on the speaker, and she tilts it a little bit, feeling the weight of the liquid inside. She picks up the beer can. It is half-empty. She holds the beer can to her ear, shaking it and listening to it.

"I want to drink this leftover beer, but I don't know... someone may have put their cigarette out in it or something," Goya says.

"..."

"Oh well," she says with a shrug.

She raises the beer can with something like

caution. Her motions are slow, bringing the can to her mouth and closing her eyes and the liquid pouring into her mouth.

"…"

"…"

Her eyes widen.

BLEK

Goya spits the beer into the yard. She spits a couple more times. David is taking a deep gasp breath.

Goya brushes her hair out of her face. She smiles. She begins to laugh.

"…"

"Just kidding." She takes another drink from the can.

"…"

"…"

David wants to title everything he does with a nihilistic title. It should be a self-referential title. It should be a self-deprecating title. He writes the titles on the speaker being used as a table.

It Doesn't Matter

Why Not

Or Something

Or Whatever

Or Anything

I Guess

"Fucked"

It Was This Or Nothing

"Serious"
You Tell Me
It Is What It Is
Or I Was Bored
Whatever

He begins to laugh to himself. These angsty titles are things he has said to return some concept or problem to the undifferentiated void of his everydays. When his clients yell at him, he just shrugs and says "whatever" to the client. Sometimes he does not want to or need to care about the complexities of something.

Goya sits beside David. While Goya talks of some distant wilderness, David gazes quiet at bike chained to a street sign at the bottom of the hill with its wheels and seat stolen. A light rain falls on the bike. The bike is alone at the bottom of the hill. It is alone in the rain.

David thinks, I want to hug that bike.

He thinks, I would cry.

He thinks, Melodrama.

He thinks, The bike would laugh.

He thinks, Goya would come over shaking her head.

He thinks, The bike will laugh more.

He thinks, Goya will probably move to a distant wilderness soon.

He thinks, Someday I will never see the bike again.

" … "

" … "

David starts talking vaguely about not trying at his job, and Goya's mind conjures a vivid image of an insideout life, an image of a hand reaching into her life and pulling her inside out and, as she lives her insideout life, wondering what her rightside-out life would look like and slowly becoming obsessed with finding her rightside-out life and questing for her rightside-out life and studying books on ancient magics and using psychedelic drugs and learning to lucid dream and meditating and cutting through the jungles to the Temple of the Cerebremancer or whatever. As the image becomes saturated with a few colors in her mind, red and yellow and blue, she finally unlocks her rightside-out life, a mirrored version of her insideout life, a mirroring of a life inside of a life inside out. Maybe Goya should be afraid of this but whatever. At the top of her perspective, there is a pulling sensation. There is some other vague, weird thought that does not logically follow from the previous thoughts. And she imagines wearing a ghost around and doing nothing or whatever ghosts do. Where is she getting these images from? Becoming aware of her daydreaming, she turns to David.

"What are you thinking about?" Goya asks.

"About the gray sky, about sinking into the mud and about hugging that three-legged chair while I cry and about destroying our friendship," he says. He scratches his head. "What's in your brain?"

"I was thinking about being serious and being taken seriously," she says.

"I was being serious."

"I believe you were, and I am not sure if I was, but I wish I was."

"..."

■ ▲ ▲ ▲ ■

"..."

Goya walks inside. She returns with a bag. It has a print of recurring patterns of shapes in shapes.

"..."

"If we are going to be serious, I think we need a safe word," David says.

"Safe word?"

"It is a code word. We will use it to communicate our emotions. It will keep us from approaching some emotional boundary, keep us from crossing some moral boundary. It will signal us to stop the conversation. It will signal us to decrease how serious we are being or whatever."

Goya smiles. She pulls two cigarettes out of her bag. She pulls a lighter from her bag. She lights one. She passes it to David. She lights the other. David laughs a breath of a laugh. She returns the lighter to her bag.

"A safe word to have a sincere conversation, too funny."

"I said it because it was funny, but I seriously think that."

"No... it's perfect. What should ours be?"

"..."

"..."

Goya grabs a pen from her bag. She leans over. She grabs David's arm. David watches calmly. She begins writing. She finishes writing. David reads it, Numbskull. It has triangles drawn on either side of the word. Its letters are capitalized.

"..."

"..."

"Now, I am thinking about how Hunter said I can buy a gun for five hundred dollars," Goya says as she stands.

"..."

"I can afford that with my next paycheck," she says, "like... seriously." And she walks inside.

Text message from David: I worry that it will be rough with you gone. I worry that I will get used to you being gone.

Text message from David: I mean I just wish you were here.

What might be a cat approaches. It steps on the porch. David watches the cat-type thing. It walks up to the window. It looks into the house longingly.

There are a few reasons he thinks it might not be a cat. It is round. It appears to be too simple. It does not seem to have enough parts, just a face and four stumpy legs and a nubby tail. That is it. It does not have visible joints. It does not have a neck to speak of. It sits. It stares into the house. It seems depressed.

"You are too cute to be depressed," David says. He walks into the house. The cat-type thing watches him through the window. It has sad eyes. After fifteen minutes of nothing, David joins a television cult until he falls asleep.

Text message from Lela: The crayon melted.

After getting paid, Goya drives to Walmart hoping

to purchase a gun and spending an hour looking at guns and picking one out and filling out all the necessary paperwork and handing her background check to the clerk.

"So, it will take a week for the background check to process?" Goya asks the clerk.

The clerk turns the forms to read them, and he makes little reading sounds under his mustache, and his eyes go back and forth across the paper, and he breathes a deep breath in to his mouth and out through his nose.

"I can tell you right now that it probably won't pass," he says, turning the form around and pointing to a checked check box that reads, I have been diagnosed with a mental illness. "They cannot sell guns to people who have been diagnosed with certain mental illnesses."

"Okay," she says, taking the paper from him and walking through the parking lot to her car and driving down the highway and pulling into the parking lot of a different Walmart and filling out another background check without checking the box called, I have been diagnosed with a mental illness.

▲ ▲ ▼ ▲ ▲

As Goya tells David about how she wants to buy a gun, he imagines Goya accidentally shooting him through the wall between their rooms.

The sequence of hazy mental images starts where he can visualize both of their rooms at once. Goya is in a nightgown, and it has a geometric-shape print.

The shapes are fluorescent yellow and fluorescent orange. She holds some hand cannon. He stands up to put his pants on or something banal. Her room fills with smoke. The images cut to where the point of view is behind the bullet. Everything is in slow motion. His daydream follows the bullet to his brain. His body falls away. It reveals blood splattered on the wall behind him.

David focuses on the red liquid, and the blood on the wall in his mind becomes the pasta sauce he is gazing at. The room tone takes on a dead-channel quality. The buzz sits on top of all other sounds in the room.

IIRRRR

David squints. He feels nauseous. He moves a wooden spoon in the pasta sauce. It pushes chunks of vegetables around in the red liquid. Goya watches him.

IRRRRRRRR

The dead-channel tone reaches its highest point of tension.

"Smells good," Goya says.

"Thanks," David says.

She laughs. He cannot figure out why she laughed.

"Have you ever shot a gun?" she asks.

He focuses on her briefly. He goes back to watching the pan, and the sauce boils, and he leans over, and he checks the size of the flame, and the flame has fingers, and the flame fingers pulse.

"Blanks for some films I worked on in college," he says. "Why?"

"I don't know, like... I've never shot a gun, but I've been wanting to for a long time."

She brushes her hair out of her face. She pulls herself up to sit on the countertop.

"..."

"I led some generic-type guy on for months because he kept saying he would take me to shoot guns," Goya says. "We broke up, because it was like... never going to happen."

"..."

"We would just play chess all the time, and I never won," Goya says. She is starting to digress.

"Months," David says. "That seems committed. That seems quite committed. I think you can just go to a range and shoot pictures of people with rented guns."

"I feel like I am really good at chess. I must not be because I never win," she says in the digression.

"..."

"Yeah... well, a shooting range doesn't seem very meaningful," she says.

"I feel like I am good at chess because I beat someone with a chess tattoo," he says following the digression.

She laughs. David laughs. They laugh for different reasons.

"..."

"Not sure if I look for emotional significance in a shooting experience." David walks away from the stove. He gets the colander ready. He gets something else ready.

"That's unbelievable to deal with," she says.

"..."

"But you're not looking for a shooting experience, David." The sauce begins to bubble, and Goya turns the stove off for David. "This is important to me."

"I would only get a gun to live out some following-in-William-S.-Burroughs'-footsteps bullshit."

"That seems meaningful."

"Yeah, I need to get a gun," he says. He continues in a nasally, William S. Burroughs voice, "Time for our William Tell routine." He mimes placing an apple on his head, and he bites his lip as though placing the idea of the apple with care, and Goya holds some invisible hand cannon, and she takes the idea of the apple in her sights, and she fakes recoiling with its implied kickback, and he moves his hand behind his head as though his brains were being splattered on the wall behind him, as though Goya just shot him in the face.

"..."

"Or whatever."

"I've been thinking about purchasing a gun, but I just feel like... it is not a good idea. Seems like a joke that turns out not to be funny. Like joining a cult."

With a magazine over her face is Goya lying on the couch. There is supermodel wearing deconstructed jeans on the cover with a featured article about the You're Worth It campaign. A little light leaks between the magazine and her face. It illuminates images, but they are too close to focus on. Fluorescent colors are on trend. Out-of-focus fluorescent colors fill her entire field of view. When she breathes out, the pages curl and crinkle. She holds the sound of crinkling paper in her thoughts, distinct like a sound effect for a film. Crinkling paper becomes her favorite sound. She can conjure this sound at any moment in her thoughts, and again she conjures the sound in her mind, and she breathes out, creating the sound with the magazine.

CREAK KUNK

As Hunter walks in, the first thing he sees is Goya on the couch sleeping, snoring quiet breaths, making tiny crinkling sounds. He leans his skateboard against the couch, of course it makes a scraping sound as it begins falling, his hand reaching out towards the skateboard, the skateboard staying just out of his reach.

THWACK

The skateboard smacks into the hardwood floor. He picks up the skateboard. Maybe, somehow, Goya slept through it. Goya lays still with the magazine over her face, so Hunter begins walking toward his room.

"Err," Goya says through the magazine.

Hunter brushes his long, black hair out of his face revealing his sparse mustache, and he says, "Sorry for waking you."

Goya does not respond, not moving, not speaking.

"..."

Hunter starts to walk away.

"Hunter," Goya says. "What's your favorite sound?"

He pauses and turns around, and he says, "Umm," and brushes his hair out of his face again. "Something frying in a skillet." He laughs.

She smiles beneath the magazine.

"…"

"…"

"What's yours?"

"I think mine is crinkling paper."

⍰⍰ ⍰ ⍰⍰

Goya comes up behind David. She stares a getting-someone's-attention stare at him. David stops focusing on his phone. He scans the room. Every horizontal surface has beer cans on it.

"Hunter and I are walking to the bluffs," Goya says.

She asks if he would like to come with. He agrees. He grabs his camera. They walk toward the bluffs. Their neighborhood is close to downtown, and most of the homes are standalone, and they have small, unkempt yards. The neighborhood is mostly impoverished households, and the occasional new home with a manicured yard stands out. A passerby nods at them. Hunter and David and Goya wave. Another passerby yells at them from across the street to ask for a cigarette.

"Sorry," Hunter says.

"Fuck you," the passerby says.

"…"

They walk between some houses to the bluffs. Hunter and David and Goya sit. Their breath vaporizes. They cannot distinguish between cigarette smoke and their breath. They look through the

29

vaporized breath at the distant mountain. It is snow capped, and it vomits a jagged forest into polluted waters below.

"Can I bum a smoke?" Hunter asks.

David is the only one with any cigarettes left. He sets his camera down. He reaches into his pocket. He pulls a pack of cigarettes out. The pack is black, and it is beaten up, and all the cigarettes are bent. David opens the pack. He hands it to Hunter. Hunter pulls one out. He lights the cigarette. He hands the pack back. David places the pack beside his camera. He leaves the lid open as if to say, They're fair game.

Vaguely in David's direction, Goya touches her mouth with a soft touch and a distracted gaze. She reaches out, grabbing the camera and bringing it to her face and pointing it at David. His hands cover his face. He makes an anxious expression behind them.

Hunter's eyes shift from David to Goya and back to David.

CLICK

The camera flashes. As Goya pulls the camera away from her face, David pulls his hands away from his face, and they reveal their faces almost in unison.

"Did you get it?" David asks.

" ... "

" ... "

" ... "

Goya smiles as she sets the camera down, and they go back to looking at the view from the bluffs. "I think we've found it," Goya says.

" ... "

" ... "

"Found what?" David asks, and he believes he

already understands, but he asks in hopes of hearing her speak. He hopes she will speak romantically. He hopes she will speak romantically about this moment.

"I wish I hadn't said that... seems silly now," Goya says.

"..."

"I don't know... like that intersection of comfort and novelty and connection with the people around you."

"It seems nice," David says, and he may have destroyed the sentiment by acknowledging it. Hunter and David and Goya sit quietly for a while.

Everything slows down, and they never realize how slow they live.

Goya lies in her bed, her face resting on a magazine. The featured article on deconstructed jeans sticks out from under her face, and it absorbs a small amount of drool from when she was napping. Her arm hangs off the bed, and she holds scissors in her dangling hand, and the scissors open and close slowly creating a distinct, soft, scraping sound that Goya repeats at a slow, steady, unmotivated tempo. She cannot think of any reasons for anything right now, even trying to use the lack of reasons as a reason and failing. She tries to sleep, but she just woke from sleeping too much.

A call just woke her, and now she cannot get back to sleep. The mouth-clicking sound from the caller's voice remains in her thoughts. The mouth-clicking voice told her that even though she did not check the box they still looked up her mental health records.

There is a gun that costs less than five hundred dollars, and they won't sell it to her. She sighs. She gets an I-have-an-idea type feeling. She holds an image in her head, the idea of a gun. It floats in her thoughts. She stands up, stepping on magazine clippings.

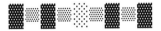

Text message from Karen: Still down for drinks?

Text message from David: My home is kind of a shitshow. I think I need to stay here.

Text message from Karen: You're going to miss some real cool brain-pouring-out-of- eyes-type stuff.

Text message from David: Shit. I guess I'll catch it the next time.

$$\dot{\Delta} \ddot{\Delta} \dot{\Delta}$$

FLUMF
TINK
The sound is followed by laughter. The sound and the laughing go into David's room. His eyes peel open. A strip of light shines along the bottom of his door. Was that a gun shot? Did Goya buy a gun? Can he really hear a sound when he is sleeping? Should he go back to sleep? Can he even go back to sleep if he wanted to? He rubs his eyes. He makes a groan. It is

low. It labels the moment, Serious.

David checks his phone. It is 11:30pm. He must have fallen asleep at 7:00pm. He laughs to himself. His hand reaches out. It turns the light on. He searches the floor. He finds his pants. The label reads, Tight Violence. He pulls one leg right-side out, and he puts them on.

People laugh outside of his door. He pauses. He opens the door. The hall extends out in one-point perspective in out extends the hall, and then David sees three people. They are dressed in fluorescent colors. They have masks on. The masks are knit with geometric patterns. The three of them are holding drinks and making chitchat.

David walks through his waking haze. He walks up to the masked people. They tell him that Goya bought a BB gun. Goya buying a BB gun instead of a real gun seems indicative of a lot of things.

David walks to the backdoor. He stands in the door frame. Hunter is standing in the middle of the yard. He holds a beer can on his head. David cannot tell if Goya is pointing the BB gun at Hunter's face or the can.

"I am sure you know how stupid this is," David says. He feels an urge to stop them, and he feels an urge to witness these events unfold as though he was not there. He reads the safe word on his arm. Numbskull is barely legible. The safe word, he mouths the word, numbskull, but the syllables do not reach anyone.

"..."

"..."

"You should get your camera," Hunter says,

holding the can on his head with both hands, and everyone agrees.

David walks to his room. He walks back with his camera. The masked people watch. David takes a couple photos of the masked people, a couple of Goya with the BB gun, a couple of Hunter with the can on his head. Hunter covers his eyes with one hand. He holds the can with the other.

"Be ready to take a picture when she shoots," Hunter says.

"Okay," Goya says.

Hunter lets go of the can, and it balances on his head.

"Okay," Hunter says.

"Three," Goya says.

"Two," Hunter says.

"One," David says.

FLUMF

Goya recoils.

TINK

Their sense of time lurches. Everyone is laughing. "Did you get it?"

⚕ Λ Λ Λ⚕

Text message from David: How was the cool brain pouring out your eyes?

Text message from Karen: You again.

Text message from David: You again again.

Text message from Karen: I thought about just replying with some sort of emoticon. That's always the funniest and most appropriate response. Maybe this one :D

Text message from David: I prefer it when people qualify things they're not going to do instead of doing them.

Text message from Karen: That's ridiculous. Goodnight.

A ghostly, dead, sleepy anxiety precedes an apathetic, avoided, moderate encounter and a negligent, slothful smog and a serialized feeling.

Text message from Karen: Thought you were goth until I saw you tagged in photos recently.

David gets dressed for work. His shirt is black. His pants are black. His shoes are black. He grabs his camera. The front door opens. David walks outside. He drinks coffee on the front porch. The cat-type thing is still there, and it still sits, and it still stares through the window, and it still seems depressed.

At the bottom of the steps, Goya lays on the sidewalk. She is on the sidewalk beside David's car. It still has a huge dent in the hood from hitting the deer-type creature, and it still has a gradient from blood and shit and piss to clean, and it still won't drive.

At the top of the steps, David sips his coffee. He watches Goya with her phone to her ear. From the gore covering the car's hood, a golden shard falls beside Goya, and she studies it. David walks down the steps.

Goya mouths words to David, I hate my life. She sighs.

David holds out the coffee. Goya grabs it. She takes a drink. David looks back at the cat-type creature, and Goya leans over the golden shard.

"You too," Goya says into the phone. "Bye." She

sits down on the curb beside the golden shard.

"..."

"I hate it when my brother tries to get me to take him seriously," she says.

"Whatever happened to wanting to be taken seriously?" David asks.

Goya takes another drink of the coffee, and she says, "My brother and I don't have a safe word, David."

David laughs. "We never use the safe word."

"It is just nice to know it is there. Now, I feel so comfortable being serious with you that I don't have to be."

"Seems nice."

"But my brother has been saying he is going to hurt himself for so long it is hard to take him seriously?" Goya furrows her brow. She picks up the golden shard.

"Seems brutal."

Across both her face-up palms, Goya holds the golden shard in front of her while inspecting it, while feeling the bony texture of the shard's branches with her fingers, while imagining it in a symmetrical pair, while realizing it is an antler from the dear-like thing David hit.

"It is brutal," Goya says, and she plays with the golden antler and with distracted motions and with her gaze directed at the golden antler and with her thoughts drifting to a place that is already fading. Goya turns to David.

"Your clothes are all black, and you have your camera, and you must be going to work," she says, and she swings the antler, and she points it at David's car, the hood smashed from hitting the deer-like creature. "Well, have fun."

"Actually I couldn't afford to fix my car," David says. Goya lowers the golden antler. "I had it towed here. I am on bike now."

"I'm sorry," Goya says.

"You didn't do anything," David says, "and I like riding my bike as long as it does not rain too much."

"That was more of an empathetic sorry."

"..."

"And riding in the rain can be a nice feeling."

"I will probably fall and bust my face open," David says. "Like, I am getting on my bike in the rain knowing it will be my last ride."

"I mean 'knowing it will be my last ride' can be a nice feeling."

"Morbid."

"..."

"Instead of going to work, I wish wearing all black meant I am dark or goth or whatever," David says.

"..."

Goya smiles.

"..."

David rides away.

Some vast, bare impression precedes an immaterial, indistinct, dim haziness and a let-down, faint recurrence and an ineffectual, avoided something.

Goya walks up to the porch, and she watches the cat-type thing. It looks into the house, and it appears to long to be inside, and it places a paw on the window. It is too cute, and she cannot handle looking at it.

"Okay," Goya says, "you can go in."

"..."

"If Hunter or David don't want you in the house, you'll have to go." Goya opens the door, and the cat-type thing walks inside, and it brushes against Goya as it passes as if to say, Thanks or something. It finds the other side of the window it was looking through to see into the house, and it sits, and it looks out of that window onto the porch with a longing-type expression on its face.

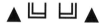

On his way home from work, David pedals.

CREAK

David walks in the front door. Goya is sipping coffee and watching the cat-type creature.

"..."

"Why do we have a cat?" David says.

"Is that a cat?"

"I mean... what else could it be?"

"I don't know," she says. "It was on the porch, and it looked sad, and I let it in."

"And it still seems sad," David says.

"..."

"..."

"I know," Goya says. "It is too cute, like... a large

part of the cuteness is that it looks sad."

The cat-type thing continues to gaze out the window.

"..."

"I want to name it Numbskull," Goya says.

David laughs. "Whatever." He pulls out his phone. "Naming a cat-type thing after a safe word for being serious seems pretty funny." He sits on the couch.

Text message from Karen: What do you do?

Text message from David: I'm a photographer.

Text message from Karen: I work at Tight Violence.

Text message from David: The clothing company?

Text message from Karen: Yep.

Text message from David: :)

Text message from Karen: Hahaha

"What does Numbskull eat?" Goya asks while lying on the floor, and the floor is covered in blankets, and she snuggles into the blanket ground, and she uses Numbskull as a pillow, and the cat-type thing is still gazing out the window.

David turns his phone's screen off, and he studies Numbskull. "Cat food?"

The moon distracts David, and he contemplates a lunar ditch for a moment.

"Okay, I'm going to walk to the corner store and get some cat food," Goya says. She stands up. "Wanna come with? I think it has stopped raining." She grabs her sweater from the couch. It has rhythmic patterns of fluorescent colors.

"Sure."

They take a moment to gather their things. They take a moment to gather themselves.

"..."

As they begin walking, David says, "I just sent my first emoticon."

Goya laughs. "That's real," she says. "That's one of those things you start to do ironically, and one day realize you're doing it all the time."

"I hate those realizations," David says as they walk into the convenience store, as the door beeps, signaling their entrance to the drippy clerk behind the counter, as the air conditioner stirs a haunted sound, and as fluorescent lights wash them in a crisp radiance.

"It's like walking in on yourself," Goya says, while she walks down an aisle, while David walks down the next aisle, and they digress to talking about the packaging they like, austere lettering and geometric patterning for the most part. Holding items of note over the aisle between them, their pace is slow, and their pace is the same, and the conversation folds in on itself.

"What were you saying about walking in on yourself?" David asks as Goya finds the cat food, and she picks up a single can, and she holds it above the aisle for David to see.

"..."

"Like walking in on yourself masturbating or going to the bathroom or –"

"Like anything, like... anytime I become aware of what I am doing, I feel an I-just-walked-in-on-myself-masturbating-type feeling." David laughs. They approach the cashier.

"..."

"What are innocent losers?" the cashier asks.

David looks around. Innocent losers? The packaging, the scratch-off cards, a non sequitur, what is he talking about?

FLOP

The cashier brushes his greasy, shoulder-length hair out of his face, and he is sweating for no reason, bold packaging layering on top of bold packaging behind him. The drippy clerk sighs, and he sniffles, and he asks, "Is that a band or something?"

"I don't know. I just like the way it sounds. I just like the feeling I get from those two words being together." Goya starts reading the packaging behind the clerk, and she is bored.

David follows the clerk's eyes to Goya's sweater. Innocent Losers hides in the rhythmic patterns of fluorescent colors. The T is an upside-down cross. Goya sets the cat food on the counter, and the clerk scans it, $1.23.

"I hope you didn't think I was looking at your boobs," the clerk says, and he makes some strange sound by breathing out of his mouth and nose at the same time.

"It's fine," Goya says handing him the money. "I

mean, I didn't think you were doing that."

The clerk nods.

"Okay bye," she says, and Goya and David leave the store, and the door beeps signaling their departure to the drippy clerk, and they leave the haunted sound stirred by the air conditioner, and they leave the crisp radiance of the fluorescent lights.

Goya and David arrive at their house. Goya prepares the cat food in a bowl. David leans against the wall, and he watches Numbskull as it gazes out the window. Goya walks over with the bowl of cat food, and she sets it down beside Numbskull.

The cat-type creature barely pays attention to Goya, turning and glancing at the cat food and returning to looking out the window.

"..."

David laughs.

Goya walks to her room.

Under a blind-shaded window, David wakes from a nap. The haze becomes images and thoughts, and he requests a video chat with Lela. He stands, and he walks past his computer. Lela opens the video window, and David is not on her screen.

"I'm sorry. I have to put pants on," David says.

"I suppose you don't have to. It would certainly change the nature of this interaction," Lela says.

"Okay, but..." He sits in front of the computer's camera. Lela tells him about her engaging and funny co-workers. What would it have been like to change the nature of the interaction? It would have been awkward.

"Talking about my work is probably boring," Lela says.

"No, it is actually fascinating. The Prince archives seem... well... important," David says. "It is hard to relate to. You are having formative experiences... When you return, you will be greater than what you were when you got on the plane."

"..."

"..."

Lela sighs. "It is so hard to look at you." She lays her head on a pillow. "I feel sad and happy at the same time. You... you look handsome."

David laughs. "I was just thinking you're really beautiful."

Lela hides her face. She sighs. She turns to look out the window. A single star is shining.

"I can't handle being in Endless Summer." She turns back to the computer. "Saying that no one is like me here seems silly."

"..."

"I mean I don't want to know anyone," she says.

"Just stay in bed... like in a blanket cocoon."

"That's so hard to see past right now." Lela pulls her pillow out of its case. She puts the case over her head. "What was your first time like?" she asks.

David smiles. "The first time I had sex?" The pillowcase nods. "It was on a beach. It was nice."

"On a beach, I'm jealous."

"We could go to the beach and have another first time."

"Why?"

"You said you were jealous. Why be bound by reality? Let's have another first time."

"..."

Lela laughs.

"I was joking, but it sounds nice."

"True..."

"Okay, David. I'm going to sleep. It is late here. I have to get into my blanket cocoon." Lela pulls the pillowcase off her head. She snuggles in her blankets.

"Okay. Sleep well."

"Talk to you tomorrow?" Lela asks. Her voice is soft.

"For sure."

"Bye."

"Bye."

David sits on the left cushion of their front porch couch with his computer on his lap, and Hunter sits on the right cushion. Goya steps out on to the porch, and she closes the door behind her, standing next to the speaker being used as a table. She moves an ashtray and an empty pack of cigarettes and two empty beer cans uncovering the list.

It Doesn't Matter

Why Not

Or Something

Or Whatever

Or Anything

I Guess

"Fucked"

It Was This Or Nothing
"Serious"
You Tell Me
It Is What It Is
Or I Was Bored
Whatever.

"Who wrote this list of bored phrases?" Goya asks, even though she can recognize David's handwriting.

David turns and rereads the list and smiles. "It was just a list of things I wanted to title everything or it was just something I thought was funny for no reason I can think of..."

Below the word Whatever, Goya adds Numbskull to the list. Her handwriting is slightly different than when she wrote Numbskull on David's arm, her letters looking a lot like David's.

Hunter begins to make his way inside, walking to the door and opening it and holding it open and asking Numbskull, "Do you want to go outside?"

The cat-type thing walks outside, looking at him and brushing up against Hunter's leg as it passes, and it finds the window it was looking through to see out of the house, and it sits in front of it, gazing into the house. Goya reaches over, and she scratches Numbskull's head, the cat-type creature seeming disinterested.

Hunter goes inside.

◬■ ◬■ ■◬ ■◬

David watches a video. A boy sits in front of a

camera. A pop song plays on blown out speakers. His face is expressionless. He lights a cigarette. It hangs in his mouth. Smoke rises from the ash. He begins to draw on his arm. The lines are crude. The lines are red. Up and down, he draws more lines on his arm. He pulls the cigarette out of his mouth to blow smoke out. Back and forth, he rocks his chair once. He puts the cigarette back in his mouth. He rubs his forehead with his wrist. He continues to draw lines on his other arm. He mouths the words to the song. As he draws lines on his neck, he accidentally drops the marker. He calmly picks the marker up. He continues drawing, left arm and right arm and neck and then his face. Red lines cover all his visible skin. If the red lines cover all of his visible skin, are they still lines? The song ends. He turns off the camera.

David stops focusing on his laptop. Goya has gone inside. Numbskull is still looking through the window.

Text message from Karen: I heard someone say, "I would let you wander off into the dark-forest labyrinth if that what you want." It seemed nice.

David looks at the wall. He stares at it for two minutes.

He finds shapes and faces in the wall's texture.

He finds a melting mountain with a horse's head.

He finds faces in faces.

He finds blankets of bodies.

There is a lightness in his arms, and he feels the lightness in his fingers. He scratches his leg.

Hunter walks back outside. He sits beside David.

"I heard you got a job at Tight Violence," David says.

"Yep," Hunter says.

"How's that?" David asks.

In Hunter's mind are inside jokes he has with a woman at work.

Four Four Four Four

Air holes

Adjusting the saturation

Infinite thoughts, but none of them are good

Blek

Bromine

Pocket salads

The ideas are not worth mentioning. It is nice being stupid with her. "It's fine," he says.

"..."

"..."

Hunter imagines shredding into work on his skateboard and gunning down the store he works at, not the employees or clientele, but the store itself, shooting Tight Violence in the heart and watching it fall over and say the only English words it knows, I'll see you in Hell.

"Our show with Scab Control is in a few weeks," David says. "Want to have band practice?"

"Sure, sounds good."

In the shed in their backyard, there are two drum kits, and Tendons is written across the front of both bass drums. A piece of paper on the ground has the Tendons set list.

Show Normalcy

Angel of Meh

Administration In blood
North of Heaven (space)
Four Seasons in the Abyss
Divine Internetz
God Hates Just You

The next morning, David goes for a walk. He talks to Lela on the phone. They talk for two hours. Lela talks about feeling like a pile of rope in a leafless forest.

"There's nowhere to be here," Lela says. She takes mental inventory of everything in her room, a twin mattress in gray bedding and a gray desk and a gray chair. "This is not a normal place," she says. "I can't hide here. There are a thousand people in the whole town and everyone lives in a mansion with a security guard."

"I just now pictured everyone living in the same mansion with one security guard for the whole town," David says.

Lela laughs. "Nah, everyone's a security guard and they live in their own mansion," she says.

"Well... the rain stopped and I told Hunter and Goya I would go to the mountain with them," David says.

"That sounds nice. I wish I could go."

"Me too..."

"..."

"Actually I wouldn't normally go hiking. It is too cold, and all the overlooks are blocked by trees. But if I don't stay busy, I will just lie in bed all day or whatever."

"No, no. You should go," Lela says. "For sure. Definitely. Have fun. Hopefully... I will talk to you later."

"You will. I will call you."

"Even if you think I'll be asleep."

A translucent, sterile perspective precedes a low trifle and a repeating, passive void and an incessant event.

"I feel like the only thing I like to do is cheat," Goya says to Hunter and David while they stand on the mountain overlook. David turns to her with a blank expression. Did Goya's internal dialogue just leak out? He cannot think of a response he does not think is funny. Hunter searches the forest from the tree line.

"What?" David asks.

"Breaking rules, not following rules I am expected to follow, at work or school or on the street or wherever or whatever... I am always figuring out how to cheat them," Goya says.

"I mean I know what cheating is."

Goya laughs. "David, like... you're sassy."

"I think my brain is broken today. I just thought you were being condescending." David laughs.

"I'm hardly ever condescending," Goya says, "unless I'm irritated."

"I am condescending sometimes," David says.

"You seem condescending, like... mostly," Goya says. She laughs. "Like you're mostly condescending." David laughs. "But it is fine."

"It's probably just that you laugh at everything,"

Hunter says.

"Yeah, I feel like I never laugh," Goya says, "unless I am nervous. I mean, I, like, laugh on the inside." Goya laughs. She laughs out loud.

David wonders, Was that a nervous laugh? What's the difference between feeling nervous and thinking something's funny? And David tries to distinguish between another feeling and another thought, and he tries to distinguish between some other things.

For Hunter, this conversation is funny because he is nervous, because he is afraid a large, vicious, woodland creature could come out of the trees at any moment, because he is afraid to die or get brutally maimed. He watches Goya looking at David. What is Goya thinking about? Has Hunter not been following the conversation? Has everyone stopped making sense?

SNAP

Hunter jumps a little, and he searches the scene until he realizes the sound was David stepping on a stick. They continue walking along the trail, the trail continuing up the mountain, mud building up on their shoes.

"Shhh," Goya whispers.

Goya is in awe of the deer-type creature and its golden antlers. The sludgy, indigo, fluorescent outlines infer its body. Its drippy, mushy head and the outlines melt for no reason. Goya feels empty, void, blank.

David and Hunter become aware of the deer-like thing too. They stare with slightly open mouths.

It senses them, and it holds its sludge head up. It turns the muck head slightly. The deer-type thing breathes out of its mouthless face. Its breath is a visible vapor. It watches Hunter and David and Goya, and they watch it.

"..."

"..."

"..."

The deer-like whatever uses telepathy to speak. The voice it projects into their thoughts is low. It is layered with other whispering voices. The whispering voices are incomprehensible. The low voice enters Hunter and David and Goya's thoughts.

"Life is here. We are here. I love you," the deer says.

"..."

It leaps into the woods. It leaps deeper into the woods. Hunter and David and Goya stand there. They watch it leave.

"..."

TUP

"..."

STUP STUP

The deerish thing runs through the forest. It leaps on to a paved street that leads up the mountain. Globs glop and roll from its ooze dome, down its back and off its tail leaving a trail of glowing indigo that fades after being away from the deer-type creature for a moment. It runs down the street. It runs down the street some more.

⋮† ▲ †⋮

The rectangle that once separated Lela's crying

and David's driving is shrinking. Inside the rectangle of everything being framed by Lela's crying, the deer-like creature lies in mud. Outside the rectangle, Lela looks ahead with a calm expression. As the rectangle becomes smaller, it crops to the goopy head and the drippy, indigo outlines of the creature's fur. It shrinks into Lela's eye. The rectangle becomes insignificant. It disappears in her eye.

Lela stands on a beach in Endless Summer. She zones out. Her faded-pink hair hangs in front of her face, and it reminds her that she is alone or different or whatever. She brushes her faded-pink hair out of her face and behind her head, and she whips it and flips it, and she puts it in a little knot on top of her head, and maybe she should just dye it if it is bothering her. She pulls a pen out and sticks it into the knot to hold it together. As the tourists on the beach creep back into her perspective, she remembers people are around. Some people are taking pictures. Some people are just standing around.

Lela begins walking toward her job thinking about her job, the long work days and the distinct lack of free time. Someone she does not know walks past her. Someone else she does not know walks past her. She walks by the library to see if it will be open when she gets off work. It won't be.

Through the only public park in town is Lela walking. It is a hundred-foot-by-hundred-foot square of grass on the shore. It is crowded with tourists. A small dock extends over the water, and a ferry is docking. The sky is clear. The water is clear. There is an island out in the water. It is a place nicer than

Endless Summer. The ferry takes people there. Most of the people are in Endless Summer for the ferry. The park is too crowded for Lela to spend time there. It is always too crowded for Lela to spend time there. She walks somewhere. She walks somewhere else. She walks along a street without sidewalks. A tender panic strobes in her head.

Lela walks behind the shops lining a boardwalk. She feels a nostalgia-type feeling. Lela sees three pale-skinned women, triplet pale-skinned women. They are hanging out in the alley beneath some power lines. They all have faded-pink hair to their waist. Their hair is the same color as Lela's hair.

One is in a black shirt, tattered around the collar, and her jeans are torn at the knee, and her feet are bare with her toenails painted black. She holds a blue lighter, and she lights another woman's cigarette with a vacant expression.

The woman having her cigarette lit leans forward to reach the flame. She is wearing a black tank top and black shorts.

Behind the woman lighting the cigarette and the woman having her cigarette lit, the third triplet hangs her head under the hood of her blue hoodie. Her faded-pink hair hangs in her face. She is seated on the ground nearby, holding a pen and looking at a piece of paper with knives drawn on it. Each knife is crude, like the stick-figure equivalent of knives.

The two other triplets join the one on the ground. They hold the pen between the three of them. They draw knives together until the paper is filled with knives. One woman brushes her hair over her ear, the way Lela often does. These women dress vaguely like

Lela. They have faded-pink hair like Lela. They have similar gestures too. Lela realizes she is staring. In a soft panic, she begins to walk past them.

One of the triplets lets go of the pen, and she looks up at Lela, and a line that would have become a knife veers across the paper. The other two let go of the pen. They look up at Lela.

Unable to handle this, directing her eyes at the ground is Lela continuing to walk away.

Text message from Lela's father: Where are you? It's time for work.

A measureless view precedes a shadowy, immense perceiving and a vain, interminable, ghostly miasma and a vacant, vaporous, bottomless, clear mental picture.

While scanning documents at the archive, Lela becomes blurry. Everything becomes blurry. She stops moving, holding Prince's organ donor card on the scanner with gloved hands, the strip of light gathering high-res information beneath the scanner's glass bed, and she looks forward, and her expression is blank.

She thinks about her well-paying job that does not involve compromising her values.

She thinks about closing her eyes.

She thinks about the people she knows in Endless Summer.

She thinks, None of these relationships seem emotionally significant.

She thinks, ...

She thinks of the women she saw with faded-pink hair.

She thinks of the herself-type women.

‡ ‡ ‡ ‡

Somewhere not there and anywhere not here, two Lela-like women touch palms. Their long faded-pink hair contrasts with the unending, dim wherever. They look calm. They look like mirrored images of each other except one is wearing glasses. Everything's colors invert for a moment. Everything's colors invert again.

⌐⌐⌐■⌐⌐⌐

Lela lies facedown in a swimming pool, her natural buoyancy keeping her afloat in the still, crystal-clear water. Past moments and new moments are indistinguishable. The present seems like an instance of the past, and instances of the past seem to be happening now, and again, facedown, natural, crystal-clear, past, new, present, and again she looks back on the time she has spent in Endless Summer. She cannot gauge her progress. Outside her head, everything seems calm. Her clothes sit beside the pool. They sit beside a chrome ladder. The pool is in her father's backyard. It is marble. It is gray. The walls of the house are bone white. She wants a total, let-down, low obliteration or something. Was that thought a song lyric? Are all her thoughts song lyrics? She lifts her head. She breathes in. Her head lowers back into the water.

‡‡ ▲ ▲ ‡‡

As Lela walks home from work, an ocean breeze flows along the boardwalk shops. The salty ocean air fills Lela's mouth and nose and lungs. To avoid eye contact with passerbys, she looks across the boardwalk to the ocean. Out-of-focus tourists and their pets meander along the boardwalk. Something catches her eye. She stops behind a car, gazing across the street.

Three triplet men with faded-pink hair sit on the boardwalk. One has long hair and scrolls on their phone. He is straight faced.

Another one zones out, the gradient in the lenses of his sunglasses fading from their hair color to blue. His right sleeve is ripped. The second triplet has long hair too. He lays his arm over another's shoulder. Smoke rises from a cigarette in his hand. His shirt is gray, a tear in the collar and a tear in a sleeve. His skinny jeans are gray, a tear at the knee and a tear at the thigh. He breathes out smoke.

The third triplet is sitting nearby. He breathes smoke into his smoke. His sleeves are cut off. A phone sits beside him.

Lela becomes aware of herself, realizing she is staring at the triplets and hiding behind a car. She skulks away, using cars and people as obstructions.

IT TOOK SO MANY OF ME TO FIND YOU

■ ‡ ‡ ■‡■ ‡ ‡ ■

A couple days later, Lela walks alone along a street without a sidewalk, and then the neighborhood fades into woods. She finds some concrete ditch run perpendicular to the street, penetrate the mass of trees. She feels a medium level of excitement for no reason. She lights a cigarette. She looks down the ditch at more ditch. She climbed down, and walked.

KRRRRRR SNAP

The distinct sound of skateboard wheels comes from around the bend ahead. It makes her miss Hunter and Goya and David. But she wishes she could find some refuge from people. She stares blankly for a moment. She takes a step. There is a slight pause.

CRACK KRRRRR

Lela takes another step. She looks around before committing to walk all the way to where the people hanging out ahead can see her. She walks down the ditch in one-point perspective.

A group of three women hang out in and around a drain. The third set of triplets Lela has seen in Endless Summer. They all have faded-pink hair. One woman skateboards up the sloped edge of the ditch. Another looks at something. The third triplet looks at the same thing. A skateboard rests on the cement beside the drain. The underside of the skateboard's deck reads, In After Times. The sans-serif letters are all capitalized.

One of the women stands, holding a skateboard, and her midriff shows below her black shirt, and her keys are clipped to a belt loop on her skinny jeans. She has a gray hat on with the bill flipped up. Under the bill reads, Lashes. Its letters are all capitalized. She raises an eyebrow above her sunglasses.

Another one sits on cement, biting her lip and draping her arms over her crossed legs and wearing a tank top, an equilateral triangle printed on the back and another equilateral triangle inside that equilateral triangle creating four triangles inside. She has a book in her hand with a finger keeping the page while she picks at something on her leg. She starts to look at something else. She starts watching the woman skateboarding. Weeds sprout from the cracks in the cement. They have poofy heads. They have white heads.

The third triplet skateboards up the side of the ditch, her arms out and her knees bent. Her right knee is scraped. Her left shin is scraped. Her faded-pink hair hangs in her face. She skates up to Lela. They look like the same person, like Lela could make them quadruplets. Lela feels a sense of connection and a distinct lack of uniqueness at the same time. The woman that came up hands Lela a flyer.

"..."

Lela does not know what to say. Maybe there is nothing to say. The triplet skates back to the other triplets.

The flyer is written in a drippy font. The heading reads, Party. It gives the time and date and location, 11pm and today and the Something House, 123 Cantor Rd. Apt. 237. Its letters are all capitalized. All the T's are crosses. All the A's are triangles.

An unbelievable, clear, hallucinatory boredom

precedes a blurry, unreal experience and a returning, vacuous obliteration and a diminished, vain, low mental picture.

Lela lies on the floor in her room. She holds the flyer to her chest. She gets tired.

She tells herself, I have found people like me.

She tells herself, I should care that I have found these people.

She tells herself, I should feel excited or scared or something.

She tells herself, I feel like an alien.

She tells herself, I am a woman with faded-pink hair, I am a woman with hair, I am a woman, I am.

She tells herself, The walls of her room look beautiful all of a sudden.

She rests her arms by her sides. She lies there. She is motionless. She has nothing to do for the rest of the day.

At the party, a poster hangs above a television, and it contains black outlines of a boy and a woman stabbing each other on a yellow background, and they have calm expressions, and they have triangles drawn on their foreheads like they partook in some Ash-Wednesday-type ritual, and below the poster, there is a gas station on the television.

CLICK

The channel changes, and there is a football game.

CLICK

Footage of smoke rise from an explosion in a city.
CLICK
Some cartoons that are geared toward adults.
CLICK
Some syndicated comedy about a group of close friends.

Two women sit on a couch, and they watch the television. They have faded-pink hair. One has a collared shirt on. It is purple. The other has a black shirt on. She puts her arm across the back of the couch. Someone behind them has the remote, and they change the channel again.

∶✝∶✝∶✝∶

Lela sits at the party, and one of the triplet women explains how Endless Summer's three sets of triplets began hanging out. She speaks in general terms. They are not actually related. The did not have the same parents. They stumbled on each other simultaneously, like all three were walking to the same point in a wherewhen but their journey was interrupted by two other identical people trying to walking into that same wherewhen. The triplet men were all about to take the same seat on a bench in the park. One set of triplet women were all reaching for the same pen that was abandoned on the sidewalk. The other set of women triplets, my set, were all walking to get the same book at the library, Parenthetical Botany by Slow Fief.

The triplet asks Lela if she has two sisters, and Lela explains that, until she found the three sets of triplets in Endless Summer, she was the only person she knew with long faded-pink hair. The conversation slows. There is a pause. And the triplet walks away.

"…"

Everyone there seems friendly enough. She is surprised at how little she feels about being there.

On an uncovered mattress nearby, two of the triplet men kiss. They are shirtless. They have long hair. One lies on the other. The one on the bottom places his hand around the back of the other's neck. The one on top grabs the waist of the other.

Lela does not know what to think. She watches the two of them. They do not pay any attention to her. They are lost in making out. Lela looks at her hands. Someone walks in. They find the men making out to be novel. They step closer. They take a photo. The doppelgängers continue making out. They do not look up.

Lela laughs a soft laugh. Suddenly she feels alone. If she left this party, no one would care. She walks to another room. Three hands hold knives, two switchblades and a fold-out utility knife pointing downward at the same angle. They have similar length blades. Lela is not surprised there are kids with knives here. Seeing all of these knives out at the same time is a bit intimidating, and this seems ridiculous, and they seem to carry the knives ironically.

Lela looks at a curtain. Slowly the ambient sounds of the party fade from her perspective. She forgets everything else. The moment takes on a film-type haze. The curtain's print contains different scenes. Each image punctuates a moment in a boy's life. Each image also has a pyramid. The curtain is covered in these images: a mom holding a baby boy beside the pyramid and the boy with a woman leaning against the pyramid and a farewell for his departing and a family mourning over a grave beneath the pyramid. All the print has faded to gray. The moon shines into the curtain. As Lela looks at the curtain for two more minutes, her mind wanders. She holds the image of squeezing David's hand in her thoughts.

Lela turns back towards the room. Even though some light still penetrates the curtain, the room is dim. She gets bored. She walks home. The rectangle grows from Lela's eye. The rectangle contains Lela's friends doing various types of nothing while she is in Endless Summer.

CLICK

Silence follows the muted click of the air rifle. A beer can sits on the fence in the backyard. Beyond the can, the shot splashes into a mud puddle. Hunter lowers Goya's BB gun. He is standing in the middle of the backyard. A cigarette hangs from his mouth. Smoke sits in the air beside his face. It is raining. The rain is light. Goya is standing on the porch. She is facing Hunter. Hunter is facing away.

"Can I bum a smoke?" she asks. Her words come out as visible water vapor.

"This is my last one," Hunter says.

SHICK SHICK

Locked and loaded, Hunter thinks. "Locked and loaded," Hunter says, and he takes aim at the can.

"You have been trying to shoot that can for a while," Goya says, and she laughs.

"..."

Everything except the can falls out of focus for Hunter. He takes a deep breath. He pulls the trigger.

CLICK

There is silence. They cannot tell where the BB hit, but they can tell that it did not hit the can.

"Only a quitter quits," Hunter says.

David wakes from a haunted sleep, and he wants a cigarette. He puts his clothes on and walks outside. He sits in a chair on the back porch and lights a cigarette.

SHICK SHICK

"My turn," Goya says. She grabs the air rifle from Hunter. Goya and Hunter walk to opposite sides of the backyard. Hunter covers his genitals with one hand. He covers his eyes with the other.

SHICK SHICK

She readies the BB gun. She takes aim. She begins pulling the trigger. She lowers the air rifle.

"I think we loaded it twice," she says. "Now it won't fire."

Hunter begins running over to take a look. Goya smiles. She readies. She takes aim. Hunter dives for cover behind the shed. Goya laughs.

"..."

"I was just kidding," she says. She lowers the air rifle. Hunter stays hidden.

"I don't believe you."

"Aww, come on Hunter." She makes an expression that is both sad and happy.

"..."

"Please, it is still broken," she says. He peeks his head out.

"..."

"..."

Hunter steps out. He runs over. David watches Goya and Hunter try to repair the BB gun.

Text message from Karen: What are you doing in real life?

Text message from Karen: It's a serious question, so you don't have to answer.

Text message from David: Smoking a cigarette and watching my roommates shoot each other with an air rifle. What are you doing irl?

Text message from Karen: That's too much to handle.

Text message from David: Yeah but... it is happening.

Text message from Karen: Seems like turning your life into a performance, like... living a fake life.

Text message from David: I mean I like them.

"Got it," Goya says. Hunter runs across the yard. He turns around and covers his eyes and genitals.

"Okay."

"Okay."

SHICK SHICK

"..."

She pulls the trigger.

CLICK

An unclear meditation precedes a sterile, reluctant

64

perceiving and a reappearing, fuzzy exposure and a sluggish, enduring, slack episode.

David looks at Numbskull. The cat-type creature looks out the window. David gets an I-give-in-type sensation, and he opens the front door, holding it open for Numbskull. It walks to the door. It brushes up against David's leg. It steps onto the porch. Hunter walks up, and David keeps holding the door open as Hunter follows the cat-type thing out.

Numbskull finds the window it was looking through to see out of the house, and it sits in front of it, and it looks into the house. Hunter descends the stairs toward his van, and David closes the door and follows Hunter.

THUD THUD

Hunter gets in the van. David gets in the van. The van is covered in monster drawings. It is a chain of monsters vomiting other monsters eventually vomiting monsters that vomit themselves.

"The print shop is right up the street," Hunter says. He grabs a tape from the van's dashboard. The tape reads, Puss Grime. The album art is faces melting into other faces. He puts the tape in a boombox sitting on the floorboard between them.

VOORRR

Hunter turns the keys in the ignition.

CLICK

He presses play. Blasting drums kick in. The van pulls forward. They are on their way to print flyers for the Scab Control show. Hunter and David's band is opening for Scab Control. The venue is called Mind Damage.

The Puss Grime tape is warped. It speeds up

intermittently. It slows down intermittently. They pull into the parking lot.

KLING CLICK KRINGLE THUD THUD

Hunter turns off the ignition. He stops the tape. From the back seat, he grabs the flyer he drew. He closes his door. David closes his door. They walk into the print shop. Hunter makes his way to a copy machine. He begins copying the flyer. David browses the shop, and he hums a simple melody.

"I can't understand why you seem so happy right now," Hunter says. His tone is sarcastic.

David realizes he seems sad generally.

He realizes Hunter was analyzing his emotional state.

He realizes something else.

He realizes printing is expensive.

He realizes the reality.

He realizes what embossed means.

He realizes laser-jet printers do not use ink.

He realizes the steady sound of a printer is pleasant.

He realizes some people still use fax machines.

David shrugs. Hunter grabs the flyers. He pats David on the back. They walk to the van.

THUD THUD CLICK VOORRR

They get in the van. Hunter presses play on the tape player. Hunter turns the keys in the ignition. Blast beats pollute their perspectives. They are bombarded with sonic violence.

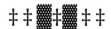

The model is tall. Her hair is black. It is cut short. She looks androgynous. She also seems conventionally beautiful. Why is David not attracted to her? He gets lost in the ideas of her.

Spider, David's focus shifts. Spider, the switch is abrupt. Spider, his focus switches from the androgynous model to the spider crawling across her face, and it is the size of her head.

SPLAT

David lifts his foot. Underneath is a page torn from one of Goya's fashion magazines. The page contains the androgynous model. Spider innards are splattered across her face and upper body.

"Woops," David says.

"..."

David looks up at Goya. She is in the middle of her room. She is cutting into a magazine.

"I think I might have ruined something you are using for one of your collages," David says.

Goya looks up from the magazine she is cutting. She picks up the page with a spider splattered across.

"I am using something on the other side," Goya says. "You're fine." She cuts into the page. She cuts out a human figure. She cuts it in half. The torso falls off. She cuts the feet off. She turns it around. It is a pair of jeans. They are deconstructed jeans. Goya puts glue on the backside of the cutout. She holds it in both hands and places it slowly and places it deliberately. She glues it to the collage she is working on.

David cannot tell why she placed it where she did. He does not care why. His perspective shifts. He looks at the whole collage. The entire canvas is covered with deconstructed jeans. His perspective shifts again. There are many collages of deconstructed jeans in Goya's room. Her walls are covered with deconstructed-jean collages. David laughs.

"I know," she says. She feels self-conscious about her obsession. She looks into a burst of deconstructed jeans.

"..."

"I have never recovered from seeing the ritual ad for Tight Violence," Goya says.

"..."

"Do people still wear deconstructed jeans?" David asks.

$$\underline{\Delta}\,{}^{\text{o'o'}}\,\underline{\Delta}\,{}^{\text{o'}}$$

The door closes behind David. He sighs.

Text message from Karen: I just thought, I can't die until my dog dies.

Text message from David: Hahaha

Text message from David: Do you remember the first time you typed lol?

Text message from Karen: I've never typed it. Just thinking about it makes me nervous.

⸎ ⸎‡━‡⸎ ⸎

SKIR

Hunter flies by on his skateboard. He feels content.

68

CLAKK

Beneath power lines along a city street, Hunter takes flight, smiling a soft smile, floating in the air above the concrete, his arms rising slowly, attempting to control his flight, his feet only reaching two feet above the ground at their highest point in the wide-low arch of his flight, his legs kicking outward, his skateboard turning slowly revealing an overworked drawing of faces in faces on the underside of the deck.

CLAKK

Hunter lands on his skateboard, the world jerking forward to catch up to him as he skates up to an automatic door. He stops. His hand waves in the style of a Jedi, and the door slides open. Hunter picks up his skateboard. He enters the store. He sees the woman he has inside jokes with.

Four Four Four Four

Air holes

Adjusting the saturation

Infinite thoughts, but none of them are good

Blek

Bromine

Pocket salads

He pulls a handful of flyers from his pocket. He approaches her.

"Hey Karen," he says, holding out a flyer for her. She looks at it. Tendons is written in a sweating font. Melting strands connect the letters. Barf Parade is written in an oozy font. Negative Slime is written in a drippy font. Scab Control is written in a slimy font. The logos are evenly spaced. Scab Control is slightly larger at the top. The details of the show are handwritten at the bottom, Thurs. at 10pm at Mind Damage.

"Oh, Negative Slime," Karen says. "My boyfriend is in that band." Hunter lowers the flyer. This is the first time Karen has mentioned her boyfriend to Hunter.

"Your boyfriend is Wes?"

"Yeah!" Karen exclaims. "You know him?"

"I am not sure if I would say I know Wes, but I know who he is, I know he is crazy..."

Karen laughs. "Yeah, he is a mess. I was going to the show anyway, but can I still have a flyer?"

"..."

He raises the flyer as if to say, Sure. Karen takes it. She turns it around to look at it.

"Did you draw these logos?" Karen asks.

"Yeah," Hunter says.

"They look awesome," she says, "but I have to go back to folding jeans... I'll see you at the show."

"Yeah..."

She turns, and she walks away. Hunter clinches the rest of the flyers in his hands.

⌐ ╚■ ▲ ■⌐ ╚

Goya runs over the details of her day in her mind. Running over the details of her day is the first detail of her day, I ran over the details of my day in my mind and while running over the details of running over the details in my mind finding there are details in my mind and something in my mind and something in

70

my mind on my mind and my mind is on my mind.

Hunter enters the room holding the BB gun. He looks at Goya. She looks up at him.

He says, "I have been reading a lot about that woodland, deer-like creature that we saw on the mountain."

"..."

"Some deer are born with the Indigo Fluorescent Protein, or IFP," Hunter says. Goya smiles.

"Was that a joke?" Goya asks.

"No... I read it somewhere," Hunter says. "The protein has other effects. They are known for being themselves and not caring what others think about them and growing golden antlers and doing what they want."

"..."

"I am going to the corner store... Do you want anything?"

"No thanks."

Goya spends twenty minutes scratching into the kitchen table with the golden antler. She lifts the golden antler. The table reads, Numbskull. Its letters are all capitalized. She puts her head on the table.

▲ †‡ ‡? ▲

David draws a couple blanks on a letter to Lela. All he can think of writing is Numbskull with a triangle on either side of the word. The word Numbskull with a triangle on either side of it means nothing to her. He sits in the park. He wants to write something Lela will find emotionally significant. He wants to write something Lela will find funny. He does not write anything for a couple hours. He wants to get at the reality of their situation. He wants to get at the reality of their relationship. He misses her. He is getting used to missing her. He grabs a pen. He begins to write.

I drew a couple blanks on a letter to you. All I could think of writing is Numbskull with a triangle on either side of the word. I thought, Numbskull with a triangle on either side of the word means nothing to you. I was sitting in the park. I wanted to write something you would find emotionally significant. I wanted to write something you would find funny. I have not written anything for a couple hours. I wanted to get at the reality of our situation. I wanted to get at the reality of our relationship. I was missing you. I was getting used to missing you. I grabbed my pen. I began to write.

x infinity

⚏ ■ ‡ ■ ⚏

"What's the occasion?" David asks. Goya hunches over a box. It is wrapped in a collage of deconstructed jeans.

"I am pretty sure it's my brother's birthday next week," Goya says. "But, like... I am not sure what day." She tapes the wrapping. "So, I am sending him a present. A half-smoked pack of cigarettes and a framed sketch of Michael Jackson and a pack of birth control pills that I thought I lost and a card for a born-again Christian that reads, Happy Rebirthday."

"..."

"I put the birth control pills in there because my brother said he never uses condoms and if he gets his friend pregnant he'll shoot himself in the head," Goya says. "Well, he didn't say it. He made a hand gesture of placing a gun in his mouth."

"..."

"I can't tell if it is just me, but it seems like everyone is talking about death. Like every conversation is thin translucent veil over a field of skulls?"

"It could just be in your head. You've been looking at these photos of that model."

"..."

"You know when you get a new pair of shoes, and you start to notice everyone who is wearing those shoes?"

"..."

"It could be like that."

"My brother is sending me text messages about stepping into oncoming traffic," she says. She sticks a bow on the package. "Probably should be more alarming than noticing people I match clothes with."

"..."

"But what am I supposed to do?" she asks.

"If you think it is a joke, it is probably fine," David says.

"I don't think it is a joke, and I also think he will be fine," she says.

"..."

"..."

Text message from Karen: Someone on the internet, someone who does not know me, told me they want to masturbate to my profile picture.

▲ ‡ ‡ ■ ‡ ‡ ▲

"I hope that Numbskull stops looking so sad," Hunter says. "Maybe we should let him in again."

"..."

David has mixed feelings. The cat-type creature will be sad no matter what... seems normal. Hunter throws his bag over his shoulder. He holds the door open for Numbskull. The cat-type creature walks to the door. It brushes against Hunter's leg. Numbskull finds the other side of the window he was looking into. It gazes out of it. It seems sad. David laughs.

Hunter steps out of the house, and David follows. It is the first warm day in a long time. The warm day reminds David that Lela is returning soon.

He imagines going with Lela and Hunter and Goya to the river.

He imagines them doing nothing.

He imagines everything being okay.

He imagines being in bed with Lela.

He imagines falling down the stairs.

He imagines himself as an old person.

He imagines Numbskull doing something other than looking through the window when no one is observing him.

David turns around, and Numbskull is still gazing through the window. Hunter descends to the street. David descends to the street. Hunter opens the rear doors of his van. The van is packed with gear for Tendons' show opening for Scab Control. Hunter throws his bag in. David stands by the passenger side door.

"It should be open," Hunter says. "After it was broken into twice in one year, I don't lock it anymore."

THUD THUD

They climb in, and they close the doors behind them.

"Do they have an extra drum rug at Mind Damage?" Hunter asks.

David shrugs.

"I guess we'll need ours," Hunter says, and he opens the door, and he gets out.

THUD

He goes back inside, and he returns with a rolled up rug, and he throws it in the back.

THUD

As Hunter gets back in the driver's seat, he asks, "Are we good to go?"

"Yeah, but I was hoping we could buy some drugs on the way or whatever."

"From TV Mike?"

"Yeah, but we don't have to."

"Sounds good." Hunter reaches for his keys. He pauses. "I told TV Mike that I would bring his box of stuff the next time I saw him. Is it cool if I run back in and grab TV Mike's stuff?"

"If it fits, I couldn't care less," David says.

THUD

"Cool," Hunter says, talking through the rolled-down window. He walks up the stairs to their house. David watches. He feels calm. Hunter disappears into the house.

David can hear the wind, and he can hear Hunter yelling the lyrics to a Puss Grime song from inside the house. Waiting here seems nice.

Hunter walks down the stairs, and he is carrying a box. It is blue. It is plastic. He opens the van's side door, and he places the box on the floor. The contents are an assortment of psychedelic curios: a skull with three ropes hanging from it with three skulls tied to each rope, a holographic picture of a wizard, a holographic picture of an owl, an infinity mirror, an optical illusion machine in the shape of a triangle.

THUD

Hunter gets back into the van, closing the door behind him.

VUURRR CLICK

Hunter grabs the keys. He turns the keys in the ignition.

"I kind of want to listen to the Scab Control tape," David says.

"I don't," Hunter says, and he grabs a tape from the dashboard. It reads, Puss Grime. He puts it in the boombox between their seats.

CLICK

Blasting drums pulverize the air around them. Hunter laughs a small laugh, and David smiles. The van pulls forward. It veers sharply to avoid a branch.

THUNK

The passenger side mirror hits the branch anyway. The mirror is on a hinge. David reaches out. He grabs the mirror. He pushes it back to where it was before the branch hit it. He lights a cigarette.

Hunter and David wait at a light. They wait to turn

left. "I know I am being paranoid," Hunter says, "but if a cop finds our stash, one of us should say it is theirs so the other person can bail them out of jail." They turn left.

"..."

"When I got caught getting stoned with Goya and Lela, Lela said all the weed in the car was hers," Hunter says. "I couldn't let her take all the blame. I told the officer it was actually all mine. We both got tickets. Nothing happened to Goya... I mean I can take the blame if we get caught."

David laughs an anxious laugh. "I can't really handle that," David says.

"I would much rather have you free," Hunter says. "You can get money from my bank account and get me out."

"That's ridiculous," David says. "I can't handle that."

"I am just being stoned and paranoid," Hunter says. They park across from TV Mike's house. It is a modest house. It is a two-bedroom house. A truck is parked in the driveway. David walks up to the door. Hunter follows shortly. He is carrying the box of curio.

KNOCK KNOCK

A dog comes to the window. It begins to bark. David looks at it, and he steps back. He stands next to Hunter. The door opens. It reveals TV Mike. He is holding his baby.

"Hey, guys," TV Mike says. He opens the door wider. He lets David and Hunter in.

"Hey," Hunter says. He holds the box of curios out.

"Oh," TV Mike says. He raises the kid to say, My arms are full. Hunter sets the box on the couch. TV Mike seats his kid. The kid's seat is suspended in a plastic ring. It is suspended by elastic bands. Toys and noisemakers sprout from the ring. The baby bounces up and down. Hunter kneels down to play with TV Mike's kid. TV Mike flips through the channels on his television. He finds a children's show. The screen is filled with shapes with universes in them. Hunter turns toward the television. The baby turns toward the television. Hunter and the baby watch the shapes with universes in them. They are beguiled. Their mouths are open.

"..."

TV Mike walks to the kitchen. David walks to the kitchen. "My coworker went to the doctor and said 'I am interested in learning about Adderall,' and he walked out with a prescription," TV Mike said. He blinks. He pulls out a cooler.

"Seems cool," David says. "Did he give you some?"

"No," TV Mike says. "I went to the same doctor and got my own prescription." David laughs. "Aren't you opening for Scab Control soon?"

"Yeah," David says. "Like when we walk out of your home, and we get in Hunter's van, and we drive to Mind Damage."

"Oh damn," TV Mike says. He opens the cooler. It reeks of weed. He weighs some out on a scale. The scale is one commonly found in middle school science classrooms. "An eighth," he says. He puts it in a bag with some Adderall. "Sixty sound good?" TV Mike asks. David is unsure of the value of the

Adderall.

"..."

"It is a good deal," TV Mike says. David shrugs. He pulls out his wallet. He hands the money to TV Mike. TV Mike places the money on the scale. He weighs the money. He zones out.

"..."

David tries to find something to look at while TV Mike is in another universe, and all he can find is a cabinet door, and he stares at the cabinet door. It is brown. The handle is brown.

TV Mike looks up at David. He hands the bag over to David.

"Sweet," David says. He places the bag in his pocket.

"Have a fun show," TV Mike says.

"Yep," David says. He walks back into the room with the television. TV Mike follows. "Ready, Hunter?" David asks.

"Yeah," Hunter says. He is still looking at the shapes with universes in them. The baby is still looking at the shapes with universes in them. David opens the front door, and he walks outside. Hunter stands. His eyes are locked onto the television until he walks outside. They wave a goodbye wave to TV Mike.

THUD THUD

They climb into the van. David pulls the bag from his pocket.

"Can you put this in the can?" David asks.

Hunter reaches into the back. He grabs his bag. He opens his bag. He pulls out a Sprite can in a koozie. He twists the top off. Lifting the top reveals a stash: three Xanax and two hits of acid on two Teddy Grahams individually wrapped in tinfoil and some weed. He stuffs the bag of weed and Adderall into the can. He twists the lid back on.

An immense, gradual drive precedes a slack, emptied, negligent exposure and a loitering, dreamy, imperceptible banality and a measureless, drowsy, delaying, enormous event and an inert, enduring vapor.

A small crowd hangs around the venue's front door, smoking and talking. Over the crowd, the sign reads, Mind Damage. The type face is neutral, and all the letters are capitalized. Hunter and David walk to the front door of Mind Damage. The venue's exterior is dilapidated, cracks webbing across the large windows and layers of graffiti and cigarette butts.

All the members of Scab Control stand in circle. The guitar player from Scab Control nods at David and Hunter, and Hunter waves in response. The guitar player is standing around the front door. Some other people are standing around the front door. "Do you want a beer?" Hunter asks.

David shrugs. "Do we get free drinks for playing?" David asks.

"I don't know," Hunter says. "But I'll get you if we don't."

"Uh... sure, sounds good."

Hunter quickly makes his way into the bar. David stands just outside the circle of Scab Control members, watching the crowd. Someone sits down against a light post, and he is wearing a box for a shoe, and the box is for a twelve pack of beer.

"You see that woman over there?" the guitar

player from Scab Control asks. "The one with the gauged ears."

"..."

David realizes he is being spoken to.

"The taller of the twins," the guitar player says.

"Yeah..." David says. He is ready to be bored.

"After you play, she will be all over your dick," the guitar player says.

"..."

David looks at her. He blinks. He looks at the building across the street. He blinks. He looks somewhere else. Thin spires of cigarette smoke stand in the windless air.

"I know for a fact she is under twenty-one," the guitar player from Scab Control says.

David feels discomfort. He lights a cigarette. He hopes smoking will substitute for talking. He breathes in.

"I mean... she is drinking on the sidewalk," the guitar player says.

David cannot think of anything to respond with. The man with the beer box shoe stands. He is dirty, and his gestures are effeminate, and he is seven feet tall, and he is bear-like. The large man crosses David's line of sight. A woman sitting next to David stands, and she gives the bear-like man a one-armed hug.

"No no no," the bear-like man says, "full-body hug. I shot a little heroin before the show."

"..."

They hug again, squeezing their arms tight and squeezing their eyes tight.

"..."

They release the hug. The woman's shirt rode up

in the hug, and she has a tattoo across her stomach that reads, Cunt. That seems intense to David. That also seems funny to him.

"We had a couple of amazing shows in Brooklyn," the guitar player from Scab Control says. David tries to remember where they are on tour from, Canada or Brooklyn or wherever.

David glances over at Scab Control's shirts and records on the merch table. Their shirts have pentagram dream catchers on them, and their records have pentagram dream catchers on them.

"When I first saw your aesthetic, I thought you were from Brooklyn," David says. "But yeah... you're from Canada."

"Well, Quebec," the guitar player says. David laughs.

"..."

David takes a breath. Pentagram dream catchers seem indicative of a lot of things. He holds the image of a triangle inside of another triangle forming four triangles inside a triangle, and it spins in a forest, and it is dark there, and David self-deprecates.

"..."

"..."

The guitar player from Scab Control turns to David. "Are you staying for the after-hours party?"

"I didn't even know there was one," David says.

"Is that the one where you need a password to get in?" the woman with the Cunt tattoo asks. David moves to let the guitar player and her talk more directly. "I am Helen, by the way," she says.

"Mark," the guitar player says. They shake hands.

"David," David says, and he waves a small wave.

"..."

"I don't think so," Mark says.

"..."

"There is a room above the bar where there is an after party," he says.

"..."

"Since you're in a band, you're invited," he says.

"Oh," David says. He zones out. He gets bored. He looks at his phone.

Text message from Karen: I just pretended to be happy for 23 minutes.

David walks inside. Hunter walks up to him. "Here you go," Hunter says, and he hands David a beer.

"Thanks," David says. Hunter takes on a grave expression. David watches Hunter quickly walk outside.

David turns around to see what spooked Hunter, and he sees Wes approaching. Wes is the only original member left in the band Negative Slime. His hair is long and wavy, and his eyes are shifty, and his shirt reads, Advocate first-degree murder, and he seems to nod constantly. David is reminded of Wes pissing on the front door the last time Negative Slime played here.

"When should we start?" Wes asks.

"Probably nowish," David says, but he does not know why he is being asked. He realizes he does not even know who organized the show.

"Okay," Wes says. "Cool," he says. "When do you play?" he asks. "I'm going to walk down the street to see another show until you play," he says. "You're the only other band like us, right?" he asks.

"I believe so," David says. In his thoughts, he holds Wes' words 'the only other band like us'. He does not know what that means. He goes along. "We play fourth or second-to-last or whatever."

"Okay," Wes says, and he climbs onto the stage. "Well," he says. "We will get started then," he says.

David opens the door. From the doorway, he tells Hunter the first band is starting. David closes the door. He walks to the merch table. He sits.

Helen, the woman with the cunt tattoo, joins Wes on stage. The guy with the beer box shoe climbs on stage. Out of nowhere, the clerk from the convenience store, the one with greasy hair that awkwardly asked about Goya's shirt, climbs on stage. Each person on stage has their own amp. Each amp runs to a pile of guitar pedals. Each pile of guitar pedals has a contact mic running from it. Each contact mic is run along the inside of its own metal bowl. Each bowl-and-contact-mic-and-pile-of-pedals-and-amp set creates their own drone. Each knob-turner's drone is ambient.

IRRRRRRRRR

A quiet nobody precedes an easy, shadowy, inactive vision and a barren obscurity and a weak, worthless feeling.

"Ready to play?" Hunter asks.

"Sure," David says.

Hunter hands a one-hitter back to David. They climb out of Hunter's van, briefly pausing in front of the chain of monsters vomiting other monsters eventually vomiting monsters that vomit themselves painted on the van.

They walk into Mind Damage. Hunter climbs on the stage. David climbs on the stage. They set up their gear. Hunter sits behind a drum kit. He holds his drumsticks in both hands. He stretches his arms. David sits behind a drum kit. There is a pause. David holds his drumsticks above his head. Hunter holds his drumsticks above his head. A hush comes over the crowd, and the lights dim.

CLICK CLICK CLICK

The brutal churning of blast beats slams the audience. Hunter and David have two visions, loud and fast.

CRASH CRASH CRASH
BA DUM DUM DUM DUM
TAKKA TAKKA TAKKA TAKKA
DUM DUM
DUMMM
TAKKA TAKKA TAKKA TAKKA
DUM DUM
DUMMM
CRASH CRASH
CRASH CRASH
BAAA
DUM DUM DUM DUM
DUM DUM DUM DUM
"AHHHH!"

BA DUM DUM DUM DUM
DUM DUM DUM DUM
CRA CRASH CRASH CRASH CRASH
BRATATAT BRATATAT
CRASH CRASH
CRASH CRASH

≙ ◼◞ ◟◼ ≙

Tendons finishes playing. David and Hunter begin breaking down their gear. They are in a strange haze. Helen walks up to David. Wes stands behind her, and he does not say anything, but he nods a lot.

"I really like your hair," Helen says.

David reads her shirt. Life is written across the front, and its letters are all capitalized, and the font is gothic, and the letters are white, and they have a red highlight. Dropout is written below the red highlight, and its letters are all capitalized, and the font is gothic, and the letters are red, and it has no highlight.

"Oh," David says, "thank you."

"   ..."

"   ..."

"Okay," Helen says. "Well, I'll let you pack your gear." She waves. She walks away with Wes.

David watches her walk away, and an ocean scene replaces all the blue in the room. David turns to his gear, and he continues packing. Hunter walks to the van carrying a bass drum. David sighs, and he hunches over his kit. He feels a presence over his shoulder.

"Hunter, is the van unlocked?" David asks.

"..."

"Or can I get the keys to take my drums out to the van?" he asks.

"..."

David turns around, and he expects to see Hunter standing there, and a woman is standing there. It takes a moment, and he puts a name without a face with this face without a name, and he realizes she is Karen. A vague recollection of meeting her at Lela's going away party drifts through David's thoughts.

"You again," David says.

"You again again," Karen says. She smiles a slight smile.

"..."

"..."

"How are you –"

"Hey, Karen!" Hunter says. He walks up, and he waves.

David grabs some of his gear, almost more than he can carry. He walks outside, leaving Karen and Hunter talking.

The parking lot is paved black, diagonal lines making spaces making rows. In the van is David stacking his gear. The snare rattles when he lays it down, and the hardware clinks.

He walks back, and Hunter and Karen are still talking. David does not say anything. Keeping his head down, he grabs the last of his gear. He walks to the van and waits for them to finish talking. The muffled sounds of Scab Control's set make their way to David. It is some nostalgic rock 'n' roll that, for David, confirms there has never been an original thought.

An unconfirmed anticipation precedes a ghostly, clouded sense and a dull vision and a miring, unending knowledge.

David stands in front of the chain of monsters vomiting other monsters eventually vomiting monsters that vomit themselves, and he is smoking a cigarette. Karen walks out of Mind Damage, and her hands hold the straps of her camouflage backpack. Her face makes a wide-eyed expression that somehow says, It is deafeningly loud in there. She unlocks her bike. She walks up to David. David gives a slight wave. She gives the same wave back, and she makes an anxious smile. David sits on the van's rear bumper, and Karen sits beside him.

They talk vaguely about expectations.

They talk vaguely about expectation management.

They talk vaguely about being young forever.

They talk vaguely about never giving up.

They talk vaguely about panic attacks.

They talk vaguely about thoughts on thoughts.

They talk vaguely about the weather.

They talk vaguely about existentialism.

They talk vaguely about never expressing a worldview.

David finds himself wanting her to hate him, even though he does not hate her. The idea of her hating him seems nice for various reasons.

" ... "

" ... "

"What's your plan for tonight?" Karen asks.

"I think I am going to hang out in my room," David says. "Probably reading and watching a movie and listening to music."

"At the same time?"

"By reading and watching a movie and listening to music, I mean I'll be doing nothing." He laughs.

Karen nods, Ahh.

"What are you up to?"

"I really don't want to go home right now," Karen says. "I am probably going to a club." She climbs onto her bike. "It is in a loft downtown. When I am there, I feel like I am in another city, like... Tokyo or something."

"Why not the after party? I thought your boyfriend and the other guys in Barf Parade were going to that."

"They are..."

"..."

"..."

"I think you and my boyfriend make me more anxious than anyone," she says.

"..."

"He is so dumb."

David laughs. He hopes she thinks he is dumb too, seems nice. He manages expectations. "The only things about him I can think of is he told me 'Your band's songs need to be longer,' and then last time Negative Slime played here he pissed on the front door."

"..."

"..."

"..."

"Well, have fun," David says.

Karen waves another slight wave, and she rides away. David sighs, and he gazes at the front of Mind Damage. The venue's door opens, and Hunter walks out with the last of his gear.

"I think I am going out with some friends," Hunter says. "You should come."

"I think I am just going home."

A never-ending, deprived introspection precedes an avoided cognition and an inactive, blurry speculation and an unclear, moderate feeling.

Hunter and David finish loading their gear back into their house. Hunter walks to his van. The van pulls away. David sits on the porch, the night's black wind blowing down the street. Not far away, the lights of downtown wash the skyline in a vomit yellow. He does not feel committed to doing nothing. What about a getting vegan hotdog? He pulls out his wallet checking how much money he has.

Text message from David: How's Tokyo?

Text message from Karen: Under populated.

Text message from David: Seems funny and terrifying.

Text message from Karen: At least the sound system is good.

Text message from David: Hahaha

Text message from David: Is there dancing?

Text message from Karen: Lil bit. Thinking of coming out? Nothing great, but I am sick of being home.

Text message from David: I am thinking about coming out. I do not know anything about that Tokyo-type place.

Text message from Karen: Six hundred and sixty-six Congress Street. Looks like a coke den. Gold trim, leather couches, and shit. Three dollars.

Text message from David: Umm... I was going to

get a veggie dog with my three dollars, but that sounds like something too.

David makes his way to Congress Street, watching passerbys and loitering with little to no thoughts about what is going on around him. Karen stands across the street. She is outside the doors to the club, and she is smoking a cigarette, and she is standing in a group, Karen and a woman with a bloody nose smoking a cigarette beneath an asymmetrical haircut and someone with hair covering their face and three people in fluorescent colors with masks knit with geometric patterns. A car goes by. Another car goes by. Karen looks up, and David and Karen are making eye contact. David makes an exaggerated sad expression. Karen smiles. Some more cars go by. David makes his way across the street. Karen walks up to a light post, and she leans against the light post. David walks up to the light post.

"Hey," he says.

"Hey," Karen says. She makes a slight gesture, directing David's attention to the group she was standing with. "This is everyone at the party... like the five of them and you and me." David laughs a small laugh. "Do you want to get a drink somewhere?" she asks.

David nods. Karen walks to her bike, and David follows her. He waits as she unlocks the bike. He looks around.

"Where's your bike?" she asks. "Or did you drive?"

"I walked."

"..."

"I live a couple blocks from downtown," he says.

91

She furrows her brow and asks, "Where do you want to get a drink?"

"There is a whole shit show of bars over there."

Karen laughs. "Yeah, we should go to Sixth Street." And she begins walking her bike.

"I was joking, but okay."

David walks alongside her, and they walk to the Sixth Street and Congress intersection. The street channels the sounds of bars and clubs. They turn on to Sixth Street.

"Look," David says, and he nods toward two people yelling on the other side of the street, and the two of them stare across the street.

"The are experiencing a public breakup."

Someone is yelling at the someone else, and the background is filled with people dancing and vomiting and selling glow sticks and stumbling and fighting and people watching and smoking. The person yelling runs their fingers through their hair, and they stop yelling, and they turn, starting to run away, and they turn down another street. The person that was being yelled at pursues. They cannot catch up. They give up.

"Running away from the past..." Karen says.

"..."

They walk along Sixth Street. The street is lined with clubs and bars. The street is blocked off at either end. It is pedestrians only at night.

A group of cops, all wearing sunglasses even though it is night, handcuff someone and throw them against a squad car, and the vomiting and pissing and stumbling and dancing and groping and smoking continue around the police.

"We should walk in the street," Karen says, and she steps off the sidewalk and rolls her bike off the curb. David follows. They weave between groups of people dancing and posturing and vomiting and crying and catcalling and smoking.

"I always love Sixth Street at this time," David says.

"I am imagining someone watching us, being super critical and bored and happy because they feel sad," Karen says.

Right now, nothing makes sense to David. He scans for a place to get a drink. He sees a neon sign. It is above a door, and the door leads to stairs, and the stairs are going down. The neon sign reads, You Will Die. Its letters are all capitalized. The neon is white. In front of the door, a man dances. He is muscle bound. He is in a full bodysuit. The suit is mesh. The mesh is dayglow yellow. It is skintight.

"We should go there," Karen says. "If there's no cover."

David laughs. He does not think she is serious, but it would seriously be funny to go in. He gets lost in his thoughts.

He thinks, I generally hate the this-film-is-not-funny-but-that-we-are-watching-it-is-funny-type irony.

He thinks, The feeling of experiencing that variety of irony would be comforting though.

He thinks, That feeling is funny.

He thinks, That feeling of that irony is funny.

He thinks, But my thoughts on that feeling are already boring.

He thinks, My thoughts on those thoughts are

already boring.

He looks around. Karen has walked off. David walks past the man in the mesh suit and walks down the stairs. A bouncer stands in front of a closed door.

"Did an awkward-looking woman with a camouflage backpack just come in a second ago?" David asks. The bouncer shakes his head, No. "Is there a cover?"

The bouncer shakes his head, No.

"Thanks," David says. He walks back upstairs.

Karen is standing at the top of the stairwell. "I locked my bike up."

"There's no cover here..."

Karen nods, Okay.

They walk into the club. Everyone in the club has blank expressions on their faces, and they dance to a simple beat, and the beat is only one bass drum sound, steady and midtempo. A large, stoic man stands on stage behind a pile of electronics on a table. His expression is also blank. He is wearing sunglasses and a jean jacket and fingerless biker gloves, and his hair is buzzed. Another large, stoic man stands beside him, and they are identical, center reflected behind the pile of electronics. The man in the mesh suit comes into the club. He walks onstage and continues dancing.

"Let's get a drink," Karen says. David steps aside to let Karen pass, and she pushes into the crowd ahead. David follows her to the bar.

"Do you want a beer?" she asks.

"Sure."

"I am going to buy you a beer."

"I could buy my own."

Karen leans on the bar. She looks at him over her glasses.

"I mean, thank you. A beer sounds great."

David stands around. Karen turns from the bar holding two beers. She hands one to David.

David asks, "Would you be interested in going near the stage and dancing?"

Karen nods. They walk through the crowd. They walk toward the stage. The man in the mesh suit spins glow sticks on strings. Karen and David stand five feet from the stage, and they watch the stage, and they are calm. David looks at her. He looks at the stage. Karen looks at David. She looks at the stage.

She starts nodding her head to the midtempo beat. David starts nodding his head to the midtempo beat. There is a gradient from nodding their heads to dancing. Their dances are simple repetitions of a single move. Occasionally they jerk. Occasionally they pose. They dance for a little while. Their smiles are soft. Their smiles are Mona-Lisa-type smiles. The bartenders announce last call.

Karen leans in to speak into David's ear. "Wanna go sit?"

"Sure."

David and Karen sit at a table in the back of the club. The table is lit in black light. A cup sits on the table, and it holds flowers, and the flowers glow under the black light.

At the next table over, two people are making out. One of their legs is shaking. David looks at the leg and then at Karen. She nods as if to say, Yep... they're making out.

"That twitching leg seems intense," David says.

Karen laughs. She starts watching people. Someone supports someone too drunk to stand on their own. Someone else is crying. Someone else humps someone else.

Karen notices an abandoned drink on a nearby table, and it is almost full. "An almost full Long Island Iced Tea," Karen says.

As David realizes which drink she is talking about, someone comes up and grabs it.

"..."

"Oh, over there," Karen says, directing David's attention to a similar Long Island Iced Tea. David shrugs. He walks over, grabs the drink, turns around.

And Karen is holding flowers in front of her face, and her hair and pink button-up shirt frame the black-lit flowers, like the flowers are her face. She has a ring on her hand. It has a large, obsidian crystal. Her fingernails are painted with patterns, and the patterns are black and white, and the patterns create an optical illusion of slight movement.

David focuses on the patterns on her nails, and their white glows in the black light. He hopes her flower face is smiling.

He sits beside Karen. She lowers the flowers. David holds the drink out to her. She holds her beer can up as if to say, I am still drinking this. Why did he get the drink if she does not want it? He takes a sip.

"How is it?" Karen asks. Without waiting for a response is Karen taking it from his hand. She takes a drink. "Sugary." She hands it back.

"Yeah..."

"And not very alcoholic."

David continues drinking it to occupy his hands.

They sit there quietly for a moment.

"..."

"..."

"Those people outside that Tokyo party were actually the only people there," Karen says. "Like there were four of us at the party."

"Seems intimate."

An unreal impression precedes a sterile, translucent exposure and an immaterial, dreamy essence and a dim, all-embracing ambiguity.

The lights come on. Most of the people in the club are leaving. David and Karen watch them shamble out. Someone comes up to them. They say the bar is closed, and they say everyone has to leave. Karen and David walk out of the bar and walk up the stairs. They can smell piss on the wind.

As all the bars and clubs are closing, people pour out of the clubs, and more people pour out of the clubs, and the streets are flooded with vomiting and arguing and stumbling and dancing and kissing and smoking. Karen walks around the corner. David walks around the corner. Karen is unlocking her bike. Next to her bike, a woman holds a white trash bag, and she is making a face that says, I'm about to vomit. Another woman stands over the bag making a face that says, I'm about to vomit first. David feels amazed. Being prepared enough to bring a bag for vomit seems intense. The two women start to vomit. Next to them, two people are making out.

Karen walks her bike to a nearby wall. She leans her bike against the wall, and she leans against the wall. David walks up, and he stands beside her. Karen begins rolling a cigarette. David pulls a cigarette pack out, and he lifts a cigarette out, and he lights it and returns the pack to his pocket. He hands Karen the lighter when she is done rolling her cigarette.

"Do you still want to be out of the house?" David asks.

"Nothing is going on now."

"We could walk to the bridge or something."

Karen nods. She looks around. She makes a subtle gesture toward the women vomiting in the plastic bag.

"..."

"Ridiculous," David says. They are smoking their cigarettes, and they are watching the puking and smoking and confronting and tripping and dancing and eating.

"..."

"..."

While Karen puts out her cigarette, she asks, "Do you still want to go for a walk?"

"For sure," David says, putting his cigarette out on the bottom of his shoe.

"It is awesome that you can walk downtown from your house," Karen says.

"Yeah..."

"..."

"..."

"..."

"Ready?" she asks. They stand on one side of a river of people flowing down Sixth Street. David nods. They start walking from one side of the crowd to the other, and the volume of the crowd layers on their perspectives, a wave of incomprehensible talking.

"This will sound lame," David yells, "but I sort of marvel at how shitty all this is, bringing a vomit bag and last-ditch efforts to get laid."

She responds with an inaudible response.

"..."

David and Karen come out the other side of the river of people, and they walk away from the crowds. They walk toward the bridge.

"Did you ever come out for the protests?" Karen asks.

David holds images in his mind of the recent protests at the end of the bridge, people camped for days and people upset about being poor and some mutual friends of David and Karen's.

"I was nearby," David says. "But I did not participate."

A pedestrian-only portion of the bridge runs along its underside. They walk along it. They stop halfway across. A cold breeze pierces David's sweater. "I thought it was supposed to be warm already." He shivers.

"Not so much at night," Karen says. "It is supposed to be warmer tomorrow."

"..."

"..."

"When I saw the protesters, I was on acid riding my bike back and forth across the bridge," David says. "Over and over, I would put a different song on my headphones and ride across or whatever."

"..."

"Did you go?"

"I came one night. I was told the cops were going to clash with the protesters," Karen says. "I rushed

99

down to see the violence." She laughs. "It was ridiculous. The police just wanted the protesters to move for a moment so they could clean up the litter."

"..."

"I wish we could get on a boat," Karen says. David turns to see what she is looking at. A few boats are docked near a hotel.

A vacuous, total, bare continuance precedes an ineffective, sterile occurrence and a sleepy, hazy phantasm and an enormous, abstract deduction.

On the opposite side of the river from downtown, David and Karen are walking along the shore under the bridge.

"What did you mean when you said, 'I think you and my boyfriend make me more anxious than anyone'?" David asks.

"I said that?" Karen asks.

"Yeah... Then you immediately followed it up by saying, 'He is so dumb.' Then I had a longing for you to think I am dumb."

Karen laughs. "You do make me anxious." She locks up her bike. "And my boyfriend is dumb. I think you and my boyfriend are like opposites. Or you are more like me intellectually."

They begin to walk toward the nearby dock.

"We are both cynical," she says. "I don't know... like in terms of dating, you are very different in my mind."

David smiles. He avoids anything implied by speaking in terms of dating. He does not want to think in terms of dating.

They walk down a path. They walk to a gate. It comes up to their waists. It is locked. Beyond the gate, a wooden dock extends over the reflection of downtown water, and two riverboats are tied to either side of the dock. David thinks about climbing the gate.

"I don't think we can get in too much trouble for climbing the gate," Karen says.

"It is nice that we were both thinking about climbing the gate."

David and Karen climb over and walk on the dock. They investigate the boats. David peers through the windows, and Karen checks the doors. The sides of the riverboats have circular paddles reminiscent of old steamboats. The backs of the riverboats are flat, and they sit just above water level.

David climbs onto the back of one of the boats. Karen follows. David sits, and Karen sits. They look at the city's downtown on the opposite side of the river. They look at the reflection of the city's downtown in the river.

"..."

Karen pulls her camouflage backpack from her shoulders, and she opens the front pocket, and she pulls a gray bag out, and she pulls a camera from the gray bag.

"Reflection shot," David says.

Karen takes a photo.

"Reflection shot," Karen says.

She puts the camera in the gray bag, and she puts the gray bag in the front pocket, and she puts her camouflage bag on her shoulders.

"..."

David thinks about how he enjoys talking to Karen.

He thinks about how he enjoys watching her talk.

He thinks about the way she looks over her glasses.

He thinks about the way she smiles behind her drink or hand.

He thinks about how her laughs tend to be quiet.

He thinks about how they tend to be only one or two breaths.

Karen looks at him. She looks back at the skyline. He looks at her. He looks back at the reflection of the skyline.

They talk vaguely about the people they are dating.

They talk vaguely about only having one thing you care about.

They talk vaguely about being unable to be that one thing for someone else.

They talk vaguely about drugs.

They talk vaguely about wanting to care and not care at the same time.

They talk vaguely about caring and not caring at the same time.

They talk vaguely about hating their brains.

They talk vaguely about their friends.

They talk vaguely about being bored.

They talk vaguely about how boredom is interesting or funny or whatever.

They talk vaguely about how their thoughts on their thoughts are already boring.

They talk vaguely about daydreams.

They talk vaguely about other types of dreams.

They talk vaguely about how being told a dream is boring.

They talk vaguely about how they think absurdity

and angst and despair are nice.

They talk vaguely about self-deprecating.

"When is Lela getting back?" Karen asks.

"Two days," David says.

"How is that going?"

"Rough," David says. "She has been gone for a few months. Talking about it seems sad."

WIRRR

"What's that sound?" Karen asks.

"I think it is a leaf blower. Probably the groundskeeper up by that hotel."

"..."

"..."

David and Karen duck down, trying to avoid being seen by the groundskeeper. David's hand brushes against Karen's leg, and his perspective is momentarily overwhelmed.

"This is kind of dreamy," David says, and she rests her leg against his. "I have an I-could-die-happy-now-type feeling."

"If you asked me to, I would drown you in the water," Karen says. "If you asked me to..." They exchange smiles.

"I think I-care-enough-to-let-you-jump-type sentiments are amazing," he says.

"..."

"But I was thinking more like, I enjoy teenage-sneaking-on-tour-boats-at-four-in-the-morning-type things," he says.

"Yeah..."

CLANG CLANG

"What's that?" Karen asks.

David peeks around the side of the boat.

"Is someone there?" she asks.

"Not at the dock," David says. "The grounds-keepers are still by the hotel."

"..."

"I think we should go," David says.

They make their way back to Karens bike, and they walk across the bridge to downtown. The street sweepers are noisy, and David and Karen cannot hear each other over them. As they walk through downtown, they do not talk. They exit downtown near David's house.

"I can feel my heart sort of drop as the night is ending," David says.

"You can come over," Karen says, "if you'd like."

"Sure."

"Really?"

"Yeah..."

The repeating, sluggish ground precedes a faint, hallucinatory breath and a nightmarish, indistinct whatever and an unclear, emptied empathy.

David sits on the couch in Karen's living room. She walks past him. She walks to her room and returns with a jar and her laptop. The jar contains a handful of marijuana. She sets the jar on the coffee table and sits on the couch.

She plugs her laptop into two speakers on the coffee table. The speakers are little pyramids. She turns on some music. It is angular, and it is mostly vocals. The voice is distorted. The lyrics are nonsensical, or it is too late to make any sense of them, or whatever.

David looks at the computer. The clock in the corner of the monitor reads 6:54am. Karen packs a small pipe and brings it to her mouth and lights it and lowers it. Some books are lying on the floor, and David reads their covers, Lords of Chaos and Technological Slavery and The Singing Knives. Karen hands him the pipe. He takes it and brings it to his mouth and lights it and lowers it. He hands the pipe back. Karen reclines against the couch's arm. She lays her legs across David's. The music takes on a cozy warmth. Everything takes on a cozy warmth.

"I feel the urge to address any expectation that we will hook up," David says.

"I don't want to."

"Awesome," he says and sighs and runs his fingers along his scalp. "I was starting to feel an extreme amount of anxiety about that for some reason."

"It is just nice to hang out with someone in an intimate way."

David nods, Yeah.

"Is it alright that my legs are here?" she asks.

"Yeah..."

She smokes from the pipe again. She holds out the pipe to offer it to him.

"I am fine," he says. "Thank you."

She closes her laptop, and closing the laptop turns the music off. She grabs the pipe and jar and stands.

"Are you going to stay here tonight?" she asks.

David glances out the window. The sun is out. He laughs.

"Sure," he says.

"Do you want to come to my bed?" she asks.

"Yeah," he says. He is not sure, but he is tired. Karen walks to her room. David follows. She puts a record on. Synthesizers oscillate over slow drumming. She climbs into bed. He follows.

He asks, "What do you think about spooning?"

She laughs. "I like spooning."

David slides an arm under her neck. He wraps an arm across her chest. He hugs her.

"I think I used that on someone recently," she says. "'What do you think about spooning?'" David softly caresses her arm. She runs her fingers between his.

They exchange stories about experimenting with homosexuality.

They exchange stories about being told stories.

They exchange stories about not talking.

They exchange stories about not moving.

They exchange stories about being terrible people.

They exchange stories about their relationships.

"..."

"You have a nice touch," Karen says and laughs. "I should not have said that."

David laughs. He pulls her close and smells her hair. He drifts to sleep. She drifts to sleep.

"..."

A hazy, persisting dream precedes a haunted equivalence and a deprived thought and a hazy, sleepy indistinctness.

David wakes an hour later. He wakes to the sounds of her roommate getting home. The roommate stumbles around in the kitchen. Karen wakes up.

"I don't think I can go back to sleep," she says.

"Yeah," David says. His voice is soft. His voice is groggy. "I should probably go home."

She rolls over. She bites his shoulder. The bite is

soft, and it is playful. David smiles. He stands and waves a small wave. She returns the wave.

The door closes behind David. He cannot think of anything to do today, and he has a lot of time until Lela arrives. He steps off Karen's porch. He walks down the street. He pulls out a cigarette. He does not light it. He rolls it between his fingers.

There is a bus stop down the street. It has a bench, and plastic walls are on three sides of the bench, and the walls are transparent, and they support an opaque plastic roof. David sits on the bench.

He looks at the graffiti on the plastic walls. Remember Me is written in capital letters with a drippy marker, and a face is drawn inside of a face on the stomach of a cyclops eating a slice of pizza with a face on it, and Sex Stains is written in all capital letters, and a skull is drawn inside a dodecahedron.

David places the cigarette in his mouth. He rubs his index finger between his nose and his eye, trying to clear any crust that built up while he slept, and there is no crust. He runs his fingers through his hair. He squints.

A bus is approaching. It slows. It halts. This bus route goes right by Goya and Hunter and David's house. The front door opens. He makes a gesture to say, I am just sitting here.

Someone steps out of the rear door, and he is wearing a khaki shirt and khaki pants and khaki shoes. He turns, and he watches David. The bus closes its doors. The stranger walks towards David. His shirt has a list of words, Swallow and Death and Vomit and Life. The letters are jagged and capitalized. The stranger pulls out a lighter.

"Do you need a light?" he asks.

David pulls the cigarette from his mouth. He holds and looks at it, and he zones out briefly.

"No," David says. "I have a lighter. I just have not lit this for no reason." The bus pulls away.

"Can I bum one?" the stranger asks.

"Sorry," David says.

"Really?" the stranger asks.

David looks at him with nothing to say. This moment seems extra vivid. The sound of the bus pulling around the corner grows loud, and the small hairs under the stranger's nose from a sloppy shave are more vibrant, and the brown crust in the stranger's pores seems more real, and all the other details jet out like peaks in a sound wave. The stranger's eyes are blue, and they are a generic-type of beautiful. The right eye has a black discoloration, and it makes the pupil appear to be oozing or to be torn open. Time elongates, and David zones out hazy in the extra time. He rubs his hand across his face.

"..."

"Okay," the stranger says. He walks away, and he places the lighter in his pocket.

The discolored eye lingers in David's mind for a moment. He places the unlit cigarette in his mouth. He breathes out, and his breath is clear. This reminds him that the weather is warmer now. The thought of Lela returning tomorrow overlays the image of the discolored eye. The image of the discolored eye fades.

He pulls a lighter from his pocket, and he sparks the flame and lights the cigarette. And embers on the end of his cigarette glow white, and the paper turns gray, and the paper rolls in on itself, and the black line forms around the ash, and smoke is staining the paper brown. He pulls the cigarette from his mouth. He watches the ash grow to over an inch. He squints his eyes and stands and does not notice the ash fall to the concrete.

David walks down the sidewalk, away from Karen's house. He does not walk from A to B, or A to C, or A to D, or A to E. He does not walk home. He walks through a park. He walks somewhere else. He walks into downtown.

A drone fills David's thoughts. It is low. It is sweeping. People crowd the streets, and the streets are silent. Everything is inaudible. The people crowd in generic ways, and they crowd like stock footage for a film, and they move in slow motion. David walks by forgettable faces.

In an alley, a piece of paper tumbles and stops and waves and tumbles again. The streets are in slow motion, and the alleys are in real time. A shade blanket covers featureless walls. The street is gray, and the sidewalks are another gray, and the walls are another gray. At the end of the alley, a building looms on the far side of an intersection. It is concrete. It is fortress-like.

Other people crowd other streets, and they are also in slow motion. Someone plays saxophone for the crowd, and the saxophone player also crowds the street in slow motion, and no one pays attention to him.

In another alley, the street is another gray. Other trash sits along the curb. A car is parked on the other side of the street. A taxi drives past on a perpendicular street.

David walks past a storefront. He walks into an alley. He hangs his head and watches the ground pass under him. Sidewalk patterns fill his perspective. He steps on trash, and he steps on cracks.

The only other person in the alley sits along a wall. He is shirtless. He sits on a bed of boxes. Both his hands rub both his eyes at the same time. He is waking.

David walks by, and the shirtless man waves at David, and the wave is friendly, and it is a good-morning-type wave. David returns the wave. He avoids a puddle on the sidewalk. The shirtless man watches David walk away.

David turns the corner onto another silent street. He slows. He stops. His attention moves to where the buildings meet the sky, and he makes a curious expression. The fortress-like building looms over David, and David likes the looming. He continues to walk. He turns another corner.

Down this alley, each consecutive block is like a smaller instance of the previous block. Around David walking, the lines of the streets, buildings, and sidewalks run parallel to each other, and they vanish at some point in the gray haze. In one-point perspective, David is himself plus nothing, and himself plus nothing is himself plus nothing (plus nothing) plus nothing plus nothing. With all the nothings, he feels calm.

Under an overpass is David walking close to the

wall. And he focuses on the texture of the concrete. David rubs under his nose with his index finger. His walk is unhurried. Everything's details fill his thoughts, and each detail's everything fills his thoughts on his thoughts. The details go through his ideas of himself, hands and reality and stoves and milk and adulthood and sunlight and other light and winter to spring and patterns of patterns. Some of the details are repeated. Some of the details record or experience other details, and these details have details inside. Some details record or experience themselves, and this creates a recursive, infinity effect. He thinks about his thoughts, and everything becomes a recursive blur. David grabs a fistful of his hair, and he pulls his hair slightly. He walks out of downtown onto a neighborhood street.

He thinks, A neighborhood street is like a deep hole.

He thinks, I go in the deep hole.

He thinks, I am stuck in my head.

He thinks, I go further in the deep hole with that boresome beast in my head.

He thinks, I am directionless and tired.

He thinks, I wish I was in bed.

He thinks, I never remember my dreams.

He thinks, I never remember when things are dreamy.

He thinks, It is dreamy in this deep hole with a boresome beast.

Text message from Lela: I just thought if I am going to be with myself, I should be with you. Seemed nice and sad. Not sure if that makes any sense.

‡‡ ▲ ‡‡

Something happens, and something else happens, and David watches a cloud. He walks across a bridge, and the bridge crosses a drainage ditch. The ditch is dry. David walks around the bridge, and he walks in the ditch under the bridge. He imagines being murdered there. This seems like a people-get-murdered-here-type place. He is glad he is alone.

The underside of the bridge is covered in graffiti. A triangle is painted between two hexagons in a field of evenly spaced lines, and Singular Anger is written in a neutral font, and a drooling mouth is painted in the palm of a hand, and the drool has a sad face in it, and Orphan is written in a different neutral font with capital letters. Five burned out candles are on the ground, and a couple of empty beer cans are on the ground. David sits beside the candles. His back is against the wall. He rests his left arm across his chest. He runs his fingers along his scalp. Just Life is written on the wall over his left shoulder.

The five candles are evenly spaced. He connects the dots into a pentagon. He closes his eyes. He opens them slowly for a moment, and they are barely open, and his phone is vibrating.

Text message from Lela: I see humans, but no humanity. Cell division against all odds. Haha I can't wait to see you tomorrow.

David's eyes open. Everything takes a moment. He realizes he fell asleep. He realizes he fell asleep in a ditch. He rubs his eyes. Waking up in a ditch resembles a generic- and funny-type bleak. David picks up a candle and inspects it briefly. He tosses it on the ground. He stands, and he gazes down the ditch. He lights a cigarette, but it smokes itself.

David walks out of the ditch. He walks down the street. He walks past some children. They are sitting on a curb. One throws a pebble into the street, and another watches a cloud, and another picks at a scab, and another sighs, and another stares at a pattern.

● ≙ ● ● ≙ ●

Horizontal lines repeat at the bottom of everything. The lines have a VHS-type warping. Everything has a recording-of-a-monitor quality. Its details are distorted. Lela still frames this rectangle of everything. In this rectangular everything, grass grows unkempt on a dirt road in the middle of nowhere.

Hunter holds the BB gun, and his shirt has a wallpaper print, and his pants have the same print. He paces back. He paces forth.

A group of bikes rests against a nearby tree. Their bike lights shine circles of light onto the dirt road. The diffuse glow of the circles quickly fades into the pitch of night.

A boombox rests beside the bikes. Music plays, and David dances simple repetitions of a single move. Occasionally he jerks. Occasionally he poses. He has a black sweater on, and his face is straight. He looks down holding his arm by his head, and he looks to the side with his arm down slightly, and his arms are at his chest, and his arms are at his sides with his eyes closed.

Hunter readies the BB gun's stock against his shoulder. He holds the BB gun perpendicular to his body and takes aim. The view down the barrel of the BB gun is a woman walking though bike light circles. She is calm. She slowly walks toward Hunter. The wind picks up, and his long hair blows in the wind. He sighs. He lowers the BB gun. He smiles a soft smile.

The woman in circles of bike light has faded-pink hair, and she is Lela. Slowly, the rectangle containing this everything comes out of her eye. Another rectangle containing everything heads towards her eye. Everything is above itself, and everything is beyond itself. Everything starts melting inside itself with itself inside. Everyone is melting in the melting everything. Everything strobes. Everything happens again. Everything happens again (Everything happens again. Everything happens again [...] and again. Everything becomes a pattern of everything.) and again. Everything becomes a pattern of everything. An image of Numbskull, the cat-type creature, covers everything. This sentence becomes this entire book. Everyone melts more. Everything melts more. It strobes more. In the melting everything of everything, grass still grows unkempt on a dirt road in the middle of nowhere.

Hunter holds the BB gun, and he shakes his head to the music. He lights a cigarette and walks down the dirt road. He walks up to Lela.

Lela and Hunter are face-to-face. She feels a nostalgic-type feeling for the present. Lela pulls out a name tag, the kind someone who works retail would wear. She pins it to Hunter's shirt, and it reads, Lela Pierce. Hunter smiles. Lela walks from one circle of bike light to another. Hunter kicks some rocks into the tall grass.

Lela walks out to the river's shore. Some of her friends wait for her in the river. They wait for her to jump. They wait for her to join them. She brushes her hair behind her ear.

KERSPLASH

She jumps into the water. She surfaces. Everyone becomes distorted. Everything becomes distorted. Lela swims out to her friends, a woman with a bloody nose smoking a cigarette beneath an asymmetrical haircut and someone with hair covering their face and three people in fluorescent colors with masks knit with geometric patterns. The water is cold, and Lela shivers. No one else minds the cold water.

Stand on the dirt road are Hunter and David talking about how they wish Goya was with them.

"..."

"..."

Headlights pierce some trees, and a vehicle is coming down the dirt road. Maybe it is the people that own the property with the swimming hole. Maybe it is someone else trespassing. Either way, everyone runs for their bikes, and David grabs the boombox, and Lela smiles at David, and the group pedals along the dirt road, and they ride between two trees, and the dirt road becomes a paved one.

Goya rubs her fingers together, watching dry glue flake from them. The dry glue becomes unusually vivid, and Goya is captivated. This is the most interesting thing going on. The flakes continue to beguile her. She feels a dread-type feeling and looks away.

Her room is covered in layers of deconstructed-jean collages. She imagines the bike ride David and Hunter and Lela and some other people are on. The wisps of glue drift about.

● ● ● ●

They ride into downtown, and the night sky is solid black. They ride along the city streets, and the city streets are empty. The buildings and lights and signs have a plastic look to them. Some of their bike lights shine ahead like spotlights. Others strobe. The strobing adds a ghostly look to the pack. They ride out of downtown.

David's boombox plays modulating sounds. They are slow. They are low. There is a moment where their surroundings sync up with the music, and everything is melting for that moment.

"Let's see how far Twenty-Sixth Street will take us east," Hunter yells. "If you think you can keep up."

David follows the pack, but he wants to ask Lela if she wants to go home. It has been so long since they have spent time together. He just wants to lie in bed with her for days. He looks up at Lela.

She pedals ahead of the pack excitedly. David gives in, and he joins the pack, and there is a gradient from faking enthusiasm to feeling enthusiastic. The group rides down the street with speed and excitement. They cross over a highway. They cross over a bridge. Downtown lights wash the east side. The light is a vomit yellow. They pedal away from downtown. David looks back.

Goya is picking up scraps for the collages. Fashion magazines litter every horizontal surface in her room. They mostly feature Tight Violence ads. She places a collage amongst other collages. It blends in, collage camouflage. The golden antler sits atop a stack of magazines. She grabs the golden antler, fidgeting with it and walking out of her room with it. It is the first time she goes outside her room today.

The road slowly winds. They continue to ride nowhere, and the background streams away behind them. Hunter leads the group, and someone's strobing bike light gives him a phantasm-like quality. Hunter speaks under his breath, "What?" Beyond the bike lights, the road fades to black. "Shit."
KRIIIII
Hunter brakes hard, and dirt is kicked up.
SKRIII
His foot scrapes along the ground. His bike slides,

and it faces perpendicular to the direction he is going, and his bike light beams outward.

CRII

He stops. The road ends. "Whew," Hunter says. He sighs.

Lela raises her arm to signal the group to stop.

"We were just getting going," someone yells from the back of the pack.

"Why'd we stop?" someone else asks.

The group gathers at the road's end, and they find something. They find the absence of anything.

"It's a dead end," Hunter says. The group decides on a new direction like a symphony tuning. David looks at Lela. She holds her helmet in both hands, and she looks at the night sky.

Goya stands beside the cat-type thing, and it is looking out of the window.

"You are ridiculous," Goya says, and she opens the door for Numbskull, and she points the golden antler out the door. Numbskull walks outside, and he walks to the other side of the window it was looking out of, and it looks inside the house. Goya steps outside, closing the door behind her and lighting a cigarette and sitting beside Numbskull.

"I don't think you will ever be satisfied."

The group turns their bikes to the direction they came from.

"I think I am going to call it a night," Hunter says, and that sounds nice to David, and it sounds nice to Lela.

"Yeah," someone says, "sounds good."

CRRCHRRCHRRCH

The group rides along. They weave between each other. They ride the empty streets.

About the Author

No Glykon is a writer, designer, and musician based out of Providence, RI. They are stretched upon the plain and covering some nine acres of ground. Two vultures on either side of them are digging their beaks into their liver, and No Glykon keeps on trying to beat them off with their hands, but cannot.